"...GREMLINS REALLY EXIST. YOU'VE JUST GOT TO KEEP WATCHING FOR THEM."

Billy couldn't suppress a smile.

"It's true, said Mr. Futterman. You think I'm pulling your leg? Gremlins were everywhere during World War Two. We used to see them dancing on the wings of our plane. They played every prank in the book. Once they snuck up to our pilot and shouted, 'You're flying upside down, you fool!' That was really a close one because the pilot turned us over in a split second."

Billy laughed. "You actually saw them?"

"You'd see them out of the corner of your eye, but just as you shot them a full glance, they'd vanish...."

Other Avon Books by
George Gipe

GREMLINS — *Camelot edition*

GREMLINS

George Gipe

Based on a screenplay
written by Chris Columbus

 AVON
PUBLISHERS OF BARD, CAMELOT, DISCUS AND FLARE BOOKS

AVON BOOKS
A division of
The Hearst Corporation
1790 Broadway
New York, New York 10019

TM indicates a trademark of Warner Bros. Inc.
Copyright © 1984 by Warner Bros. Inc. All Rights Reserved.
Published by arrangement with Warner Bros. Inc. Library of
Congress Catalog Card Number: 84-90893 ISBN: 0-380-86610-0

First Avon Printing, June, 1984

AVON TRADEMARK REG. U. S. PAT. OFF. AND IN
OTHER COUNTRIES, MARCA REGISTRADA, HECHO EN
U. S. A.

Printed in the U. S. A.

WFH 10 9 8 7 6 5 4 3 2 1

Special thanks to the people who helped make my job
Gremlin-free:

Elaine Markson

Kathryn Vought

Dan Romanelli

Mike Finnell

Joe Dante

Brad Globe

Geoffrey Brandt

Judy Gitenstein

Ed Sedarbaum

CHAPTER ONE

In his cage tucked in a far corner of the Chinese man's back room, the Mogwai dozed fitfully. Soon the old man would come in, stroke him gently, speak briefly in that strange-sounding language, set him free to wander among the musty books and artifacts for a while, and then, best of all, feed him.

As a Mogwai, he was nearly always ready to eat, though he had learned to control his hunger. Such was the built-in adaptability of the Mogwai. He was so adaptable that even though confined to the cage and small room, he felt no desire for freedom. In fact, his mind was his escape mechanism, a perennially active entertainment center which he could use to visit any time or place—at any time at all. His mind was not like the human mind, a perverse instrument which so often refused manipulation, but played tricks or dealt its owner doses of duplicity. The Mogwai's mind, in sharp contrast, was a constant source of pleasure to him.

Mogturmen, the inventor of the Mogwai species, had

1

seen to that. Centuries ago on another planet, Mogturmen had set out to produce a creature that was adaptable to any climate and condition, one that could easily reproduce itself, was gentle and highly intelligent. Exactly why Mogturmen embarked on this venture is not known, except that such inventors flourished during an era of widespread experimentation in the field of species creation—an era, it should be added, that passed into disrepute following later, unsuccessful attempts to introduce cross-pollination among certain species of crawling carnivores.

At first, Mogturmen's experiment had been looked upon as a great success and he was hailed as the genetic hero of three galaxies. The first sets of Mogwai turned out as planned, although the gentle little beasts had a few drawbacks not foreseen by their creator. Their vast intelligence seemed to interfere with their ability to communicate (Mogturmen said it was because they thought so much faster than they could verbalize), and for some unaccountable reason they were repelled by light. Discounting these deficiencies, the galactic powers ordered the Mogwai sent to every inhabitable planet in the universe, their purpose being to inspire alien beings with their peaceful spirit and intelligence and to instruct them in the ways of living without violence and possible extinction. Among the planets selected for early Mogwai population were Kelm-6 in the Poraisti Range, Clinpf-A of the Beehive Pollux, and the third satellite of MinorSun#67672, a small but fertile body called Earth by its inhabitants.

Soon after these first departures it was discovered that Mogturmen's creatures were highly unstable. To be exact, fewer than one in a thousand retained the sweet disposition and charitable aims built into it by the inventor. Instead, something went wrong. Very wrong. The Mogwai himself knew of the unstable Mogwai, being well versed in the historical background of his species. He preferred not to think of the complications that had developed, but it was nearly impossible not to. It was, after all, part of his heritage. Closing his eyes as he relaxed in his cage awaiting his supper, he mused briefly on the wars, landslides, and famines that had taken place on Kelm-6, Clinpf-A, and even here on Earth because of his creator's miscalculations and willingness to disseminate an untested creature. Small wonder Mogturmen had been punished by having his . . .

The Mogwai pushed the thought from his mind. True, Mogturmen had failed in the overall, but he himself was one of the successes, the one in a thousand who still embodied all the good things put there by his high-minded inventor. Yet his existence, he knew, had no long-term benefits for society. Gentle as he was, he was a distinct threat to those around him. Just a few drops of water, a morsel of food at the wrong time, and—

The Mogwai made a little guttural noise, unhappy with himself for allowing such unpleasant thoughts to enter his trained mind. Why was he even considering the possibility that he might bring about some disaster or other? The Chinese man seemed to understand the rules (although the Mogwai was at a loss to explain how he knew them other than by the fact that Orientals seemed to understand the inexplicable almost without trying). He kept the room dark, water-free, and fed the Mogwai well before midnight. Few strangers were admitted. The Mogwai was never subjected to journeys such as those he had been forced to endure with his previous owners, among whom were a medieval peddler and a sixteenth-century smuggler who sold stolen gems.

No doubt about it, the Chinese man was the best caretaker of them all. But why then was the Mogwai filled with a sense of malaise at best, of impending doom at worst? Perhaps, he mused, it was because he had had it so easy for so long. Thinking back, he wondered if he had the strength to deal once again with a new outbreak of . . . them.

What do you mean, of them? he asked himself, suddenly realizing that "they" and he were virtually the same. Except that Mogturmen's miscalculations were built in to them.

And built in to me as well, he thought, feeling guilty. I just happened to be one who escaped. As he had done so many times in the past, he began to wonder what had happened to the others, how long they had survived, how much trouble they had caused.

No, he thought, forcing his mind to erase the coalescing picture. That's not to think about. I will take a mental tour instead . . . a tour of the beautiful Catelesian fire streams.

He closed his eyes, and his Mogwai mind, ever obedient, began to show him the vivid colors generated by the boiling rivers of the subplanet Catelesia. It was one of the Mogwai's favorite mental images, although when he felt a minor surge of aggression, he enjoyed watching mind-battles between the armored worms of Ucursian. His favorite Earthly visions included the sun-darkening flights of the passenger pigeon (which he understood had ended a century before) and scenes from the San Francisco earthquake.

He was curled into a ball, thoroughly enjoying the mental spectacle of the Catelesian fire streams, when the Chinese man entered. A small plate held in his thin fingers, the frail gentleman with skin like old leather shuffled quietly to the side of the table and stood looking down into the cage at his furry friend. On the plate was an assortment of Oriental delicacies left over from Han Wu's restaurant next door— a partial egg roll, rice, broccoli, and twice-fried pork scraps. To all this the Chinese man had added a small rubber washer he had found in his handy room closet.

Aware of his master's presence, the Mogwai stirred, opened his eyes, then pounced to an expectant standing position as the food's aroma suddenly reached him.

Smiling benevolently, the Chinese man opened the box from the top and reached inside to gently lift the Mogwai

onto the table. He deposited him next to the plate and nodded.

"You may enjoy yourself now, my friend," he said softly,
patting the Mogwai gently on the head and then taking a
step backward.

The Mogwai looked down at the plate. Sure enough, a
foreign object was there again. Yesterday it had been a piece
of soft chewy wood; the day before a couple of foamy white
chips he had seen the Chinese man take from a packing
crate. Sniffing at the black rubber doughnut, the Mogwai
analyzed it instantly and knew it would not hurt him if he
ate it. He also knew it would be tasteless at best, perhaps
bitter, virtually nutritionless, and very hard to chew. But
the Chinese man so enjoyed seeing him chew up non-edible
substances that it seemed churlishly uncharitable to disap-
point him. Getting the black object down would take only
a minute; he could then enjoy the rest of his meal as dessert.

Snapping up the washer, he pulled it inside his mouth
and started to grind away, first using his back teeth as a
vise to break the dry object in half. As he suspected, it was
tough and tasted rather like petroleum—not his favorite
flavoring agent—but the Mogwai enjoyed seeing the
expression of amazement and happiness crinkle the old man's
features. Less than a minute later, the washer swallowed if
not digested, he was busily and eagerly attacking the rice
and egg roll. Glancing up briefly, the Mogwai saw the
pleased smile lingering on the Chinese man's face and was
glad he had taken the trouble to eat the washer.

Humoring the old man, after all, was a small enough
price to pay for the peaceful life he led.

CHAPTER TWO

For a long moment Billy resisted the urge to deliver a good swift kick to the side of his perverse Volkswagen. Then he lashed out, driving his boot solidly against the rusting spot where the rear fender met the car's body.

He was immediately sorry. Not just because he was rewarded with a jolt of pain in his toe. The car, a '69, was old and usually provided him with reasonably dependable transportation. The heating vent resisted all efforts to open and close according to Billy's will, but had to be either opened all the way or jammed completely shut. There were various shudders and groans that tried Billy's patience, but as they were all "intermittent" (a term used by garagemen when they were unable to find the trouble's source), he and the car somehow adjusted to each other.

But why did it always seem to conk out when he was late for work? Last night had been just as cold, perhaps colder than this morning. He hadn't especially wanted the pizza, and he certainly experienced no joy in being the one selected to go get it. Why hadn't the bug coughed and sputtered and died then?

He sighed, looked at his watch, and winced. If he could be shot directly out of a cannon into the bank, he would be only a minute late. He glanced about him. The streets of quaint Kingston Falls, population 6,122, were deserted, as they always seemed to be when you needed a lift or were looking for company.

Some might have called it a boring town, but having lived all his twenty-one years here, Billy liked it. He and Kingston Falls somehow seemed right for each other, having down-to-earth qualities in common. When his mother used to say things like that, the Billy Peltzer of a few years ago had often grown sulky, dispirited, and occasionally hostile. Now he realized that he *was* average. A B − or B +, depending on the taste of the feminine onlooker. His hair, dark and worn as long as the bank executives would allow, framed a longish face, a pair of dark earnest eyes, and a wide expressive mouth. His skin, he thanked the Lord, had passed the acne stage; either that or the zits were in a state of remission.

Definitely not muscular, he was too well filled out to be called wiry. His was the body that even a high school football coach would have difficulty assigning to a position. He was too small for the line, a bit too chunky for the whippet-like receivers, not quite strong enough for running back. And so, because Kingston Falls put more emphasis on participation than winning, Billy Peltzer spent two years in the school's defensive backfield. The high point of his career came not when he intercepted a pass and ran it back for a game-winning touchdown, but when he recovered a fumble that salvaged a tie—all that stood between Kingston Falls and a totally winless season.

After graduation he didn't go to college because he simply didn't know what he wanted to be in life and it seemed a shame to have his folks shell out good money while he decided. Following in his father's footsteps would have been like tracking a squirrel through the forest. Part inventor, part traveling salesman, Rand Peltzer had a resume that resembled the parts list for an aircraft carrier. Billy knew he didn't want a similarly nomadic existence, yet he was so hard pressed to define his goals that his friend Gene Grynkiewicz—now nearly through engineering college—once suggested that he try to become a day watchman at a drive-in theatre.

Instead, Billy took a post–high school aptitude test, which revealed that he would do well working in a bank. The test did not say how well he would do if he continued to arrive late, however.

"Broke down again?"

The voice, a familiar one, belonged to Murray Futterman, the garrulous neighbor around the corner who was now seated behind the wheel of his bright red snowplow. Whenever it snowed Futterman hopped on his plow and helped clean the streets, partly as a public service and partly, Billy suspected, because it gave him a better opportunity to jaw with people.

"You need a jump, Billy?"

"No, thanks," Billy replied. "It's not the battery. I just put a new one in. I think it's the connection. Or it's just made up its mind to be stubborn for a while."

Futterman pulled on his brake and descended from the snowplow's fur-lined seat. Inwardly, Billy groaned, knowing he had no time to waste. Futterman meant well, but he could use ten minutes telling a thirty-second story.

"Thanks, Mr. Futterman," Billy said quickly, walking away from his car and toward the street in the hopes of sidetracking the well-intentioned neighbor. "I'm gonna walk. I'm already late for work now."

He might just as well have spoken in Sanskrit or performed a few bird imitations. Nodding genially as he brushed past him, Futterman looked closely at the Volkswagen. "No-good foreign cars," he said, shaking his head. "They always freeze up on you."

Billy hesitated, not yet desperate enough to just start walking to work in the cold. Futterman was harmless and occasionally even helpful. For a long moment he stood looking at the car, his straight black hair hanging limply across his forehead. Well into his fifties, Futterman looked younger, yet because of his garrulous nature and fuddy-duddy attitude he somehow seemed older as well.

"Doesn't happen with American machinery," he said. "Our stuff can stand up to anything."

No sense arguing the point, Billy thought. Forcing a tight smile—which he hoped Futterman would take as an apology for his buying such a defective foreign product and drop the subject—Billy opened his mouth to reiterate his dilemma, gesturing up the street as he did so.

The words died in the wake of Futterman's next verbal onslaught.

"See that snowplow?" He smiled. "Fifteen years old. Hasn't given me a day of trouble. Know why?"

Obviously it was a rhetorical question. Again Billy's mouth opened but no words came forth.

"It's because it's not some foreign piece of junk," Futterman answered himself. "A Kentucky Harvester. You'll never see a snowplow as good as that one. Company went out of business because they were too good. Hear that, boy? Too good!"

Billy shrugged. He tried to look sad, not a difficult maneuver in light of the fact that he might be fired in a few minutes.

"That's real nice, Mr. Futterman," he said. "I mean, it's nice it's such a great plow and it's too bad they went out of business. But I gotta go. Really."

"Hop on, I'll give you a lift," Futterman offered.

Billy weighed the situation. Nothing else on the road was moving, and as most people had not yet shoveled their sidewalks, walking was going to be slow. At least Futterman's snowplow could get him to the bank faster than he could move on foot. If—

Futterman homed in on Billy's hesitation. "We'll go straight to the bank," he promised. "That's where you work, right?"

"Yessir."

"Come on. I'll open her up full and we'll be there in no time at all."

Billy hopped up next to Futterman and they started off. As they did so, Billy groaned.

"What's the matter?" Futterman asked.

"Mom must have let Barney out," Billy said. "Now he'll follow me to work."

Sure enough, in an instant the yellowish brown mutt with the large ears—he was somewhere between a beagle and an Irish setter—had leapfrogged across the heavily drifted snow until he was next to Futterman's snowplow. His rheumy dark eyes looked up lovingly at Billy.

"Want me to stop so you can take him back?" Futterman asked, his hand reaching for the brake.

"No, it's all right," Billy said. "I can tie him under the counter at the bank. Mr. Corben won't like it, but if Barney's quiet maybe we can get away with it until lunchtime."

Futterman nodded and gunned the snowplow forward. "What's wrong with your car?" he asked.

"I'm not sure," Billy replied glumly. "It's intermittent. Sometimes it works fine, even in freezing weather. Other times it won't start, even when it's nice."

"Sounds like gremlins to me."

"You mean all those cars used to act like that?"

Futterman laughed. "Guess you're too young to recognize the word *gremlin* as anything but an American Motors car," he said.

"What else is it?"

"A little devil," Futterman said. "They love to fool around with machinery. I saw a lot of 'em in World War Two. I was a tail gunner on a Flying Fortress. Bet you didn't know that."

Billy shook his head even as he tried to remember whether one of Futterman's endless ramblings had once contained that information. Looking at Futterman now and doing some quick arithmetic, he was amazed that the man was old enough to have taken part in a conflict that had ended nearly four decades ago. He was old, of course, but somehow Billy automatically coupled World War II veterans with men in rocking chairs or nursing homes. Compared to them, Futterman was very much alive.

Billy said the diplomatically correct, and as it turned out, accurate, thing. "You must have been a teenager."

Futterman nodded. "Eighteen when I went in, nineteen when it was over. But I saw a lot of life in those twelve months."

"I'll bet."

"Most important thing I learned was that gremlins really exist. You gotta keep watching for them."

Billy couldn't suppress a smile.

"You think I'm pullin' your leg," Futterman deadpanned. "But it's true. Like I said, they like to fool around with machinery. With all them planes flying, World War Two was their meat. Let me tell you, those gremlins were everywhere during the war. I mean, all over our ships and planes. I think that's why our machinery's better than that foreign stuff. In the war we learned to deal with gremlins and make our equipment better. For some reason, gremlins didn't go after the Japanese and Germans the way they went after us."

"Why was that?" Billy asked.

"Don't know for sure, but I think it's because we—our side—had a better sense of humor. You know how human nature is. It's like, well, you only play tricks on people who'll laugh, right? After a while, you don't play tricks on people who get all ruffled, 'cause it's no fun. That's why the gremlins took after us. Half the time we'd end up laughin' at what they'd do."

"And what did they do?"

"You name it. Now I was a tail gunner, right? They'd knock my sights out of line so I'd miss. Or they'd chisel tiny holes in the glass window so cold air would get in. They'd even slide down the gun barrel and jam the trigger as I was about to fire. Or they'd stick a pin in my rear just as I was about to fire."

Billy laughed. "You actually saw them?"

"Well, yes and no," Futterman replied. "You'd see them out of the corner of your eye, but just as you shot them a full glance, they'd duck out of view."

"Sounds like you were making them up, Mr. Futterman," Billy said candidly.

"No. They were there. Other guys saw them and would swear to it. Now Jackson—he was my navigator—he used to see them outside the plane all the time, dancin' in the slipstream of the wing. Or they'd chew little bits of rubber out of the de-icing boot on the wing's leading edge so we'd pick up ice. Sometimes they'd make sputtering noises in the pilot's ear so he'd think one of the engines was missing. They could even imitate our voices. Once they snuck up to our pilot and shouted, 'You're flyin' upside down, you fool!' That was really a close one, 'cause the pilot turned us over in a split second. You shoulda seen how the coffee cups and maps and people went sailin' every which way."

"But that could have been dangerous," Billy said. "From the way you described them, I thought the gremlins were just playful."

"Oh, they were. They didn't mean to put us in dangerous

spots like that, but some of their pranks turned out that way."

The snowplow crossed the intersection of Carver and Clark, a normally busy corner now nearly deserted except for a few cars nearly buried in drifted snow. Looking at his watch, Billy noted that he was ten minutes late, but he was comforted by the fact that with luck he'd make it before the bank opened to its customers.

"Before the war was over, we'd learned to deal with all kinds of 'em," Futterman continued. "The strato-gremlins were the worst. They used to show up above ten thousand feet. Spandules were middle-aged gremlins and fifinellas were females. There was also jerps and bijits. Each kind was different. There was even a song we used to sing . . ."

Fearing the worst, Billy looked away from Futterman, noting with mixed emotions that Barney was trotting behind them, apparently determined to follow them no matter how far they traveled.

A moment later the rasp of Futterman's snowplow engine blended with his off-key singing voice.

"When you're a thousand miles from nowhere,
 And there's nothing below but the drink,
 It's then you'll see the gremlins,
 Green and gamboge and gold,
 Male and female and neuter,
 Gremlins both young and old.
 White ones will wiggle your wingtips,
 Male ones will muddle your maps,
 Green ones will guzzle your glycol,
 Females will flutter your flaps,
 They'll freeze up your camera shutters,
 They'll bite through your aileron wires,
 They'll bend and they'll break and they'll batter,
 They'll jab toasting forks in your eyes.
 They'll—"

A giant convulsion of the snowplow stunned Futterman to silence and nearly threw Billy off the side. A second explosion, accompanied by an arc of red fire, caused the engine to shudder.

"Darn," Futterman rasped. Reaching forward to turn the ignition key, he lifted himself off the seat, pulled the hood latch, and grabbed a wrench from beneath the seat in one fluid motion. "Don't worry, I know what it is," he apologized. "Won't take me but a minute or two to adjust that darn thing."

Billy slid to the ground, gave Barney a pat, and called across the flat hood to Mr. Futterman.

"I'll cut across Mrs. Deagle's," he said. "Thanks a lot for taking me this far."

"Won't take me a second to get this working," Futterman repeated. "It's the only thing wrong with this snowplow. Doesn't usually act up, but I guess all this talk about gremlins brought it on."

"Yeah," Billy laughed. "Thanks again."

Leaving Futterman with his head thrust deeply into the engine well, Billy started to trot across the vast expanse of Mrs. Deagle's lawn, a carpet of virgin snow marred only by a few squirrel tracks. Barney followed.

As he moved along the edge of the property toward a break in the iron fence, Billy noted that once again Mrs. Deagle's place was the only piece of property in this, the main square of Kingston Falls, with no Christmas lights. Even the Union Savings and Trust Bank, his place of employment, sported a double line of holiday lights, which twinkled in bright ironic contrast to that firm's new get-tough policy with its customers.

A beeping horn and crunch of car chains against packed snow diverted Billy's attention from further thoughts of disaffection concerning his employer.

"Get outa the way, you dumb cat!"

From the rolled-down window of the Kingston Falls police car protruded the thin, weasel-like face of Deputy Brent. In the passenger's seat sat Sheriff Reilly, a husky, friendly-faced man with thick dark hair.

"Move, you stupid rat with legs," Brent yelled.

The few pedestrians near the scene paused to watch—Billy; Dr. Molinaro, on his way to his office; and Father Bartlett, a white-haired elderly priest. Beneath the front wheel of the police cruiser crouched a large gray tabby cat, its refusal to move caused by either fear or stubbornness. As Brent continued to shout at the cat, a stream of happy chatter emanated from the car radio, contrasting sharply with his venom. "Good mornin' to all you late risers," the unseen voice warbled. "Rockin' Ricky Rialto here with a list of school closings. But first, let's listen to a Motown Christmas classic, the Jackson Five bringin' you some chestnuts roastin' on an open fire—"

A protracted blast on the horn overwhelmed the ebullient announcer. Simultaneously, Billy darted quickly into the street and grabbed the cat.

"Thanks." Sheriff Reilly smiled.

"It's one of Mrs. Deagle's," Billy said.

"If I'da known that," Brent groused, "I'd have kept right on drivin'."

Reilly nodded, rolled up the window, and indicated that Brent should continue driving. After checking to make sure Barney was behind him, Billy started a diagonal path toward Mrs. Deagle's front door, the squirming cat tucked firmly in the crook of his arm. Even as he did so, he noticed the edge of a living room curtain fall and her sharp, unsmiling face disappear into the dark recesses of the house. Before he arrived at the front door, it opened to reveal Mrs. Deagle, clad in a singularly unattractive housedress and obviously taken by surprise, judging from the lopsided position of her metallic auburn wig. Her lips were pursed, her expression as formidable as that reserved for an IRS agent.

"I told you not to walk on the grass," she said sharply.

Billy cast a quick glance behind at his footprints in the snow. "I didn't walk on the grass," he responded. "I walked on the snow."

"Don't be smart," Mrs. Deagle shot back.

Billy shoved the cat at her, his eyes locking on her face for only an instant. Unlike most old people, whose faces shone with character and wisdom, Mrs. Deagle's expression generated only sadness and revulsion within him. Large, tacky earrings dangled from her ears, and her eyes were outlined by thick mascara-covered lashes through a heavy layer of ghostly white powder. Yellow teeth contrasted bizarrely with purplish red lipstick smeared below and above the thin lips of her mouth. With her sharp, nervous gestures, she resembled an evil mannikin or puppet, the sort of creature Billy had seen in TV cartoon shows.

"Well, I brought your cat," he murmured softly. "It was nearly run over by the police car."

Mrs. Deagle took the animal, dropped it quickly to the floor behind her.

"The way you were carrying her, it's lucky she can still walk," Mrs. Deagle rasped.

Billy shrugged.

"All right. Get off my porch. I hope you're not waiting around for a reward."

"No, Mrs. Deagle," Billy replied. "I guess a thank-you was even too much to expect."

With that, he turned and started off the porch with Barney. As her parting shot, he half heard Mrs. Deagle shout something about making sure Barney didn't befoul any of her precious shrubs. Mostly his mind was occupied with thoughts of self-loathing. "Dummy," he said aloud. "You should have known better than to bother. . . . Dropping the cat in her yard would have been good enough."

And would have gotten him to work a few minutes earlier—or less late, he thought. As he turned the corner of Mrs. Deagle's property, he began to run, a movement that caused Barney to do likewise. The sudden acceleration brought the dog into contact with a large ceramic snowman, the only frivolous object the old woman allowed on her property. Crinkled and spotted with tiny fracture lines, the snowman's head had started listing to its right several years before; now, as Barney brushed the bottom of the figure, the head leaned sharply downward, hesitated, and then rolled onto the snow.

Peering at the departing figures from her dining room window, Mrs. Deagle inhaled sharply as the ceramic head of the snowman disappeared into the snow.

"Those destructive little beasts!" she hissed. "I'll get both of them for that."

She watched silently as young Billy Peltzer and his dog went into the bank, a look of determination slowly replacing her expression of horror. Then, righting her wig before the dining room mirror, she made the decision that had eluded her so far this morning—whether or not to brave the elements in order to take care of some business.

"Blast the snow," she said now. "It'll be worth getting my feet wet to teach that young punk a lesson."

CHAPTER THREE

It was always so difficult getting something truly different and exciting for his family, Rand Peltzer mused, and every Christmas it got worse.

Rather than grow despondent, however, he accepted selecting the proper gift as a challenge. Which was the way he looked at his life in general. Rand considered himself a survivor, a grown-up boy from the poorest section of town who, without benefit of college or any other specialized training, somehow had managed to marry the finest woman in Kingston Falls and support a family reasonably well. True, he had to scramble, but wasn't that part of life's fun? People laughed at him when his inventions failed to perform as they should, but didn't that make it even more enjoyable when they did work?

Now, although bothered by his inability to find the ultimate present for Billy, he was happy. He loved Christmas and everything it stood for—the bringing-together spirit, the stepped-up economy, a feeling of mellowness, and especially the opportunity to be nice to people without their looking at you oddly.

How he arrived in Chinatown he was not exactly sure. He had no recollection of ordering a cabbie to "take me to Chinatown," or even of deciding that he should take himself there. Probably, as he meandered through shop and mall and stall in search of the elusive unique present, he had arrived in Chinatown almost by osmosis. He had never shopped here before, although he had visited as a tourist. But why not? Why shouldn't this be the place where he found it?

Whatever *it* was.

With a slightly puzzled expression on his round face, Rand resembled any other middle-aged shopper. A genial-faced man who might once have been quite handsome, he still possessed an attractively thick head of ruffled gray hair and penetrating green eyes. Below the neck he had aged less gracefully, the burly chest yielding to a thick waist that stopped just short of being a beer-belly. (Although some of his less diplomatic friends used that term occasionally.) One might have imagined him as a professional football player, say a lineman, who retired in 1965 and had been losing the battle of the bulge grudgingly. Dressed in a tweed jacket, corduroy pants, and a gray pullover sweater, he was obviously a man who put comfort over style.

"There's got to be something here," he muttered.

He surveyed the articles on the counter of the Chinese curio shop, a glittering array of souvenir-type items. There were ashtrays, tie pins, pen and pencil sets, even Chinatown toilet paper; above him tinkled mobiles from which dangled acrobats, gargoyles, unidentified artistic shapes. On the walls were clocks and dart boards, posters and plaques, paintings and etchings, but nothing that appealed to him. Nothing, he knew, that would bring that light into Billy's eyes he loved so much.

"Help gentleman?"

With typical (to Rand Peltzer) Oriental furtiveness, a tallow-faced Chinese woman had suddenly appeared from beneath the counter by the simple process of standing up. Rand started, nearly dropping the brass ashtray he had picked up.

"Yes," he said. "I'd like something for my son. Something different."

The woman pointed to a stereo, then to a watch when Rand shook his head.

"He like mechanical things?" the woman asked.

"No. He's an artist. Cartoonist. Maybe you got some sort of gizmo an artist could use."

"Gizmo?"

"Yeah," Rand replied, with sudden inspiration. "Maybe something like a combination easel and brush holder, or . . ." His eyes drifted toward the ceiling as he began to feel his inspirational juices flowing. "Or maybe an easel you can fold up and carry in your pocket. You know, for the artist who travels a lot . . ."

"Gizmo?" the woman repeated, holding a rechargeable battery for Rand to see.

He shook his head, starting for the door as he continued to ponder the problems of constructing a portable easel.

"One minute," the woman called out.

Rand hesitated as she darted from behind the counter through a small door leading to the back room. No sooner was she gone than Rand became aware of another presence.

"Mister want something different?" asked a new voice.

It belonged to a very thin Chinese boy. He had long legs, which made him appear taller and no doubt several years older than he really was, which Rand guessed to be about nine. He was dressed in a faded Los Angeles Dodgers jacket, a wrinkled Springsteen T-shirt, washed-out torn Levi's, and high-top sneakers, an outfit, Rand observed inwardly, that made him look like a walking advertisement for unclaimed-freight auctions. Still, there was something about him Rand liked and trusted.

"That's right," he replied, his glance alternating between the huge dark eyes of the kid and the doorway through which the woman had departed. "Something unusual, something nobody else has." Then, realizing that such a description fit only a very few items, such as the Hope diamond, he amended himself. "I mean, it doesn't have to be expensive or the only thing of its kind, but I'd like it to be . . . well, different, you know."

The youngster nodded. "Follow me, please," he said.

"Can't you just tell me what it is?"

"No, sir. It defies description."

Oh-oh, Rand thought. So it "defies description," does it? If the kid had picked up that phrase at such a tender age, he must be a truly precocious con artist. Perhaps he was the bait for a gang of muggers or kidnappers. Good sense warned Rand to give up his quest as soon as possible. On the other hand, when had he ever listened to his own good sense?

The old woman reappeared, dragging a huge inflatable— and now quite inflated—red dragon, which would have filled all but the largest bathtubs.

"Gizmo?" she asked.

"No." Rand smiled, backing toward the exit. "But thanks anyway."

A moment later he was on the street, the Chinese youngster at his elbow. "Trinkets," the boy said disparagingly. "You want something different and she offers you trinkets."

As a salesman, Rand had learned long ago never to knock the other fellow's product. In time this young man would learn the same lesson, he supposed, and now was an appropriate moment to give him a subtle bit of wisdom. "That was a very nice dragon," he said. "A lot of people might enjoy that. It just wasn't for me."

"A trinket," the kid repeated. "A big trinket. Follow me and you'll see something really different."

Rand did so, although he cautioned himself to be warier than usual. The avenue was bustling with activity, but he scanned the passing faces with careful scrutiny to catch a nod or signal directed by or at the youngster. As they moved down the length of the block, he saw nothing unusual. Tradespeople passed quickly, each involved in his or her own thoughts; a couple of nuns, giggling nervously, rode by in a rickshaw; several young men who looked like college students carried on a brief conversation with a young Oriental woman, trying desperately to match her world-weariness with a coolness of their own. Soon they were standing next to a stairway leading into a cellar. "Here," the youngster said.

"No wonder you have to drag people in off the street," Rand muttered, looking around carefully.

The kid opened the door at the bottom of the stairwell, indicated that Rand should follow. Taking a deep breath, Rand did so.

Inside, it was no shop of horrors, but neither was it a shop brimming with exciting items. The main source of illumination seemed to be hundreds of candles, which burned singly or in groups from every flat surface in the cluttered room. Above dangled the usual Oriental mobiles, the metal ones creating their jangling music as the tiny slivers touched one another. Rand examined a truly beautiful chess set with huge men carved to resemble Japanese warriors and peasants. For a moment he thought Billy would appreciate the artistry of the set, perhaps even be able to use it as a model for some of his cartoon figures. Then he shrugged. The chess set simply did not say "buy me."

Turning to locate the youngster, he saw an old Chinese gentleman instead. He was seated on a sort of platform, puffing gently on a long pipe. Long gray whiskers adorned the lower portion of his face, and on his head was a black skullcap. Dressed in a flowing brown tunic, he seemed almost priestly seated up high. Rand entertained that thought for only a moment, however. The man, for all his formality and air of ethereal detachment, was simply another salesman like himself. Only their environments differed. This man sat in his shop all day while Rand patrolled the world outside. Having arrived at that conclusion, it was logical that Rand take the next step. Moving closer to the man, he opened his briefcase and pulled out a complex-looking object approximately a foot long.

"Excuse me, sir," he said. "I followed a young man in here who told me there might be something truly different for me to see."

The Chinese gentleman nodded slowly. "My grandson," he said in a surprisingly deep and resonant voice. The expression accompanying the two-word reply was a mixture of fondness and skepticism, confirming Rand's earlier notion that the kid was a precocious con artist.

Never one to be discouraged, Rand had already decided to make his pitch. Looking around at the curio shop, which was cluttered with the usual array of frightening Oriental masks, ancient witchcraft tokens, rotting skulls, and dusty books on the occult, he made a sort of sweeping gesture. "Now, sir, if I may say something," he began, "this is a very nice shop. But what you could use, in addition to this wonderful inventory you already have, are some new and modern items. Like this."

He held up the object he had taken from his briefcase. A formless thing, it resembled a tuning fork to which clung a variety of smaller contrivances, gadgets, and appendages.

"Now let's say you get on the train or bus for an important

business appointment," Rand began. "No sooner are you seated than you realize you forgot to brush your teeth. And your mouth feels like the government's been using it to test deadly chemicals. Normally, you'd have cause for alarm, but not if you've got one of these—the Bathroom Buddy. It's my own invention, just another product from the inventing laboratory of Rand Peltzer, the man who makes the impossible possible and the illogical logical."

Ignoring the Chinese gentleman's total lack of interest, Rand slid one arm from the side of the object, producing a sort of crude toothbrush. He then pushed a button, which in turn caused a spray of watery white paste to spurt out so hard it hit the nearby wall, then dribble slowly onto the floor.

"No problem," Rand said, pushing the OFF switch.

The device continued to spew off-white gunk down the length of the object and into the palm of Rand's hand, burbling thickly as it did so.

"No problem," Rand repeated. "It cleans up easily. And when it works, it's just one of ten highly useful parts of this Bathroom Buddy. Of course, I'm prejudiced, but I think you could use a few modern gadgets like this in your shop. How about if I put you down for a dozen? Believe me, even in a place like this, which isn't exactly Sears Roebuck, they'll be gone in a week."

As if to punctuate Rand's climactic promise, the Bathroom Buddy emitted a single loud noise, something between a belch and an explosion of wet cement, sending forth a thick geyser of gluey glop which eventually came to rest on the inventor's left lapel.

"Still has a few bugs in it," Rand said weakly.

The Chinese man broke then. Like Mount Rushmore suddenly coming to life, the lips parted, revealing a set of impressively huge teeth, and gales of laughter began to shake him. First he undulated sideways, then up and down.

A trembling finger emerged from beneath the tunic and finally homed in on Rand, an accusing crook that bounced lightly as the old man shook with laughter.

"Tee-hee-hee . . . Thomas Edison," he giggled. "Thomas Edison."

Embarrassed but inured to the experience by past mishaps, Rand chuckled good-naturedly, especially when he noticed that the young shill had witnessed the demonstration and was also laughing. For a moment Rand merely faked his own laugh, waiting patiently for the moment of derision to end. As he did so, however, he became aware of a third voice in the choir of laughter. It was higher than those of the old man and boy, rather unearthly, a cross between the gurgle of an infant and shriek of a parrot.

"Wait," he called out. "What's that?"

It took a moment for the old man and boy to contain themselves. When they did so, their sudden silence isolated the alien voice, emphasizing its strange intonation as it continued to giggle in the background.

"I've never heard anything like that," Rand muttered, looking from one Oriental to the other. They responded to his implied question with evasive expressions. The old man seemed to have developed a sudden fascination with a piece of paper on his desk; the boy, less subtle, merely turned away. Meanwhile, the bizarre laughter continued to echo from a small room just behind them.

"Boy, that must be something," Rand said to no one in particular, moving toward the doorway of the room.

As he reached the entrance, he turned to look at the youngster. "Is that it?" he asked. "Is that the reason you brought me here? Is that the 'different' thing?"

The boy looked at the floor, intimidated by the sharp glance from his grandfather.

"Yeah, I guess it must be," Rand replied to his own question. "I'd sure like to see who or what owns that laugh."

Hesitating at the doorway, he paused as a sense of propriety gripped him. The back room, after all, was private, and regardless of his curiosity he felt it necessary to have their permission to look there.

In response, the old Chinese gentleman shrugged.

"Thanks," Rand said.

Pushing his way through a set of beaded curtains, he entered the inner sanctum, waiting a moment for his eyes to adjust to the darkness. Finally he was able to make out a table on which several dozen shoe boxes, each containing bits of assorted trinkets, were piled. Near them was a small box, about a foot square, draped with a piece of burlap. From behind the burlap came soft sounds—no longer the high-pitched gleeful giggle of a minute previously but something unearthly nonetheless. Moving to the edge of the table, he reached forward, now aware that the two Orientals had followed him and were standing at the doorway, their figures casting elongated shadows into the room.

Gently, almost reverentially, Rand lifted the burlap curtain.

"Wow," he said softly.

He had never seen a creature like it before.

"What in the world is that?" Rand asked.

"Mogwai," the old Chinese man replied.

"Mog—what?"

"It's what he calls himself. It took me a while to find out. I have no idea what it means."

"Mogwai," Rand repeated. "Sounds like something from another planet. Too hard to remember and pronounce. As far as I'm concerned, you're just plain Gizmo."

The creature looked balefully at Rand, a low sound emanating from its closed mouth.

"What's he doing?" Rand asked.

"Singing," the Chinese youngster replied. "He only does that for people he likes."

Rand smiled. "What's he eat?" he asked.

The old man returned the smile. "Anything."

"What do you mean, anything?"

"Anything that can be chewed. Yesterday he ate a rubber washer. He's also eaten cardboard and packing chips. But I think he most enjoys the things we like."

"Candy?" Rand asked, suddenly remembering that he had a Milky Way bar in his jacket pocket.

"Oh, definitely," the Chinese man replied.

Rand found the bar and unwrapped it. Pushing it gently into the cage, he watched intently as the creature sniffed it, then devoured the soft mixture of chocolate and caramel in three or four large bites.

Delighted, Rand found himself applauding. Swallowing heavily, the Mogwai seemed to return a glance that said "thank you."

"How much do you want for it?" Rand asked.

"Mogwai is not for sale," the old man replied.

"Aw, c'mon," Rand persisted. "My son'd love it. And we'd give it a good home."

"I am sorry."

"Listen, I gotta have it. This is what your grandson brought me to see, isn't it?"

"No. I send him out to interest customers in other items of my shop. But not Mogwai."

"But that's the only thing you have that's different. The rest is just curio stuff, the standard souvenirs and—"

"Trinkets," the young man interjected.

"Not exactly," Rand added, seeing a pained look in the old man's eyes. "You've got a nice place. That chess set out there is wonderful. My boy doesn't play chess, though. This here Gizmo is perfect. I'll give you a hundred bucks."

"Thank you, no."

Rand removed his wallet, hoping that the sight of the money itself would change the man's mind, or at least make him realize how serious he was. Fingering a couple of fifties, Rand added another, then another. The old man continued to shake his head.

"Two hundred-fifty," Rand said, spreading the bills across the palm of his hand, like a poker player displaying a royal flush. "Take it. Please."

The old man withdrew his eyes from the money, revulsion and desire blended in his features, a dieter confronted with a juicy meal that he wants and does not want.

"Two-sixty," Rand persisted. "It's all I've got."

"Take it, Grandpop," the young man urged.

"No."

"We need the money. The rent—"

"No," the old man repeated. "Mogwai is not like other animal. He is a very special creature. With Mogwai, comes much responsibility."

"Hey, I'm a responsible person," Rand interjected. "I go to church every Sunday. Well, a lot of Sundays. I pay my taxes, take the garbage out. What's wrong with me?"

"It is not you. It is humanity. I'm sorry, but I cannot sell Mogwai at any price."

With that, the old man turned and left the room.

Rand sighed, slowly pushed the money back into his wallet, noting that the young man continued to eye the bills wistfully.

"You can't reason with him?" he asked.

The young man took a deep breath, walked slowly to the doorway, and looked out at his grandfather, who was now seated near the front of the store, staring stoically at the passersby. Returning to Rand, he looked at him in the manner of an employer assessing someone applying for a job.

"Listen, mister," he said. "The old man's right. This is a very special creature. The person who has him has to be extra careful . . . do some strange-sounding things . . ."

"Like what?"

"Well, there are rules, you see. You gotta keep him outa light. That's why it's so dark in here. He hates light, especially bright light."

"O.K. I think I can handle that. We have a nice dark basement and Billy's room—"

"And don't get him wet. Keep him away from the water."

"No light, no water. I guess a day at the beach is out of the question."

The kid looked at Rand pointedly. "I'm serious, mister," he said.

"Sure," Rand replied. "It's just that animals need water to drink, right?"

"This one doesn't."

"You sure?"

The youngster nodded emphatically. "I'm telling you," he said. "Light may kill him and water may kill you."

"What?"

"That's what my grandfather says. Don't ask me how he knows. But those are two important rules. If you don't think you can do that, say so. It's only 'cause we need the money so bad that I'm even thinkin' about selling you Mogwai."

"Sure, I understand." Rand nodded, reaching for his wallet again.

"I almost forgot the most important thing," the boy continued. "The thing you can never forget is . . . no matter how much he cries, no matter how much he begs, never, ever feed him after midnight. You got it?"

Rand swallowed, forcing back a sudden impulse to laugh at such a quaint set of rules. Maybe the old man was senile and the kid just plain crazy, but his heart was set on bringing that little animal home to Billy. If that meant playing the game with this kid, he'd do it.

"I got it," he said seriously. "No light, no water, no food after midnight."

He started to hand the money to the boy, then thought better of it.

"Where'll I meet you?" he asked.

"Out back. In five minutes."

Rand nodded. Whistling softly, he stole another look at Gizmo and then walked briskly out of the curio shop.

CHAPTER FOUR

It was 8:54, six minutes before the bank opened for business, when Billy pushed through the EMPLOYEES ONLY door and began the ridiculous task of trying to look unobtrusive while arriving a quarter hour late with a wet dog in tow.

Luck was with him briefly. Tugging gently at Barney's collar, he managed to make it to his window, locate the leash he kept in his drawer, and secure Barney out of the way without his breaking into a barking fit. Whipping out his nameplate, he placed it—upside down—on the counter, brushed a bead of sweat from the corner of his eye, and exhaled wearily. Only then did he see the object that he usually looked for first when he entered the bank.

Today she was dressed in blue, a form-fitting but conservative dress that complemented her flashing green eyes and dazzling dark hair. Billy, like so many other young men—and older men too, for that matter—had fallen madly and totally in love with Kate Beringer the first time he laid eyes on her. She was twenty, a perhaps too-intense woman of that age, a champion of the underdog. Considering himself an underdog, that suited Billy just fine, of course, but so far he had found Kate pleasant but somewhat unapproachable. Perhaps it was because she was so smart, never at a loss for words, that he feared being shot down by her should he move too quickly. And so he moved nearly imperceptibly. "By the end of the century," he once said to himself as he analyzed his longing for her and what to do about it, "by then I'll have asked her for a date."

As he began to arrange his money drawer, he noticed Kate moving toward him. Arriving at his window, she reached out to turn his nameplate right side up, smiling briefly as she did so.

"Morning, Kate," Billy said. Now, with her so close, he could smell her scrubbed freshness, see the fine hairs on her arm as it tapered to a beautifully slim wrist.

"Billy," she said, her voice warm but not intimate, "will you sign a petition?"

"Sure," he said.

He reached for a pen.

"Don't you want to know what it's for?" she asked with a touch of pique.

"Not really," he replied. "If you think it's a good idea, it's O.K. by me."

It was the wrong thing to say.

"I'd like you to agree with me that it's a good idea," she said archly, "and there's no way you can do that unless you know what the petition's for."

Billy nodded. "What's it for?"

"We're trying to have Dorry's Pub declared a landmark."

"Why?"

"Mrs. Deagle's threatened to close it when the lease expires later this month."

"She's threatening to close down everything when their leases expire," Billy murmured. "She told my dad the same thing. 'Course, he forgets to make payments every once in a while. What's Dorry's problem?"

"It's another of Mrs. Deagle's personal vendettas," Kate replied. "She says Dorry's is a dive. An eyesore. A bad influence on the neighborhood."

"But that's where my dad proposed to my mom," Billy said ingenuously.

"That's where everybody's dad proposed to their mom. Or vice versa," Kate said.

Billy smiled, fantasizing that he might propose to Kate in the same place. His courage aided somewhat by the notion, he said: "You...ah...That's a beautiful dress. You look very pretty today....Not that you don't look pretty every day..."

Kate smiled, flattered but anxious that Billy sign before Gerald Hopkins got to the window and started asking questions. She thrust the petition beneath Billy's pen and watched as he wrote his name. A moment later, Gerald Hopkins was at their side.

"What's going on?" he asked.

At twenty-three, Hopkins was already fast approaching middle age. Gerald's mind, in fact, seemed to have attained that goal and only awaited his body to catch up. The bank's junior vice-president, he was tall, slender, and good-looking in a somewhat sneaky way. Perhaps because he smiled too quickly and his eyes darted nervously from side to side—those were the things that gave him away—he laid bare his ambition to become an important man in as short a time as possible. Young people—most of them, at any rate—distrusted Gerald, but that did not bother him as long as Mr. Corben and other grown-ups continued to compliment him on his efficiency, drive, and initiative. They, after all, were the ones who made the decisions.

Kate, ignoring Gerald's question, started for her window.

For a moment it seemed that Gerald was about to follow; then he turned abruptly to Billy.

"Mr. Corben and I want to see you," he said.

Billy shrugged, walked slowly behind Gerald into the sumptuous but very formal office of Roland Corben. Around the walls of the oak-paneled room were portraits of every United States president, generals George Patton, Omar Bradley, William Tecumseh Sherman, John Pershing, and, looking decidedly underdressed in a toga and a bit embarrassed, Julius Caesar. Beneath this panorama of greatness were bookcases, each locked and filled with soporific-looking, legal, identically bound books except for a long bottom row filled with the complete works of Horatio Alger, Jr. Every time he was summoned into Mr. Corben's "vault" (as Kate termed it), Billy's eye fell on the end Alger volume, which was entitled *Luck and Pluck.* He wondered if Mr. Corben had read it as a boy. Perhaps Gerald Hopkins had read it only a few weeks ago.

Seated judgelike behind his mammoth desk, a gold nameplate in front proclaiming his identity, was Roland Corben in a perfectly fitting three-piece gray suit. In his early sixties, he was the epitome of the word *distinguished,* his neatly trimmed white hair framing a face that was lightly tanned and only slightly wrinkled. If he smiled, Mr. Corben might have been almost handsome. As it was, he usually frowned, a movement that collapsed and pinched his features like someone pulling the drawstring on a leather pouch. His habit of putting his thumbs and fingers together to form a sort of prayerful tent had become a trademark of both him and his protégé, Gerald.

"Seventeen minutes and thirty-three seconds," Corben said now in ex cathedra tones. "That's how late you were, William."

"I'm sorry," Billy stammered.

"Punctuality is the politeness of kings," Corben said fatuously. "Do you know who said that?"

Billy hesitated. For a fleeting moment he was tempted to suggest that the dull aphorism was coined by Gerald Hopkins, but then he thought better of it. No sense making a bad situation worse. Instead he shook his head.

"It was Benjamin Franklin," Gerald interjected.

"Louis the Eighteenth," Corben corrected, intimidating Gerald with a baleful glare. Returning his attention to Billy, he added: "If King Louis the Eighteenth could be on time, so can you."

"Yessir," Billy said. "Except that King Louis never had a temperamental Volkswagen."

Gerald snorted derisively.

"We didn't call you in here to listen to excuses, Peltzer," Gerald said. "Your job carries a lot of responsibilities. One of them is to be here on time."

"Well said, Gerald." Corben nodded, obviously impressed with young Hopkins's didactic tone.

"Thanks, Mr. Corben." Gerald smiled.

"Straighten your tie," Corben shot back.

"Yessir."

He did so. Corben watched him briefly before directing his glare once again at Billy. "See that this doesn't happen again," he said. "If your car's temperamental, get a new car. Or leave earlier so you'll be prepared for problems."

Billy nodded enthusiastically, just as if Mr. Corben had come up with a miraculous solution to his dilemma. Then, as he turned to leave, he heard Corben harrumph.

"Yessir?" he asked.

"Your shoes, William," Mr. Corben growled. "They're brown."

Billy looked down, nodded once again. No doubt about it, his shoes were indeed brown.

"No one wears brown shoes with dark blue trousers," Corben intoned.

"Oh, thanks. I'll remember next time," Billy replied as respectfully as possible.

He was allowed to slink out then, but his troubles were only just beginning. The doors of the bank having been opened to the public during his trial and conviction, there were perhaps a dozen customers in the process of doing business, most of them withdrawing money for Christmas purchases. One of the group was Mrs. Deagle, who in pushing her way to the front of the line suddenly found herself next to Mrs. Harris. Harris, a genial middle-aged woman, was known to have had a bad year in that both she and her husband had lost their jobs and had medical problems. She seemed almost jovial today, however, as she tugged at Mrs. Deagle's coat sleeve.

"Mrs. Deagle," she said in a voice loud enough to be overheard by Billy. "My husband got another job."

"Oh?" Mrs. Deagle replied sharply. "What's that supposed to mean to me?"

"It means we'll be able to make a few back payments—soon as Christmas is over."

"What's Christmas got to do with it?"

"Well, there's presents to buy, you know . . ."

"And in the meantime, I wait. Is that it?"

"No, not exactly. I just thought that since things are lookin' up for us, you might be willing to wait a while longer."

"Mrs. Harris," the old woman said. "This bank and I have the same purpose in life—to make money. Why should we have to wait around until you decide to pay your legal obligations?"

Mrs. Harris frowned. "But we don't have the spare cash now. It's Christmas."

"Then you know what to ask Santa for," Mrs. Deagle replied, dismissing her with a wave of her hand.

She moved toward Billy's window, the bodies parting in front of her like the Red Sea obeying Moses. Under her arm she carried the severed head of the ceramic snowman, which, seen close up, looked tacky and ugly. Yellowed and pockmarked from the weather, the object's mouth hung open in what seemed more a crazed stare than a happy smile.

"Hello, Mrs. Deagle," Billy stammered. "What can I do for you today?"

"You mean, in addition to what you've already done!" she announced grandly.

"I'm sorry," Billy said. "I don't understand."

"This is what's left of my imported ceramic snowman," she nearly shouted. "Your dog broke it this morning."

Billy had no recollection of the incident but was at too decided a disadvantage to protest. "Gee, I'm real sorry," he said. "Just tell me what I owe you . . ."

To his surprise, she replied: "I don't want money."

"That's a switch," a phantom voice to Billy's right whispered. It was Kate, looking straight ahead at her own customer but totally enmeshed in Billy's dilemma.

"I heard that, young lady," Mrs. Deagle rasped, glaring at Kate. "You'd better watch out. I'm on to you, scheming and plotting behind my back." Suddenly her accusations seemed to include everyone within earshot. "I know what's going on, what you think, what you'd like to see happen. But it'll never work, because I'm one step ahead of all of you."

Kate, returning Mrs. Deagle's glare, waited patiently until the old woman looked back to Billy.

"Now then," she said. "Since you've admitted your guilt in breaking this, and before a bank full of witnesses, what do you propose to do?"

"I don't know, Mrs. Deagle," Billy muttered. "I mean, if you don't want money, what can I do? Do you want me to clean up your yard or—"

With an angry gesture, she cut him short. "I want your dog," she said.

"Barney?"

"Such a stupid name. Yes. The ugly mongrel that follows you around. I want him."

"But why?" Billy asked.

"Because he's a menace to this town and I aim to see that he's punished." An evil smile broke across Mrs. Deagle's face, revealing her singularly unattractive teeth. Excess lipstick clinging to her teeth made it seem as if she had just finished a bloody meal. "Yes, I'd like to punish him," she said. "Do you know that in the old days they used to put evil animals on trial and punish them? They hung an elephant once, by his neck until he was dead."

"Guess who the star witness against it was," Kate whispered, her voice discreetly lower this time so that the content of what she said was heard only by Billy.

Stifling a laugh, he looked directly at Mrs. Deagle. "I'm sorry you feel he's a menace," he said. "I don't see how you can say that."

"He snapped at the Hagen boy. And my nephew Douglas."

"They were trying to burn off his tail with a propane torch," Billy said, causing a ripple of laughter from the customers nearest the arena of battle.

Mrs. Deagle dismissed Billy's defense with a wave. "He's always barking and growling at my cats, scaring them half to death."

"Well, cats and dogs just don't . . . get along so well," Billy replied. "You've seen the cartoons . . ."

"I hate cartoons," Mrs. Deagle grated.

Billy looked away, suddenly conscious that he was facing a double jeopardy now. Having heard his name, Barney had arisen from his sleeping position and was now trying to jump onto Billy's lap. The leash, fastened not too tightly about his neck, was slowly coming loose as Barney tugged at it. The rasping sound of his claws against the bank's polished wood floor caused Billy to break into a cold sweat. Why didn't the old woman leave him alone? Why did his normally obedient dog pick this time to get playful? Pushing gently at Barney not only did no good; it made Mrs. Deagle think he was preoccupied with something on his lap, which inflamed her to new outreaches of anger.

"Pay attention," she shouted. "I'm telling you, I want that dog. I'll take him to a kennel where he'll be put to sleep. It'll be quick and painless... compared to what I'd like to do."

More to distract her from Barney's restless maneuvering beneath his chair than to find out, Billy asked: "What... what would you like to do, Mrs. Deagle?"

Her response was immediate. "I'd like to say, 'Here, Barney...,'" she began. "'Come here, nice Barney, so I can strangle you with my own bare hands....'"

It was over in a split second. Freeing his neck suddenly from the leash, Barney hurled himself onto the edge of Billy's chair and toward the sound of his name. With only a brief bounce on the counter top, his next destination was Mrs. Deagle's shoulders, on which he came to rest with both floppy, and still slightly wet, front paws. Face to face with her enemy, Mrs. Deagle shrieked and dropped the ceramic head, which promptly shattered into a thousand bits and splinters. Barney took the occasion to lick her face, starting at the cleft in her chin and continuing until his tongue became enmeshed in the wiry dankness of her auburn wig. He then started to gag, the first violent heaves throwing him and Mrs. Deagle to the bank floor in a tangle of arms, legs, and paws.

"Help! Help!" she screamed.

Instantly the twin figures of Gerald Hopkins and Mr. Corben appeared, each bumping the other in his eagerness to assist the bank's greatest benefactor to her feet.

"William!" Mr. Corben shouted accusingly. "What is that dog doing here?"

"He followed me, Mr. Corben," Billy replied weakly. "I couldn't help it and there was no time to take him home because I was already late—"

"Peltzer, this is a bank, not a pet store," Gerald offered.

Mr. Corben nodded agreement, then turned his attention to the disheveled Mrs. Deagle, who stood adjusting her hair and trying not to look undignified. "My dear lady," he murmured solicitously, "are you all right?"

Taking the cue, Mrs. Deagle placed a fluttering hand over her breast. "My heart," she whined. "I can't take this kind of shock . . . I'm not supposed to have any excitement. . . ."

Billy looked at Kate. Her expression, which he read perfectly, seemed to say, "Well, if you're not supposed to have excitement, why do you run around causing trouble?"

"Barney wouldn't have hurt you, Mrs. Deagle," he began.

"Lies and excuses," she shot back. "You're just like your father. I've been listening to his excuses for months. How he 'forgot' to make a payment. He's a loser, a crackpot and a loser—do you hear that?"

Billy shook his head, started to protest, but Mr. Corben intervened.

"Please, Mrs. Deagle," he soothed. "You said yourself you're not supposed to have any excitement."

"I can tell him what I think of his no-good father and no-good dog," she snapped. "That's not excitement. It's a public duty!"

Gerald laughed appreciatively.

"I'll get that mangy beast," Mrs. Deagle continued, the

blue veins in her neck standing out starkly against the pow-
der-bleached paleness of her throat. "Someday when you
least expect it, I'll get even."

Barney, not comprehending the threat in the least, wagged
his tail in response.

With one final, hateful glance at the entire group, Mrs.
Deagle propelled herself out of the bank.

"If I ever see that dog in the bank again, you're fired,"
Mr. Corben said, turning on his heel and heading for his
office.

"Yessir." Billy nodded.

Gerald Hopkins shrugged and smiled scornfully. "I hope
he's bankbroken," he sniggered. "If not, your time may be
here sooner than you think."

As Billy started back toward his window, he reflected
darkly on the fortunes of this day. If the downward spiral
continued at the same rate, by evening he would be in a
degree of trouble experienced by few mortal men.

CHAPTER FIVE

The Mogwai, nearly asleep only minutes after finishing the delicious candy bar given him by the mysterious burly stranger, thought at first that the disoriented feeling was part of the prelude to the dreamland he often experienced following a hearty meal. The box was moving so slowly, so subtly, he barely noticed it. Then he heard the voices, soft and sibilant, as if the speakers were making a conscious effort to be quiet. Accompanying these symptoms were a rise in unfamiliar background noise and a sudden change in temperature. A cry of terror caught in his throat and then burst forth. He was being moved!

Now the voices outside the box spoke quickly, as if panicked, and the movements of the Mogwai's tiny home were quick and jolting, all pretense at secrecy having been abandoned. Tossed back and forth in the box, the victim of some terrible upheaval, he tried to cry out to the Chinese man. Again and again he tried to form and pronounce the words of the strange language he had heard so often, but because of problems built into his species by Mogturmen, he was unable to emit more than a shriek of gibberish.

"Woggluhgurkllll...," he called out. "Mevvaf-frummlldrd..."

Just when he began to think his body was about to shatter from the turbulence and dizziness he was experiencing, the box came to rest. The floor was at a slant but at least the earthquake was over. Two loud metallic slams, a grinding sound, and an engine roar followed, then a gentle, contin-uous rocking that would have been comforting had he not been utterly terrified. The tears came a few minutes later when he faced the probability that he would never see his Chinese man again.

"Don't worry, Gizmo," a deep soft voice soothed. "It's gonna be all right."

The edge of the burlap was lifted from outside, admitting the sudden flash of a neon sign through the openings in the box. The Mogwai screamed, threw his hands to cover his eyes. Abruptly the burlap fell and the voice said: "Sorry, old buddy, I didn't realize...I guess what he said was true....But don't worry, I'll be careful. We all will."

It had happened again. He knew it would, of course, since by Earth life standards he was virtually immortal. These beings lived such brief lives. Why couldn't they hang on longer so that there would be less upheaval in his ex-istence? He had been with the Chinese gentleman nearly forty Earth years, had seen him bend from a healthy and strong young man into a frail specter of his former self. Fortunately, the man's mind remained active and alert; they understood each other. The Chinese man knew the rules, even a few words of the Mogwai's language, and seemed to sense much more.

These transferals always threw him into such a fit of depression. He tried not to think of the numerous times he had barely escaped death because his "owner" knew nothing at all about his needs—or, knowing his needs, simply didn't care to see that they were provided for. Even worse were those who discovered his powers and—how was it possible these humans could be so dense?—actually used him as a source of amusement. That they were amused only briefly before having to face the ultimate terror was of little solace to him. He merely wanted an enlightened caretaker, someone who understood or was as responsible as the old gentleman.

This burly man who was now transporting him heaven knows where did not seem exactly responsible to the Mogwai. For one thing, he kept calling him "Gizmo" over and over, as if trying to have him accept that as his name or description. Yet the man knew his was Mogwai—the Chinese man had told him so. Was it the first harsh reality of his new situation that he would have to be called Gizmo? It sounded truly terrible.

There were worse things, of course. Thinking back as they bumped gently along, he remembered the China Sea crossing just before he had encountered his owner-friend of nearly forty years. *They* had gotten loose then—there had been no way to prevent it. He shuddered. What would have happened had he not been rescued by the Chinese man just a few minutes before the ship was torpedoed? Before that was the incident at the Royal Air Force base. Incident? A near-tragedy of epic proportions! Somehow an extended joke had been made of the thing, but Mogwai knew differently. What would he do if it happened again? Probably nothing very much, as had been the case in the past, because he was largely powerless to act once it started. That's why the Chinese gentleman had been such an exemplary guardian; without being told, he seemed to know how important prevention was. Even better, he realized that Mogwai did not mind strictures or avenues of freedom being closed off. That's why the past decades had been comparatively hazard-free. The Chinese man had enough responsibility for both of them.

"Gizmo, Gizmo, Gizmo, my friend," the burly man sing-songed above the sound of the car, "you and me and Billy are gonna have a terrific time together."

Gizmo (yes, his Mogwai adaptability had already made him accept his new name) sighed, pulled his great umbrella-like ears over his face, and tried to sleep. A new life was beginning for him and he just didn't want to think about it.

CHAPTER SIX

Somehow Billy got through the rest of the workday, the worst part of which was the succession of triumphant leers from Gerald Hopkins every time their paths crossed. Barney fell asleep under the counter and was good as gold until lunchtime, when Billy took him home. Mr. Corben went to a luncheon given by the Tri-County Businessmen's Association and didn't return until nearly four o'clock. He seemed to have forgotten the incident involving Barney and Mrs. Deagle. Kate, as beautiful as ever, was Billy's only continuing source of visual and—as he contemplated asking her for a date soon—mental pleasure.

By closing he was in a better frame of mind, although he did not relish the idea of walking everywhere until his car decided to let him rejoin the human race. On the other hand, walking at Christmas time was pleasant in that the town was colorfully decorated and most people seemed in happy moods. Kingston Falls's main square was lined with lights when Billy closed the bank door behind him and started home. His plan was to mosey along, looking in store windows in the hope he would see something different and interesting for Mom or Dad. In recent years they had become tough cases as far as Christmas shopping went, Mom claiming she "needed nothing," but she was always delighted when package-opening time came. Dad, of course, either had everything or was in the process of inventing it. He enjoyed the thought behind a nice present, though.

Crossing to the town square, Billy walked among the rows of Christmas trees, enjoying their fresh pine smell. His mind still preoccupied with the day's turbulent events, he was the perfect target for Pete Fountaine's joke. Dressed as a Christmas tree, complete with blinking lights, dangling ornaments, and silver tinsel, thirteen-year-old Pete stood perfectly still near the other trees until Billy was inches away, then reached out and grabbed his arm. Billy jumped.

"Hi, Billy," Pete laughed. "Got you, huh?"

Billy laughed. "Yeah. Guess I was thinkin' about something else." He regarded Pete from head to toe. "How's business?" he asked.

"Don't ask me." Pete shrugged. "Pop sells them and I just act like one."

As they strolled along the edge of the tree-lined square, Pete dutifully recited his pitch whenever they approached a potential buyer. "Christmas trees, get 'em here," he called out. "All sizes and shapes. Get one just like me." As a frozen-featured man walked quickly by, Pete added: "Hey there, sir . . . Bet you could use a Christmas tree . . . huh?"

The man, staring at the ground, ignored him.

"Bet he's got an aluminum one," Pete said in a loud voice. "Or he puts lights on his cat."

Billy smiled briefly until the cat reference made him think of Mrs. Deagle and her threat to destroy Barney. Was it possible her life was so bitter she would actually consider doing such a thing?

Pete's father, an exact replica of him with thirty years added on, gestured to his son. "Help Mr. Anderson load this into his station wagon," he said.

Billy grabbed the tall tree and, with Pete, went to the car. Mr. Anderson, an elderly gentleman, opened the back and they placed the tree inside.

"Thanks, Billy," Pete said.

A psychologist, looking at Pete's eyes and listening to the tone of his voice, would have known instantly that young Pete was expressing gratitude for more than the tree errand. Now at the pimply-faced, gawky, and totally insecure stage and filled with conviction that no one really liked him, least of all older teens, Pete's admiration of Billy verged on hero worship. He was the older kid who actually treated Pete like a human being. Not that his father was unkind to him, nor was he picked on by his contemporaries. They merely treated him like something that was just there. Billy, on the other hand, seemed interested in him. If he wanted to, Pete felt he could tell him a personal problem, ask his advice, and not be regarded as either a jerk or a potential social offender.

Now, with business a bit slow and Billy at hand, Pete decided the time was right.

"Hey, Billy," he said. "You're pretty old—"

"That's right." Billy smiled. "I get my first retirement check next week."

"I mean, you've got lots of experience, right?"

"Experience with what?"

"Well, with girls."

"Sure."

"You ever ask a girl out?"

"Sure. That's usually the best way to go out with them— to ask."

"Yeah," Pete murmured. "How did you do it? I mean, what did you say?"

Billy shrugged. "It depends on the girl and situation," he said, trying to sound worldly but not blasé. "You gotta be firm. Confident. Make it sound like you're doing her a favor by asking her out."

"Really?" Pete's eyes were wide and bright with this new piece of knowledge.

"Sure. You can't get all gushy and nervous. Never let on how much you really like her."

"I get it." Pete nodded. "Maybe you should zap her with a few insults first."

Billy laughed. "That may be carrying it a bit too far. You got somebody in mind?"

"No, not really," Pete lied. Then, amending himself, he said, "Well, maybe there's somebody. . . ."

Billy laughed. He reached out, trying to find a place near Pete's shoulder to pat without getting jabbed by pine needles. "Let me know how it turns out," he said.

"Yeah," Pete answered, waving as Billy stepped off the curb and headed down the block.

Billy smiled, recalling their conversation as he walked. Why didn't life get easier? To Pete he was a wise and cool young man, capable of dealing with life in general and women in particular. To himself he was hardly more proficient than at thirteen; words still got twisted in his mouth and thoughts muddled in his brain before he could articulate them. And yet the very notion that Pete considered him worldly and wise buoyed his spirits to the point where he decided to drop into Dorry's Pub.

It was unlikely that Kate would be there yet; she usually went home to change before reporting for work. Even if she didn't arrive before Billy finished a mug of beer, however, he considered it important to take the initial plunge of going inside. Once or twice in the past he had done so but had emerged in a depressed mood after seeing the attention lavished on Kate by the older men at the bar. Not that she returned their overtures. She was friendly, even joked with them, but was never intimate. That should have pleased Billy. Instead he concluded unhappily that if she rejected those sharp-tongued, sophisticated, successful men, what chance did he have?

Tonight he was determined to brave his own insecurity. Going inside, he stood at the entrance foyer, waiting for his eyes to adjust to the darkness. Laid out as an old-fashioned Irish pub, Dorry's was dimly lit, with small wooden tables and sawdust on the floor. The long bar was already crowded with young and middle-aged men, as well as a scattering of women. In the corner a pair of video games colorfully and noisily zapped aliens or threatened the player's electronic hero with instant fragmentation.

Locating an empty table, Billy sat down, ordered a beer from none other than sandy-haired Dorry Dougal himself, the genuine Irishman who operated the pub. Ten minutes later, beginning to feel relaxed, he took out the drawing pad he always carried with him and began to sketch. Soon the lines evolved into recognizable forms—a muscular warrior battling a giant, horrifying dragon with a face too similar to Mrs. Deagle's to be mere coincidence. In the process, the warrior was defending a young princess with an uncanny resemblance to Kate Beringer. Despite the bad lighting, Billy was pleased with the results he had gotten and was admiring the effect when a sudden shadow falling across the picture brought him back to reality.

"Terrific," a sardonic voice said. "The world needs more unemployed artists."

It was Gerald Hopkins. In deference to its being after hours, he had unfastened the two bottom buttons of his three-piece suit and loosened his tie slightly. Without being invited, he dropped into the chair opposite Billy and smiled in a superior manner. "Speaking of unemployment, guess who almost applied for it today."

"I give up," Billy said coolly.

"You." Taking a long beat so that it could sink in, he then continued. "Mr. Corben had second thoughts, though. He gets all sentimental about the holidays."

"Imagine that."

"Yeah," Gerald sneered. "I would have fired you in a second."

"Merry Christmas to you, too," Billy deadpanned.

"You think it's mean of me to even think about firing somebody, right?" Gerald demanded. "Well, let me tell you something. It's a tough world out there. To get ahead you have to be tougher. That's why I'm junior vice-president at age twenty-three. In two or three years I'll have Mr. Corben's job. And when I'm thirty, I'll be a millionaire. When you're thirty, you'll probably be only twenty-eight."

Billy shrugged. "Well, you have my blessing, Ger," he said evenly.

"Don't call me that. My name's Gerald."

"Sure, Ger."

At that moment Kate passed nearby with a tray and drinks, wearing an apron on which DORRY'S PUB was emblazoned in large green letters. Gerald spun his head and snapped his fingers in her direction. With a tight smile, she moved to the table.

"I'll have an Irish coffee," Gerald ordered. "But don't pour the Irish whiskey in the coffee. Bring it in a separate glass and I'll do it."

Kate nodded, looked at Billy. "You all right?" she asked.

"Fine," he said.

Glancing at the drawing in his lap, she turned her head sideways and smiled. "Do I sense some hostility there?" she murmured slyly.

"Hostility but no talent," Gerald countered.

"I think it's good," Kate said.

"Then you're still into comic books," Gerald sneered.

Billy, somewhat embarrassed by Kate's praise and intimidated by Hopkins's arrogance, tried to change the subject. He succeeded only in blurting an obvious statement that Gerald gleefully pounced on.

"I guess you're working tonight," he said to Kate.

"No, dummy," Gerald interjected. "She's modeling aprons."

"Every weeknight," Kate said, ignoring him. "So Dorry won't have to pay an extra waitress."

"No pay?" Gerald said. "You work for free? Suppose everybody did that! It's ridiculous. Maybe there's a young mother out there who could use the money."

"Dorry's got to save as much money as he can or Mrs. Deagle will close down this place pretty soon. So everybody's pitching in to help. It's not a matter of keeping a paying job from someone else. If this place closes down, a lot of jobs will go."

"I think it's great," Billy said.

"It's dumb economically," Gerald muttered. "If a business can't make it without help from charity, it deserves to go under."

"I'll get your Irish coffee," Kate said, turning to leave.

"Wait a minute," Gerald said in a softer tone. "You don't have to get all bent out of shape because I'm practical. Actually, it's a very nice thing you're doing."

"Thank you," Kate replied.

Gerald reached out to touch her arm. "Hey, Kate," he said. "You haven't seen my new apartment."

"I haven't seen your old apartment," she countered.

"That's right," he retorted. "The lights were out."

Seeing the fire in her eyes, Gerald laughed elaborately. "Just kidding," he said. "But why don't we have dinner tomorrow night, just the two of us?"

"I'd love to, but I've got to work."

"Tell Dorry you're sick. He won't be able to dock you."

Kate smiled mirthlessly, shook her head no, and left. Gerald watched her with smoldering, lustful eyes. Then he looked at Billy in a conspiratorial manner. "You think she's got something going with Dorry?" he asked.

"Dorry?" Billy laughed. "He's in his forties, maybe old enough to be her grandfather."

"Why else would she work for free?"

"You ever hear of the Christmas spirit?" Billy challenged.

"Only the kind that comes in a bottle." Gerald smiled.

"I'm sorry for you."

"Don't be."

Billy swallowed the last of his beer, threw a dollar on the table, and stood up. "That's for Kate," he said. "And thanks a lot for the drink, Ger."

"I told you never to—"

But Billy didn't hear the rest. He was already halfway to the door. As he reached out to push it open, he spotted Kate coming out of the back room and into the bar. She smiled warmly at him and winked.

It was chilly outside, but during his walk home Billy hardly felt it.

CHAPTER SEVEN

Lynn Peltzer always felt an extra twinge of nervousness around Christmas time. It hadn't always been that way. Growing up in a suburb of Pittsburgh, she had been a fairly normal child of a middle-class family. Christmas excited her because she usually received some new clothes and a few special things. In addition, she enjoyed picking out presents for other people, anticipating their joy as they opened them. Though not especially religious, she also enjoyed the holiday because it seemed symbolic of new hope, kindness, and generosity.

Not until she met Rand Peltzer did she begin to associate Christmas with danger.

Neither he nor she had intended it to happen that way. Nearly a quarter century before, when they were married, both of them had had high expectations that someday Rand would have his face on the cover of *Time* magazine. He had not gone to college, but when he patented a simple device that made it easier for laundries to locate their customers' clothes, he seemed to be on his way. Taking a smooth-talking friend's advice, Rand quit his job in the sporting goods department of a large store and "invested in himself," as he put it. His lifelong desire was to be another Thomas Edison, and to that end he forthwith applied himself. The money ran out soon, most of the inventions gathered dust, and eventually he was forced to find a job selling other people's wares, but Rand never really gave up. Working in his spare time, he continued to conceive and construct new instruments to benefit society.

The problem was that they were usually tested first on Lynn, and almost always as Christmas presents.

The first year Lynn received an automatic, "painless" ear-piercing device for use in the home. It sent Lynn to the hospital emergency room Christmas night and it was well after New Year's before she could remove the bandages from her earlobes. The next year an improved fingernail polish remover caused something strange and crusty to grow on her nails and remain there for several months. Other devices, such as pineapple parers, automatic shoe buffers, cleaning poles capable of reaching anywhere, and fish cleaners, all came neatly wrapped at Christmas, were duly tried, failed, and recalled for "improvements." Most, fortunately, never saw the light of day again. A good sport, Rand shook his head and endured the jokes generated by his failures, but the light bulb of inspiration never left its permanent spot above his head.

Lynn wondered what it would be this year. Her wonder was not alloyed with dread but with uncertainty. It would be nice to prepare herself if that was possible.

The real problem, she supposed, was that she simply couldn't tell Rand to just stop inventing things and trying them out on her. She loved the big guy and if he ever gave up this quirky habit, it would kill her. Such feelings of love, however, did not cause her to flinch less as the annual day of present-giving approached.

"It'll be all right," she said aloud to herself, adding optimistically: "Last year was easy with the tomato dicer. We had the ceiling cleaned in minutes, washed our faces, and that was that."

Removing the meat loaf from the oven, she caught a glimpse of herself in the glass door. With her styled gray hair and face that was marred only by "character lines" (no sense calling them wrinkles just yet), she was remarkably well preserved for forty-seven. She was reasonably content with life and well aware of the fact that whatever excitement was due her had probably happened already, but she often wondered how things would have turned out if she had been the breadwinner instead of Rand. He was tenacious, but she was a fighter. He traveled circuitous routes; she bored straight ahead. Sometimes Lynn wondered how she would have handled herself if, not having been born several decades too soon, she had been drafted into the army and asked to fight for her country. Surprisingly, the idea intrigued rather than repelled or frightened her.

"Too late now," she said, looking at the clock.

Billy was already late for dinner, even considering the fact that he had to walk home. As for Rand, there was no telling when he would walk in.

A moment later she heard the front door open and, a beat after that, the clatter of an object hitting the floor of the living room. Those crossed swords again, Lynn thought with a sigh, putting the meat loaf on the counter and moving to the hallway.

Billy was in the process of picking up the swords and restoring them to the shaky holder, which had been designed by Rand in a moment of inspiration. ("Anybody can drive a nail into the wall and hold up those swords," he had argued. "It takes a genius to create a decorative holder that doesn't damage the plaster.") No doubt about it, Lynn mused as she watched Billy delicately restore the balance of power against the wall, that holder is beautiful and doesn't hurt the wall. But it sure makes a racket when one or both of those swords hit the floor, especially when it happens in the middle of the night.

"Hi, Mom." Billy smiled, taking off his jacket, aiming it for a chair, then taking it to the hall closet.

"Dinner's ready," she said.

"O.K.," he said. "I'll be there in a minute."

"Before you go . . ."

He waited, framed in the doorway. Her expression told him that something was wrong—not tragic but definitely unpleasant.

"I got a call from Mrs. Deagle this afternoon," Lynn began.

"Oh." Billy walked to the kitchen.

"I know she's a terrible person, Billy, but it seems you go out of your way to make her angry."

"No, I don't, Mom. She's just mean and out to get me. She'd like to get everybody."

"She says you broke her ceramic snowman."

"It was broken already. Barney must have bumped it. Did she tell you I saved one of her cats from being run over by a car?"

"No."

"See? She only tells you the bad stuff."

"Nevertheless—"

The sound of the front door opening interrupted their conversation, which would have been drowned anyway by Rand's booming voice. "Silent night, holy night!" he sang, giving the old song an uncharacteristically upbeat tempo. "Fa la la la la, la la la la!"

"Let's not talk about it now," Lynn said softly. "Not in front of your father."

"We still have a minute," Billy said, smiling, "while he puts the sword back."

As if in echo, there followed the sound of the front door closing and the crash of metal a moment later. Rand's singing immediately became louder, undercut by the sound of the sword being returned to its shaky position against the wall.

"Sleep in heavenly peace! Fa la la!"

Smiling and ebullient, Rand entered the kitchen, his arms loaded with packages. After putting them carefully on the kitchen table, he gave Lynn a kiss, Billy a hug, and Barney a pat on the head.

"Have a nice trip?" Lynn asked.

"Not bad," he replied. "Miracle, the company that makes the Kitchen Companion, might be interested in the Bathroom Buddy. It's got one or two problems I have to iron out, though."

Lynn suspected there wouldn't be a sale. They would muddle through, however, and Christmas wasn't the time to worry about long-range economics. You could drive yourself crazy. It was nice having Rand home and, for the moment, that was all that mattered.

He picked a package off the table and thrust it at her. Automatically, Lynn flinched, then took it.

"It's just a poinsettia," Rand said. "Not a real present. You'll get that later."

"Oh, thank you," she murmured, putting the potted flower on the sink. "It's beautiful."

"What's in the other packages?" Billy asked.

Rand walked back to the table. "These are presents for you and your mom that can't be opened until Christmas," he answered. "This one can't wait."

He gently lifted the burlap-covered box.

"What is it?" Billy asked. "Is it alive?"

"Turn off the lights," Rand said. Then, realizing that the kitchen's light came solely from a bright overhead incandescent lamp, he shook his head. "Never mind. It'll be easier if we go in the living room."

"He must have gotten me a pet bat," Billy laughed, as they left the kitchen.

Placing the cage on the coffee table, Rand surveyed the living room lighting. "Still too bright," he said. "Where's that light dimmer I made?"

Lynn swallowed a bit nervously. "I put it in the drawer," she explained. "It was making sounds all by itself, and when it was out, the lights kept blinking on and off."

"You don't know how to work it," Rand said, reaching into the drawer.

"Never mind," Billy said. "I'll turn the lights down."

Rand waved him back into his chair. "Listen," he announced in a soft but firm tone, "I go to the trouble of making these things so we can relax. They're labor-saving devices, see? What's the point of having them if you keep on doing things the old-fashioned way?"

With that, he pointed the flashlightlike device he had located at the nearest lamp.

Shattering with a loud popping noise, as if it had been the target of an unseen sniper, the bulb died instantly, its remains tinkling onto the end table, which was suddenly gripped by darkness.

"That's no problem," Rand murmured. "That bulb was about to go anyway."

"I'll clean it up later," Lynn soothed. "First let's see what's in the package."

"Yeah," Billy seconded. "This will be the first time I've ever gotten a present that glows in the dark."

Kneeling next to the end table, he reached out and gently

lifted the burlap. The creature was predominantly brown and white, about eight inches tall with long pointed ears and huge brown expressive eyes. Standing upright like a human being, its body was covered with fluffy fur except for bare spots at the ends of the ears, the extensions of its four-fingered hands, and a quadrilateral space for a moist pug nose and wide mouth resembling that of an elderly gentleman enjoying the luxury of not wearing his dentures. A low noise emanated from the animal, something haunting but softly urgent.

"What is it?" Billy asked, amazed.

"Your new pet," his father replied.

"It looks like something from Australia," Lynn said, moving closer to the cage. "Or Red China. They have a lot of animals there that can't get visas."

Barney looked sideways at his new companion, backed away a few steps. It looked so soft and gentle, but from dealing with squirrels, he knew that the cute ones had the most devilish tricks. A low growl rose involuntarily from his chest.

"C'mon, Barney," Billy laughed. "Be a good boy. He's not gonna hurt you."

Returning his attention to the strange animal, Billy put his finger gingerly through the holes in the box to touch it. Surprisingly, the creature did not flinch or cower. Its fur was warm and downy, like that of a Persian cat.

"Where'd you find him?" Billy asked.

"Some old junk store in Chinatown. Had to lay down a bundle for him, too."

Lynn looked closely at the creature. "Did he come with papers?" she asked.

Rand shook his head.

"Well, suppose he has rabies or something," his wife persisted. "Doesn't he need shots? Is he housetrained?"

"I guess we'll find out soon enough," Rand muttered.

"Honey, I didn't have time to check that out. I was worried they wouldn't let him on the plane. As it was, I had to smuggle him aboard in my garment bag. Don't worry. He'll be all right."

But Lynn was not to be assured so easily. "What if he's some kind of rat or something?" she sniffed.

Billy, tickling Gizmo's chin, looked askance at his mother. "No, he's too cute to be a rat," he said.

Lynn shrugged. "He's cute, all right. But I sure hope he's not carrying something. And speaking of that, how can we be sure he's a he?"

"The Chinese fella told me it's a he," Rand replied.

"A he what?" Billy asked. "Didn't he say what kind of animal he is?"

"Yeah. He's a Mogwai . . ."

"What's that?"

"I don't know. It's something in Chinese, I think. Anyway, we'll call him Gizmo, O.K.?"

"Why not?" Billy said. "That's as good as anything, and since we don't know what he is, it sure fits."

Gizmo, more at ease now around his new family, had started to hum in his unearthly falsetto tone. The three were delighted and amused by the sound, Billy breaking into applause. Only the four-legged creature remained aloof and in the background.

"Well, Merry Christmas," Rand said.

Billy gave him a hug. "Thanks a lot, Dad," he said, smiling. "It's really a wonderful present."

"Glad you like it, son."

When she saw Billy lift the creature from the box and cuddle it to his chest, Lynn couldn't resist the urge to capture the moment on film. Reaching quickly into the drawer, she brought out her Instamatic camera, slid back a few feet until she had Gizmo and Billy neatly framed, then glanced out of the viewfinder.

"O.K., smile!" she said.

As Gizmo reached up to lick Billy's cheek, Lynn pressed the button. As the flashbulb went off, Gizmo let out a wild shriek, threw himself over Billy's shoulder, and, whining piteously, scrambled beneath the sofa.

"What happened?" Lynn asked.

"Forgot to tell you," Rand replied. "The little fella's scared of bright lights. That's why I turned the lights down, but I forgot about the flashbulb."

As he talked, he fumbled beneath the sofa until he found Gizmo's foot. "C'mon, boy," he soothed. "It's O.K. It'll be all right. We won't do that again. Promise."

Gentle urging finally calmed Gizmo to the point where he allowed himself to be slid from the cool dark comfort beneath the sofa. His humming had stopped, though, and he shivered slightly.

"Still a little scared, I guess," Billy said. He stroked Gizmo's head gently.

"I should've told you about the light," Rand said. "There's a couple other rules to remember about this guy. At least that's what the Chinese boy said. Number two is to keep him away from water. And number three is, never let him eat after midnight."

Lynn broke into laughter. "That's the craziest thing I've ever heard," she said. "What difference could it make when he eats?"

"Don't ask me," Rand replied. "I'm just tellin' you what was said to me."

Lynn stood up. "O.K., we'll go along with that. I just hope he doesn't have to eat filet mignon every night."

"No, he eats anything," Rand said. "No restriction on that. As a matter of fact, the boy's grandfather said he even ate cardboard, that white stuff they pack boxes with, and a rubber washer. He probably has a stomach like the town incinerator."

"He ate a washer?" Billy repeated.

"That's what the man said."

Billy reached into the magazine rack adjoining the sofa and found a crumpled piece of cardboard. Rolling it into a ball, he offered it to the furry creature.

"Here, Gizmo," he said. "Try this for a snack."

Gizmo sniffed at the pulpy white mass. Many years before, on a whim, he had decided to humor the Chinese man by eating a tasteless object. He had enjoyed seeing the old man's pleasure and, fortunately, it was a pleasure that was not perpetrated on him very often. That was because the Chinese gentleman had a sense of responsibility and self-control. Rapidly assessing his new situation, Gizmo doubted seriously that these people would be able to restrict themselves quite as well. If he gave in to them now, before long they would have him eating every insipid piece of junk they could find, just to have a laugh. No, clearly this was the time to train these new owners and train them right. Turning aside, he refused to have anything to do with the cardboard.

"I guess he's not hungry," Billy said. "Either that or the Chinese man was pullin' your leg."

Lynn returned from the kitchen holding a small slice of meat loaf in the palm of her hand. "Let's see what he does with this," she said.

Gizmo sniffed, quivered with anticipation a moment, then snapped up the delicious morsel and forced himself to chew slowly so as to savor it. By the time he swallowed the mouthful, his contented hum had returned.

The family seemed pleased. Gizmo was pleased, too. At least with this group he'd never swallow another petroleum-based product again.

CHAPTER EIGHT

The few days remaining before Christmas passed quickly, except for the youngsters of Kingston Falls Junior-Senior High School. Because of a heavy early snowfall in November, which had canceled classes for nearly a week, the pre-Christmas vacation had been shortened by two days, which meant that classes seemed to drag on interminably. If the kids didn't like this state of affairs, Roy Hanson liked it even less. Getting their attention was difficult enough under the best of circumstances; breaking through the wall of lethargy so close to Christmas was another definition of impossible.

Still, one had to try. That was part of the challenge of teaching, and if there was one thing Roy Hanson liked, it was a challenge. The first black instructor at an exclusive private school in the county, he had left there three years ago to become only the second black teacher in Kingston Falls. Now, at thirty-four, he was recognized as one of the best biology and natural science instructors in the area. Tall and stockily built, he was a teacher with whom few students messed. Corporal punishment in the public schools was a thing of the past, of course, but at times Hanson could be so aroused by an uncooperative student that some wondered if there might not be a one-day revival. Keeping the class members a bit nervous—particularly the potential trouble-makers—was part of Hanson's strategy, and it generally worked. Soon he had no undercurrents of cross talk to compete with and certainly no overt wisecracks. That was exactly the way he wanted it.

There were limits, of course. He could command their attention but not necessarily their interest. Recognizing this, he decided to abandon their study of the circulatory system of the frog in favor of an illustrated talk he had worked up dealing with "new" animals. It was a pet (so to speak) topic to which he had dedicated considerable research. Someday he hoped to sell it as an article or monograph in a scholarly magazine. One thing was sure: if he could raise these students from their lethargy with it, it had to have something.

"We hear a lot about animals becoming extinct," he began, "but what we don't hear much about is some new animals which have only recently been discovered. In 1812, a scientist named Georges Cuvier announced that every species that existed on earth had been discovered already. But he was wrong."

Pressing the slide-changing button, he produced a photo of a deerlike animal with long wavy horns.

"Anybody know the name of this animal?" he asked.

No one did.

"It's called an okapi, and it's a close relation to the giraffe. Man didn't see his first live okapi until 1900."

He changed the slide. "Anyone know the name of this animal?" he asked.

No one did.

He told them about the mountain nyala, pygmy hippo-potamus, Komodo dragon, Andean wolf, Congo peacock, kouprey, coelacanth, and long-nosed peccary, all of which had been discovered—or rediscovered—during the twentieth century. No one knew anything and no one volunteered any questions.

Except Pete Fountaine.

"Mr. Hanson?" he said.

Hanson nodded, silently thankful that someone had gotten more out of his lecture than twenty minutes' worth of daydreaming.

"Yes?"

"Is it worth anything if you discover a new animal?"

It was, Roy Hanson thought, a surprisingly good question. Embarrassingly, he didn't know the answer.

"I really guess it depends," he replied. "I suppose if you found one animal that the government or a zoo wanted very badly, you could sell it for a good sum. Most scientists are more interested in the glory that goes with such a discovery, though."

"That would mean money, wouldn't it?" Pete persisted. "I mean, they could go on TV and recommend pet food and stuff."

The class giggled, Roy Hanson smiled, and Pete beamed at having created a joke without having to brave the teacher's wrath.

A mild chain reaction was caused by Pete's question. One student asked where you could go in the hopes of finding a new species; another asked how you could tell if an animal was "new" or just something strange he had never seen before. It was all academic, of course, since there was practically no chance a person would casually encounter a new species. Such spontaneous interest in a topic was rare, so rare that Roy Hanson encouraged the discussion to go on until the bell ended the class.

"Tomorrow we'll get back to the frog," he said, smiling when the class emitted a predictable groan.

As he turned his attention to some papers on his desk, he caught a glimpse of Pete Fountaine about to leave. He smiled and gave him a little wave.

Pete smiled slightly in response, the most that he would allow himself lest some other student accuse him of playing up to the teacher. Outside, he continued to feel good about the attention he had gotten and discussion he had generated. He was feeling so good, in fact, that he decided to go visit Billy Peltzer after putting in a couple of hours as a Christmas tree.

For the past few days Billy had gotten up early and returned home as soon as he finished work at the bank. The reason, of course, was Gizmo. He was such a fascinating creature Billy wanted to be with him every minute. He was vulnerable, too. Once, while shaving (with Gizmo watching contentedly), Billy had accidentally turned the mirror so that it caught the hallway light and reflected it back at Gizmo. Shrieking loudly as the beam of bright light blinded him, Gizmo had toppled from the edge of Billy's desk into the waste can—falling on his head.

By the time Billy got to him, the tiny creature was bruised, bleeding, and quivering with shock and fear. He was in such a bad state that even Barney, still chafing with jealousy, whined in sympathy. Billy wrapped the wound in a bandage, talked soothingly to him for a long time, and eventually lulled him to sleep.

The next day Gizmo was markedly better. Billy was glad, for he would not enjoy taking Gizmo to a veterinarian who would have no idea what sort of animal he was.

"Watch Gizmo for me, will you, Mom?" Billy called as he left the house for work.

"Why?" she asked. "He's in the cage, isn't he?"

"Yeah, but with that cut on his head and all . . ."

"O.K. I'll drop in every once in a while and see how he's doing," she promised. "And we can keep the hot line open to the vet."

"Thanks, Mom."

He arrived at work early, a habit he'd taken up since the incident with Mrs. Deagle. The door to Roland Corben's office was open, but no one else seemed to be in the bank. Hearing a rustle of paper, he hung up his coat and looked around for the source of the sound.

"Billy?" he heard Kate's voice whisper.

She was in Corben's office. On the desk was a large map of Kingston Falls, detailed enough to include every street, home, and business. Some of the buildings were marked in red, all included in a section bounded by a dotted black line. Kate was staring down at the map, her lips tight and eyes blazing.

"Have you seen this?" she asked.

Billy shrugged. "Kingston Falls," he murmured. "Yeah. I've been there."

She didn't appreciate his flippancy. "Look at the places in red," she said.

"What's it mean?" he asked.

"Those are the homes of people who are renting or leasing from Mrs. Deagle. Most of them are people who are out of work, laid off, or just can't afford to keep up the payments. And Mrs. Deagle is taking advantage of that."

"How? She can't evict all those people at once."

"The heck she can't."

"But then who would pay the rent?"

"She doesn't need the rent money. It looks like she's interested in a takeover. Here." Kate put her finger on one of the squares. "Your house is in red, and so's mine."

"Yeah. But Dad's not that far behind in the payments. Just one or two."

"Neither is my family. In fact, we're in O.K. shape."

"So what does the red mean?"

"I think it means property she can take over in a hurry if she wants to. Something about options."

"But what's she gonna do with all of them?"

"She wants to own everything..."

"Why? What for?"

"I heard them talking in the office a few days ago," Kate whispered. "Mrs. Deagle's been having meetings with the president of Hitox Chemical. She wants to sell them the land."

"So they can build a plant here?" Billy murmured, aghast. Kate nodded.

"It's like a big Monopoly game to her," he said. "We're just pieces of paper to buy and sell."

"You got it," Kate replied. "We've got to stop her, Billy."

"You and me?"

"For starters. Somebody's got to do something."

"Yeah, but what?"

"That's what I say—what?" a familiar voice asked.

The response to Billy's query came not from Kate, but from Gerald Hopkins, who had entered quietly while the young couple were bent over the map. As they turned to look at him, their expressions surprised and discomfited, he was in his glory. For the moment, at least, they were in his power.

"Snooping, eh?" He smiled.

Kate and Billy merely stared at him, there being no logical way they could deny their action.

"Mr. Corben doesn't like snoopy employees," Gerald said as he slowly took off his coat and hung it in the closet. Enjoying the game of cat and mouse, he looked at Kate through narrowed eyelids. "But maybe I don't have to tell him," he added meaningfully.

Kate didn't answer.

"You busy tonight?" Gerald asked.

"I'm busy every night," she replied. With a toss of her head, she stormed out of the office.

Gerald watched her go. Then, turning to face Billy, he forced a smile.

"I like her," he said. "She's tough. Just like me."

"Just like you, Ger," Billy repeated derisively.

"I told you not to call me that."

"Sorry, Ger, I keep forgetting." Billy smiled as he strolled out of the office.

He and Kate had little chance to discuss the problem the rest of the day, although Billy thought about it quite a bit. Did it mean his family would be thrown out on the street? If so, where would they ever find a place as nice as their present home? Depressed at the end of the working day, Billy went directly home, hoping to find some solace in Gizmo or the new cartoon strip he was working on.

Arriving home, he first went upstairs to check on Gizmo, who was sleeping peacefully, a happy smile on his face. Feeling a little better, he returned to the kitchen to find something good to eat.

The refrigerator didn't offer much that interested him. He sighed.

"Have an orange," his mother suggested.

Billy shrugged, took an orange from the refrigerator, and moved gingerly toward the unusual-looking appliance that sat on top of the counter.

"I think you can use it now." Lynn smiled, no doubt sensing his nervousness. "Your father tinkered with it last night and it peeled an orange perfectly."

"One orange," Billy said, grinning. "Out of how many?"

"Don't ask," she said.

Shrugging again, he opened the top of the device, across

the side of which was inscribed *Peltzer Peeler-Juicer,* flipped the switch to PEEL, and placed the orange in the stainless-steel bowl provided for it. Closing the lid, he pushed the START switch.

The appliance immediately began to shake and make gurgling noises. Billy moved several feet away, experience having taught him that Dad's machines often had a way of giving one an impromptu shower. This time, however, it seemed to be working. From the bottom of the device a perfectly dry spiral of rind slowly unwound itself.

"Hey," Billy exclaimed. "It peeled it perfectly."

The machine shut itself off and Billy opened the lid.

Nothing was inside.

"Where's the orange?" he demanded, turning the machine on edge, shaking it, hitting its sides.

"It's supposed to be in the top," his mother said.

"No," he replied. "It's not there. The darn thing peeled the orange and then ate it itself."

"Maybe that's what it's supposed to do," Lynn laughed. "It's an automatic orange-eating machine."

They were still giggling a moment later when a knock sounded at the front door.

"Anybody home?" Pete Fountaine asked, poking his head inside.

"Sure, come on in, Pete," Billy said.

"I brought you that tree your ma said she liked the other day," he said, dragging a Scotch pine behind him.

After replacing the sword, which had fallen right on cue, they set up the tree and studied it.

"Maybe I'd better see if I can get this trimmed before your father gets home," Lynn said. "I think he's been fooling around with something that hangs the tinsel automatically, and I'd rather not have him try it out."

"Would you like us to help?" Pete asked politely.

"Not necessary. Thanks, though," she said. "Why don't you go upstairs and look at Gizmo?"

"That's right." Billy smiled, snapping his fingers. "I've got a new pet."

"Oh, yeah?" Pete said. "What is it?"

"I don't know. Nobody knows."

"Come on," Pete said skeptically.

"I'm not kidding," Billy insisted. "Come on upstairs and see for yourself."

Halfway up the steps, Pete said in a confidential tone of voice, "I called up Mary Ann Fabrizio last night. Asked her for a date."

"Yeah? How'd it go?" Billy asked.

"Well, I was all ready to be smooth and confident, just like you said. But when she answered, I couldn't remember my name."

Billy laughed.

"So I said 'wrong number' in a real high voice and hung up," Pete continued. "Maybe I'll try again in a couple of days. Give her time to forget the voice."

"Well, good luck," Billy said. "Just try to remember that you're doing her a favor."

"Yeah. If I can remember my name."

They entered the darkened room and made their way to the bedstand, on which Gizmo's cage sat. Pete, who shared a room with his two brothers, was impressed with all the privacy Billy had. For one thing, there was a double bed, all for himself. And Billy could arrange things just the way he wanted. Walking slowly, taking it all in, Pete was fascinated by the walls, which were covered with comic strips, medieval drawings, Frazetta paintings of warriors. On the dresser was a miniature suit of armor, and farther on, a big drawing table covered with pens, pencils, erasers, a large green paper cutter, paintbrushes soaking in cans, and a stack of drawings with an elaborate title page reading *The Secret of the Dragon's Lair*. Below it Billy had signed his name. Pete's mouth dropped open slowly.

"Golly," he said. "You're really good."

Billy smiled.

"Thanks. It'll look even better when I smooth out those colors."

Somewhat embarrassed at the praise, Billy was thankful that Gizmo let out a high-pitched chirping noise, attracting both his and Pete's attention. The television set next to the bed was on, showing an old movie with Clark Gable as a racing car driver, and Gizmo was watching with intense interest, almost as if he were a human being.

"Holy cow, what's that?" Pete whispered.

"It's my new pet. We call him Gizmo."

"Where'd you get it?"

"My dad brought it back from Chinatown."

The two boys went to the edge of the bed, Pete kneeling so as to get a better look at the furry creature.

"You keep him in the cage all the time?" he asked.

"No. Just while I'm at work. We're afraid he might get into things. You see, he's very delicate, can't stand light and—"

The telephone rang. Billy answered it and was delighted to hear the sound of Kate's voice. As she proceeded to tell him some more scuttlebutt she had picked up at Dorry's Pub concerning Mrs. Deagle's plan, Billy gently lifted Gizmo from the box and held him in his lap. Pete moved closer so he could stroke the animal and listen to the contented sounds he made.

"What happened between you and Gerald after I left?" Kate asked finally.

"Nothing much. I called him Ger a few times, that's all."

He handed Gizmo to Pete and leaned back against the pillow, enjoying this moment with Kate. He liked being her

secret ally in the war against Mrs. Deagle, even if he had
no idea what to do to thwart her takeover plan. Kate had
plenty of ideas, however, most involving petitions and getting the story to newspapers and television people. As he
listened to her, Billy kept one eye on Pete and Gizmo. To
give him some privacy, Pete had moved toward the drawing
board and window, but as it was dark out, Billy saw no
cause for alarm.

"Why don't you drop by the pub when I get off and we'll
talk some more about it?" Kate asked.

"Well—" Billy stammered, suddenly realizing that she
was very nearly asking him for a date. "What time?"

"I get off at eleven," she said.

"Sure, O.K.," he murmured.

"If that's too late, it can keep," she added. "You don't
sound too hot on the idea."

"Oh, no," he replied. "I was just surprised."

"At what?"

"Never mind. We'll talk about it later."

"O.K.," she said. "If you can't make it, it's all right."

"No, it's—"

He saw the situation developing in the same sort of slow-
motion action they use to show football and basketball
replays: Gizmo seated on the drawing table top . . . Pete
stroking him . . . the edge of Pete's jacket sleeve catching on
the paint can with soaking brushes inside . . . the can tipping . . . a drop of water falling to the floor . . . then another,
larger mass of water slopping over the rim . . .

Toward Gizmo's back!

"No!" he heard himself shout.

It was too late. As the water struck the tiny creature's
back, Billy shouted "Accident!" into the telephone, hung
up, and hurling himself across the room, tried to wipe the
beading water from Gizmo's body.

A high-pitched scream told him the damage had already

been done. His eyes wider than ever, his spine arched and mouth open, gasping, Gizmo rolled over and over on the drawing board. A crackling sound, like a forest fire, seemed to be coming from his body, forming a hideous counterpoint with his pitiful cries.

"What did I do?" Pete shouted, practically in tears.

"It's the water," Billy yelled back. "It's not your fault. He can't be around water."

Indeed, Gizmo appeared almost ready to burst. Five huge spots had formed on his back where the water had landed, and now they were growing, bloodred and yellow, like mountainous blisters. Spreading and popping like miniature volcanoes, the membranes tightened and stretched until one of them finally burst. A small furry ball popped out, landing on the desk top. Pete and Billy retreated, fascinated and horrified. Another ball popped from a second blister, then a third, fourth, and fifth. The crackling diminished then, as did Gizmo's cries of pain. Billy wondered if he was dying.

In another minute it was all over. Gizmo, his breathing gradually returning to normal, lay quietly as the blistered areas on his back bonded together and began to disappear, like time-lapse photography of a wound healing.

"Thank goodness," Billy breathed. "I think he's all right."

"But what are those things?" Pete asked.

The five balls had already started to grow and form themselves into shapes similar to Gizmo. Soon it was obvious that more Mogwai had been created.

The two boys watched astounded as the creatures grew. "This is better than 'Twilight Zone,'" Pete murmured.

"I just wonder what my folks are gonna say," Billy muttered darkly.

"Maybe they're good to eat," Pete offered.

Now the five newcomers were half as large as Gizmo, who sat watching them with large tearful eyes. Once or twice he glanced at Billy reproachfully, then looked away sadly. Billy wondered if Gizmo was surprised by the incident, or if he had known or sensed that there was a possibility of its happening. Perhaps it had happened before.

Even as they grew, Billy could tell that something was different. The new Mogwai had slightly different coloring than Gizmo, but that wasn't it. There was something strange about the expression on their faces and in their eyes. Though younger than Gizmo, they seemed less innocent. There was a craftiness there Billy had never seen in Gizmo's large brown eyes.

"Can I have one?" Pete asked, interrupting Billy's thoughts.

His first inclination was to say yes. Why not? If one of Gizmo was enough, six was certainly an excess. Yet Billy had no desire, having been careless once, to compound his error. Snatching up the paint can and mopping up every bead of water, he watched as the five new Mogwai continued to approximate Gizmo's size.

"I guess not," he said finally. "This may be a nightmare, you know. Until we find out, I think it's best to keep them all here."

Pete nodded thoughtfully. "Maybe we should take one to Mr. Hanson and find out if it's a new species or not."

"That's a good idea," Billy replied.

"We could be rich and famous."

Billy wasn't so sure. Everything had happened so fast. Suppose instant reproduction occurred again? He remembered the "Star Trek" episode in which the cuddly creatures known as tribbles practically took over the entire spaceship. He had a quick vision of Mogwai stopping up the pipes of his home, lying wall-to-wall in every room and hallway, a blanket of squealing animals crying out for food even as they continued multiplying. Suppose more of them made them dangerous in some way? If they took over neighbors' homes, would the police arrest Billy for starting the problem? And, on a more immediate level, what explanation could he give Mom and Dad? He had been careless and violated the Chinese boy's admonition. To Pete, the new arrivals added up to being rich and famous. To Billy, they spelled nothing but trouble.

CHAPTER NINE

After Pete left, Billy sat on the edge of the bed for a long time, trying to think as he watched the five new Mogwai reach maturity. Logic indicated that he should report what had happened to his parents immediately. He had not done such a terrible thing, after all, nothing more than relax his vigilance for a moment. The Chinese boy said to keep Gizmo away from water. But the Chinese man also said Gizmo ate rubber washers and cardboard, information that turned out to be false. How could he have known that such a minor oversight could lead to the creation of five new creatures?

Although logic was on his side, Billy nevertheless needed time to think. For a brief while, at least, he wanted to see if he could solve the problem himself. Pete had made one good suggestion. As soon as possible, one of the Mogwai should go to Mr. Hanson for scientific study. He wondered if some laboratories or zoos might be interested, also. Surely in a world filled with thousands of stray cats and dogs it would be possible to find a good place to unload the five new Mogwai.

He was already sure of one thing: he did not like the new additions very much. They seemed combative, uncontrollable, and, compared to Gizmo, aggressive. When they finished growing, Billy found a large cardboard box and put them inside, but they indicated their displeasure at confinement by gesticulating angrily, baring their teeth, and sticking their tongues out at him. The leader of the new group seemed to be a slightly larger one with a thick white stripe of coarse fur standing up from its head.

"I'll call you Stripe, O.K.?" Billy whispered, trying to strike up a friendship with the new Mogwai.

In response, Stripe knocked over an ink bottle with a quick swipe of his paw.

As it drained down the side of the drawing board, Billy noted with horror that some of the liquid had spilled onto Stripe, Gizmo, and one other new Mogwai. Silently and nervously he watched the ink spots to see if anything happened. A few moments passed and nothing changed; apparently only water made them reproduce.

"At least that's one break," he sighed with relief.

Not long afterward, when it became obvious the new arrivals were hungry, Billy went down to the kitchen and brought up some cold chicken for them. Unlike Gizmo, who ate in a slow and civilized manner, the new Mogwai slurped and tore noisily at the food, spitting out gristle and letting saliva drain from the corners of their mouths. Filled, they belched grossly and then began to play with each other by spitting bits of food.

"Hey, Gizmo," Billy said, "isn't there some way you can help me make these guys behave?"

Gizmo's sad eyes told him more than he cared even to suspect.

Fortunately, his parents had gone out for dinner. That meant he could delay his explanation and at least have time to form an idea of how difficult the new arrivals would be. He learned immediately that food made them drowsy; after gorging themselves and playing briefly, the five new Mogwai curled up in the box and went to sleep.

Gizmo, like Billy, remained awake, watching them. His expression was a mixture of apprehension and sadness, the same emotions he had worn during his first half hour in the Peltzer home. Billy wondered how much he knew. Was the downward curl of his mouth caused by knowledge or merely jealousy? He would have given a week's pay to be able to have a meaningful conversation with his furry friend, but of course that was impossible.

Pondering the problem, Billy drifted off to sleep. But not to rest, for his mind provided him only more anxiety. In one nightmare, the Mogwai had continued growing until they were as large as his house; in another, which followed immediately, they were spitting fire and hurling bits of flame no larger than jelly beans, which clung to people like napalm.

Billy awoke with a start, experienced a moment of relief, and then became aware of a new terror. The room was completely dark. The small lamp on his desk and another on his drawing board, both of which had been on when he fell asleep, were off. No light entered the room except a thin parallelogram of illumination from outside. Was it possible that both bulbs had blown simultaneously? Even as he tried to convince himself such was the case, Billy knew the odds against it were astronomical.

In the background, from beyond the first layer of darkness, he could hear a rustling sound, a muffled voice, the sort of noise you hear at a surprise party, when everyone is huddled in corners trying not to laugh or move. It was eerie. For a long moment he lay unmoving on the bed, his ears straining to pick up a recognizable sound. At the same time, he moved his eyes from side to side as his vision adjusted to the darkness, hoping he could discover what was going on.

A minute passed and he relaxed. He had awakened, he told himself, in a fearful and susceptible mood created by the nightmares. Other than that, he was alive and well in his own room. Taking a deep breath, he swung himself off the bed and toward the desk lamp.

Suddenly he collapsed and found himself lying facedown on the rug. His legs were paralyzed!

A chorus of hysterical giggles unlike anything he had ever heard before filled the room. Whatever it was, *they* had caused it.

Dragging himself to his desk, Billy reached up and turned the switch. To his relief, the light went on. Pulling himself to a sitting position, his back against the wall, he looked across the room and then down at his legs.

They were taped together!

He could hardly believe his eyes, but the evidence was clear. Three neat bands of silver tape—one at the ankles, one just below the knees, and a third just above the knees— encircled him. Had he slept that soundly? Or, an even worse thought, were they such dexterous sneaks they had been able to tie him up without his feeling a thing?

Grabbing at the tape, he freed himself, stood up, and looked around. The room seemed different, but he could not figure out exactly how. Moving gingerly, he leaped and did a midair pirouette as something touched his arm.

The object fluttered to the floor. It was nothing more than an old comic strip from the newspaper. But what was it doing—?

Billy looked up and gasped.

The entire ceiling was covered with the array of comic strips, medieval drawings, and Frazetta paintings that he had collected and pinned to one wall of the room. As he surveyed the dangling articles, which in the semidarkness resembled peeling wallpaper, he heard the unearthly giggles again.

"All right," he called out. "It was a great joke. You can come out now."

Going to the wall switch, he turned on the main light and promptly heard the giggles change to cries of pain. Reacting quickly, he flipped the switch off and went to his drawing board.

The addition of the second small light provided enough illumination for him to study the entire room. In one corner two of the new Mogwai sat, one on either side of Gizmo, as if guarding him to make sure he didn't ruin their little jokes. A quick look around, even under the bed and in the closet, failed to turn up the other three. Billy fixed the two newcomers with what he hoped was an intimidating glare.

"O.K., where are your pals?" he demanded.

They looked at one another, twitched their pug noses, and chattered lightly in Mogwai language, studiously ignoring Billy. Gizmo directed a glance at the door, for which he received a couple of not-so-playful pats from his brothers. Or were they sons?

Billy had no time to ponder it. Striding to the door, he turned the knob and pulled.

The door did not open.

Looking downward, Billy soon saw the reason: beneath the door had been jammed bits of erasers from his drawing board as well as rolled-up globs of silver tape. Now Billy was filled with a sense of urgency, if not downright alarm. Their tying him up, turning off the lights, and rearranging his clippings from wall to ceiling were clever pranks, but if they had designated two of their group to lock him in his room, the other three must really be up to something!

Tearing at the tape and erasers, he freed the door and started into the hallway. Thoroughly impressed with the guile of the new Mogwai, he moved carefully, his eyes alert for hidden wires or anything else that could trap him or cause him to fall.

The rest of the house, of course, was in almost total darkness. Proceeding slowly, he turned on small lights as he moved down the hallway and stairs. His first surprise came soon, when he stepped on a plastic cup that had been placed on the steps along with several dozen other pieces of china. The cup rattled to the bottom of the stairway, setting off a chain reaction of giggles from the first-floor area.

Turning right into the living room, Billy spotted the first Mogwai under the sofa, gleefully shredding the evening paper. It was so intent on its work that Billy walked past without attracting its attention. Another Mogwai was in the kitchen, delicately arranging packages on the cupboard shelves so that the slightest touch would send them toppling. The third was in the den, curled up on the sofa watching a rerun of "Gilligan's Island."

Billy breathed a sigh of relief. Although there was some indication of their rooting through things, he could detect no grand scheme or signs of wholesale sabotage. All he had to do now was round them up and clean the mess they had made. But how? The Mogwai moved at a slow pace, owing to their short legs and small size, but five of them were too big an armful.

"Barney's transporter," he whispered, snapping his fingers as the idea struck him.

It was still in the back of the basement, the large plywood box with handles and a lockable lid they had purchased during one period of Barney's life when he absolutely refused to go to the vet's without a struggle. Looking inside, Billy judged it would be large enough for five Mogwai, although sleeping peacefully would require a bit of cooperation. With the top opened, Billy tiptoed up the stairs and slipped into the den.

Catching the first one was easy; it had fallen asleep while watching television. Grasping him firmly beneath the tummy, Billy dropped him into the box, closed the top, and proceeded into the kitchen. That one, the Mogwai he called Stripe, put up more of a battle, but soon he was safely inside the transporter. After grabbing the paper-shredder from beneath the sofa, he retraced his steps to the bedroom where, to his surprise, nothing had changed.

A minute later all five Mogwai were safely in the box. They chattered noisily at him, but he was undismayed. "You can say anything you like," he said. "Nobody will hear you, anyway, because I'm going downstairs to clean up the mess you made."

Only after he had patrolled the entire house and set everything in order did Billy happen to glance at the clock. It was midnight! He'd missed his date with Kate.

"Darn," he muttered.

He wondered if she'd even come close to hearing an excuse such as the one he would have to give if limited to nothing but the truth—that he'd been taped up and otherwise harassed by five strange beings who had been born that very day when some water fell on Gizmo's back.

Somehow he had the feeling she just wouldn't buy it.

Arriving home shortly after one o'clock, Lynn and Rand were both exhausted. The hall light was on but no light came from beneath Billy's door.

"I guess he went to bed hours ago," Rand said, yawning.

He brushed his teeth quickly and undressed, eager to experience their bed's softness. Having already folded back the covers, Lynn gave him a little kiss as she went into the bathroom. Rand stretched, sat on the bed, lifted his perennially aching feet, and slipped them between the sheets.

Suddenly they encountered something cold and hard, causing him to recoil so violently he nearly fell onto the floor.

Billy was up early the next morning, despite sleeping only fitfully. Immediately after being locked in the transporter, the five new Mogwai had tried for nearly an hour to intimidate him with their threatening-sounding gibberish, but he had managed to outlast them. Stripe, the final holdout, had finally given up the ghost with a final snarl and all of them had fallen asleep.

They were somewhat restless but quiet when Billy got up, dressed, and went downstairs.

His mother was in the kitchen, having already made the coffee and set the table for breakfast. She smiled a greeting at Billy, then turned her head slightly sideways.

"Why did you do that last night?" she asked.

"Do what?"

"Put the rack from the oven in our bed."

Billy looked blank for a moment.

"Only you could have done it," Lynn said. "I didn't do it, and your father was so shocked I'm sure he didn't do it."

"Oh."

"What's that mean?" Lynn asked.

"It means I have to talk with you and Dad."

"He's in his workroom."

Rand was at the bench in the incredibly messy basement area that served as his workroom. Years ago he had staked it out and paneled the walls himself, promptly lining them with portraits of Thomas Edison, Elias Howe, Alexander Graham Bell, Samuel F. B. Morse, Guglielmo Marconi, and perhaps his greatest hero, Whitcomb L. Judson. Once, when Billy had asked who he was, Rand had waxed eloquent. "These other men made great contributions and were rewarded with fame," he said. "And there's no doubt the phonograph, sewing machine, telegraph, and wireless have benefited our society. But where would we be without the zipper? That's what Judson gave us, my boy, only they were called 'universal fasteners' or 'slide fasteners' back in the 1890s when he invented them."

Now, bent beneath a giant blueprint of the Bathroom Buddy pinned to the wall above the desk, Rand was tinkering with the strange-looking object which could solve all one's morning grooming problems, providing, of course, one had several engineering degrees and lots of patience.

Billy knocked lightly and entered.

"Just added a new feature to the Bathroom Buddy," Rand said, not looking up from his work. Launching immediately into his sales pitch, he held up the object. "Say you're a few minutes late before that big meeting. You reach up and touch your chin, and . . . Oh, no! You forgot to shave. Now what?"

"Do a lot of people forget to shave before big meetings?" Billy asked ingenuously.

"Sure," Rand replied. "It can happen."

"But then you'd have to forget to shower or take a bath, too, wouldn't you?"

"Not necessarily. Some people shower or bathe the night before, so they'll save time."

Billy nodded.

Looking pleased with himself, as if he'd won a major point in the battle against ignorance, Rand flipped a switch. A tiny double-edged razor appeared from a slot in the side as if by magic.

"Hey, neat." Billy smiled.

He reached out to take the Bathroom Buddy, holding it as if to shave. Then, noticing another button on the side near the razor, he said, "I guess this is for the foam, huh?"

"No—I mean, don't!"

It was too late. Billy had already touched the button, causing a jet of white cream to head for the ceiling. Nearly dropping the Bathroom Buddy, he leaped aside as the spray ricocheted back down at them.

"That's the shaving cream button," Rand said. "But I haven't figured out how to lower the pressure yet."

"Oh."

"Don't worry. I'll get it."

"Yeah, Dad, I'm sure you will."

During the brief pause that followed as Rand wiped the excess foam off his invention, they both remembered something important.

"Oh, Dad—"

"Son—"

"There's something I have to—" they both began.

"Go ahead," Billy said.

"I just wanted to ask why you put that thing in our bed," Rand said.

"That's what I came down to tell you about," Billy explained.

"Well, go ahead," Rand urged a few seconds later, when it was obvious his son was somewhat at a loss for words.

Billy sat down in the workroom's only chair and slowly explained what had happened the night before. His father listened, at first with an incredulous smile, then with growing horror. "You mean the Chinese boy was right?" he asked finally. "That's what water does?—makes them multiply?"

Billy nodded.

"And now we have six?"

He nodded again.

"It's crazy. Animals don't multiply like that."

"I know."

"Where are they now?"

"In my room. I have them locked in that transporter we got for Barney."

"Good."

"They're very anxious to get out," Billy said. "If we try to keep them there all the time, the noise may drive us loony."

"Maybe I'd better have a look."

A minute later, Billy's parents watched as he opened the top of the transporter. Inside sat the five new Mogwai, Stripe in the forefront, their faces innocent and liquid-eyed. Except for a subtle glint in their eyes, they seemed every bit as gentle as Gizmo, as friendly as Barney.

"They're cute." Lynn smiled.

"Yeah," Billy said. "But they're not the same as Gizmo, Mom."

"They're not? How are they different?"

"They're mischievous."

He related what they had done last night in addition to putting the oven rack in his parents' bed. Even Billy had to admit that their actions sounded more like harmless pranks than deeds with malevolent possibilities.

"Maybe they were just nervous and excited," Lynn offered. "After all, it was their first night on earth."

"No, Mom," Billy countered. "There was something about them, something scary."

"Is it still there?"

"Not exactly," he said. "But it is, in a way. You see, they must have decided they didn't like being cooped up in the transporter so they're putting on a good show for you and Dad."

His parents laughed. "Are these dumb animals or college professors?" she asked.

"They're not stupid, Mom. That's why I think we'll have a lot of trouble if they stay here."

"What do you suggest?"

"I don't know. Today Pete's gonna ask Mr. Hanson if he'll study them. Maybe he'll take one and be able to tell us what they are."

"Why not just drop them off at the Humane Society?" Rand asked.

"Because if they're a rare species, they may be valuable," Billy replied.

"Well," Lynn said, "if they're going to be here even a few days, I'll not have them cooped up forever in that box."

"But you can't let them run loose, either," Rand said. "There's the shower, dishwasher, bathroom and kitchen sinks—all those things give out water. If they turn on one of those, we'll be up to our armpits in those gizmos."

"All right." Lynn shrugged. "They can stay in Billy's room for the time being, but not in the box. And just in case they get out, I'll shut the bathroom doors and watch them, O.K.?"

Billy nodded.

Lynn went to the box, opened the lid wide, and reached in to lift Stripe high above her head. His wide mouth forming a benevolent smile, Stripe gurgled cutely, the perfect picture of domesticity.

"He's darling," Lynn said.

Indeed he was, Billy thought. But not during the brief moment when, Lynn and Rand looking at each other, Stripe was able to direct a secret glance at Billy.

Was it a sneer? Something close to a wink? Billy wasn't sure, but he couldn't help feeling apprehensive about the days ahead.

CHAPTER TEN

It was ironic, Gizmo mused sadly. Once again he had become a pariah, if not an object of outright loathing. The process of alienation was a familiar one, but he had been spared it for nearly four decades—since the China Sea crossing, in fact. How strange it was that a gentle and adaptable creature such as himself should be subjected to prejudice only by his own species.

It was at times such as this that he nearly hated Mogturmen, his creator. His genetic miscalculations assured that minority Mogwai, of which Gizmo was one, would be instantly recognized and hated by the majority. Physically they all looked approximately the same; the massive differences were internal, involving character, ambition, desire for peace. So indelibly were these differences etched in the personalities of every Mogwai that there was no hiding or disguising them. Stripe was barely an hour old when he knew Gizmo was one of *them*.

"So," he said coldly, "we've encountered one of the eternal ones. You are that, aren't you?"

Gizmo did not have to respond. Stripe knew the answer even as he asked the question, and it infuriated him.

"It's not fair that you should be allowed such a long life and we such a short one," Stripe hissed in Mogwai words.

"It was an accident of Mogturmen's creative process," Gizmo replied softly.

"You also have more knowledge than we," Stripe charged. "More life and more knowledge. Why don't you share both with us?"

"It's not possible."

"And you're glad it's not possible."

Gizmo shrugged.

"What is the reproductive secret?" Stripe demanded. "You saw how we got here, so you must know."

"Why do you want to know?" Gizmo asked.

"We want there to be more of us. If we're doomed to short lives, at least we can spread our species, enjoy the company of our massed millions."

"It's not a good idea," Gizmo murmured.

"We'll find it out, sooner or later," Stripe hissed.

"I won't tell you," Gizmo said firmly.

Stripe balled his short pointed fingers into something resembling fists. "I want to kill you," he said coldly. "But I can't. Something is holding me back."

"It's the one responsible emotion Mogturmen was able to keep in us," Gizmo explained. "We're incapable of killing each other."

"You have other information we need," Stripe continued. "There's something that can kill us in large doses, cause us pain in smaller doses. What is it?"

"You will find out soon enough."

"Chetz-wubba!" Stripe rasped, swearing in Mogwai. "Why must you be so secretive?"

"It's my only weapon."

"There is another thing we must find out," Stripe persisted. "We are capable of becoming larger and more powerful. What causes that?"

"I can't tell you."

"You can't, or you won't?"

"I won't."

"It's foolish of you to withhold that. Why not use it for yourself at least?"

"Because then I would become one of the majority, with a brief and violent life."

"We'll find out what it is," Stripe promised. "It's a simple thing. Intuitively I know that. It can elude us only so long."

"Perhaps much longer than you think," Gizmo countered. "Perhaps it will elude you for your entire lifetime."

Stripe ground his teeth angrily. "Tell us now and we'll go easy on your friends."

"No. When you change you'll forget. I've seen it happen before."

"Very well," Stripe muttered. "Be uncooperative if you want. But we're going to find out what we need to know to escape these puny bodies and create more of us. And when we do—"

Gizmo managed to face the infuriated Stripe with a determined look. "I think you're going to spend the rest of your lives in this room under very careful supervision," he said evenly. "My new master is a very responsible young man. He's absorbed the Chinese man's wisdom and I seriously doubt he'll give you the opportunity to enjoy your wicked ways."

As he recited the speech, Gizmo did not truly believe his own words, but they sounded persuasive enough.

"But there are the others," Stripe shot back. "They will be careless, especially now that I've instructed my four partners to be judicious in their choice of pranks. Fortunately, your new master corrected the mess we made last night. Seeing that could have put the others on their guard, but now they will let us roam free."

Gizmo sighed. What Stripe said was probably true. His only hope was that time was on his side, that these new Mogwai would expire in captivity before they could do any damage.

A few hours later a smiling Stripe trundled into Billy's room and shook Gizmo awake.

"Clorr is dead," he said simply.

"Now there are only four of you," Gizmo replied. "Why does that seem to make you happy?"

"It's the manner in which he died," Stripe said. "Ever since we arrived here, I've felt an instinctive fear of the occasional flashes of bright light we've been exposed to. This afternoon, when the lady let us explore the house, Clorr went onto the back porch and was locked out. Before he could get back in, the sunlight destroyed him. So now we know an important secret of staying alive, which explains why this room is so dark."

Gizmo sighed. "Yes, it's true."

"My intuition tells me there are three mysteries I must solve, and one is solved already," Stripe gloated. "Next we must find out how we can reproduce. Third, we must learn how to become more powerful. Are you sure you don't want to tell me everything now and save both of us a lot of trouble?"

"I'm sure," Gizmo replied.

"All right," Stripe said, his eyes narrowing. "When we find out on our own, it will make what we do even more enjoyable. And all you'll be able to do is stand by helplessly."

With a sneer, he curled himself into a ball and closed his eyes. He was soon asleep, but Gizmo, his mind racked with memories and fears for the future, found no solace the rest of the afternoon.

"Boy, you really are a jerk." Gerald smiled as Billy set about preparing his change drawer for the day's work.

He didn't bother asking what he had done to deserve the epithet since it was obvious Gerald was going to tell him. The puzzling thing to Billy was why Gerald had waited until Kate had gone on an errand to start haranguing him. Usually he enjoyed having an audience.

"Just give me the bottom line, Ger," he said now, noting with satisfaction that his nemesis still flinched with anger whenever he used the nickname.

"O.K.," Gerald laughed. "The bottom line is you really are a fool for standing up Kate."

"Did she tell you that?"

"Not exactly," Gerald said. "I was in Dorry's last night about eleven. Kate was there so I asked her if she needed a ride home. She said no, thanks, Billy was coming by. Fortunately, I'm a very tough and persistent customer. Otherwise I'd have taken no for an answer and slunk home. But not Gerald Hopkins. I hung around . . . and she waited . . . and waited . . . And the madder she got, the sweeter I talked. Finally she let me drive her home."

"Boy, she must have really been stranded," Billy retorted.

Gerald ignored it. "Anyway," he concluded, "now that I've broken the ice, anything can happen. And I aim to see that it will."

"Maybe when Kate comes back," Billy said with a smile, "I'll say that you told me it already has."

The retort caused a sudden rush of fear to glaze Gerald's eyes. Then the fearful expression was superseded by one of craftiness. "No, you wouldn't say that," he said confidently. "That would hurt her and you're too much of a jerk to do that."

"Beware of wounded animals, Ger," Billy replied evenly.

Kate returned soon after that, but owing to a rush of early customers there was no opportunity to talk. (Not that she seemed so inclined, staring only at the customers in a businesslike manner.) Then, in midmorning, Billy's depressed mood was exacerbated by the appearance of Mrs. Deagle, who pushed her way to the front of the the line so she could go directly to Billy's window. After dropping her deposit slip silently in front of him and watching him enter it, she smiled wickedly.

"I thought you might be interested in knowing that I've set a little trap for your nasty dog," she said.

"A trap, Mrs. Deagle?"

"Nothing as crude as a bear trap," she said sarcastically. "They're illegal and I respect the law, even if you and your mutt don't. No, my trap is a lot subtler. I doubt if he'll even know when it happens. But don't be surprised if he starts acting kind of . . . well . . . let's say, crazy."

"What have you done?" Billy demanded.

"You'll find out," she said. "I know it's going to work because I went to a lot of trouble. It wasn't easy finding someone who hated dogs as much as I do. Especially someone who's invented a perfectly wonderful way to destroy them—from the mind out."

"I could have you arrested," Billy said angrily. "In fact, Mrs. Deagle—"

She interrupted him with a gasp loud enough to draw the attention of Gerald Hopkins and Mr. Corben.

"Oh, dear!" she added, half smiling when she noticed they were already on the way to her rescue.

"What is it?" Gerald demanded.

"This young man accused me of trying to cash a bad check," Mrs. Deagle stammered, her acting very hammy but obviously believable to Gerald. "He threatened to have me arrested."

"Is that what you said, Peltzer?" Gerald asked coldly.

Without giving him a chance to answer, Mrs. Deagle turned to a man behind her in the line. "Didn't you hear him say he'd like to have me arrested?" she prompted.

The man, a comparative newcomer to Kingston Falls, was not intimidated by her imperious attitude. "He didn't say he'd like to," he replied. "He said he could."

"That's bad enough," Gerald interjected.

"What did Mrs. Deagle say?" Mr. Corben asked.

"I don't know," the man replied. "Her back was toward me, so I could only hear his side of the conversation."

"I demand an apology," Mrs. Deagle sputtered. "As a matter of fact, I demand that you fire this impudent loser. He's no good to this bank, anyway."

Mr. Corben hesitated. His expression seemed to imply that even if Billy were not guilty of insulting the woman, this might be a good opportunity to fire him. Young Hopkins had been after him for several days, denigrating Peltzer and his work every time he had the chance.

"She threatened to put out a bear trap for his dog," Kate interrupted from the next window. "I heard the whole conversation."

"I said no such thing," Mrs. Deagle retorted, horrified.

"Then why did I enter the check for deposit?" Billy asked, regaining his composure. "If I thought it was a bad check, would I have done that?"

Mr. Corben nodded slowly, looked at Mrs. Deagle. Clearly the burden of proof had switched from Billy to her.

"I did not say I put out a bear trap," Mrs. Deagle stammered. "It's another kind of trap. I mean . . ."

A long pause followed. Then Mrs. Deagle reached forward to grab her deposit slip.

"Never mind," she said. "If you want to have impolite,

stupid people working for you, that's your business."

Her nose high, she clomped out of the bank.

"Now then . . ." Mr. Corben said, indicating that the bank's business was to continue as usual.

After Gerald fixed him with an angry gaze and departed, Billy glanced at Kate. His expression said, "Thank you." Her response seemed to say, "You're welcome, but I did it only in the interest of justice, not for you."

Nevertheless, at the end of the working day she did not seem particularly hostile when Billy caught up with her as she left the bank. At least she didn't call for a cop, Billy thought.

"I'd like to tell you what happened last night," he said.

"It's not necessary," she replied. "As several people have told me recently, I'm a little crazy about Mrs. Deagle's 'takeover' plan. It's foolish of me to think everybody's as concerned as I am, particularly late at night when it's nice and warm inside."

"But I wanted to come meet you," he protested. "I was all ready to. And then something terrible happened."

Her expression changed from skeptical to concerned. "Your folks are all right, aren't they?"

He nodded. Beginning slowly, he said, "You're going to think this is the dumbest excuse you've ever heard, but I swear every word is true."

"Go ahead," she said.

As quickly as possible, he told her about the Mogwai dilemma, from the first appearance of Gizmo to the last prank of the five new animals. She listened without a single interruption, her expression interested but noncommittal.

"And that's it," he concluded. "Those Mogwai got me so screwed up I just lost track of time."

She smiled slowly.

"You're right," she said. "That *is* the dumbest excuse I've ever heard."

"But it's true! I swear it!"

"Listen," she said, "there's no disgrace in falling asleep. I do it all the time, but I must admit I'm very good about keeping dates."

Trying desperately to think of some way of making his story more plausible, Billy heard the familiar voice that solved his problem. It was Pete. Ignoring Kate, the youngster grabbed Billy's sleeve and said a bit breathlessly, "Come on. Mr. Hanson's waitin' for us. He'll look at one of those things now."

"Don't you have to be a Christmas tree?"

"Yeah, but Dad said I can do it later."

"Would you like to see proof that I'm telling you the truth?" Billy asked, looking at Kate.

She smiled. "If this were April first, I'd say no," she said. "But all right. Let's go."

They hopped in Billy's bug, now back among the living, and were at his house five minutes later. Lynn, waiting for him at the door, greeted Billy with a sad expression rather than her usual smile. "One of them is dead," she said.

"Not Gizmo—"

"No. One of the new ones."

She led them to the back porch, where a tiny, flattened circle of fur was all that remained of the dead Mogwai. It looked like a football that had been deflated.

"It got out on the porch and then I must have shut the door and locked it out," Lynn explained. "It couldn't have been there long enough to have starved to death."

"No," Billy agreed. "The Chinese boy said the bright sunlight kills them."

"I don't know what to do with it. What do you do with a dead Mogwai?"

Billy shrugged. Pete, kneeling next to the tiny corpse, prodded it gently with the end of a ball-point pen. "It looks like it's really dryin' up fast," he observed. "I'll bet if you leave it here a couple days, there won't be anything left but a little fuzz."

"Don't touch it, Mom," Billy said. "At least not till we get back from school. Mr. Hanson, my old science teacher, is gonna examine one for us. Maybe we'll know more after that."

Lynn was only too happy to go along with his wishes concerning the dead Mogwai. She was less agreeable about his decision to take one out of the house. "Do you think that's wise?" she asked. "If it got away—"

"We won't let it get away," Billy assured her. "Besides, how are we gonna find out what they are if they stay cooped up all the time?"

A minute later the four of them were in Billy's room, looking at the four curled-up balls of fur in the corner and, about six feet away from them, the wide-awake Gizmo.

"Here, Kate," Billy said. "This is Gizmo. He's the best one. Would you like to hold him?"

"Er..." she said a bit hesitantly. "Sure."

Holding the soft creature, which almost seemed to smile at her, Kate was alternately enchanted and horrified. The animal was unlike anything she had ever seen or even read about. That, coupled with the fantastic story of how they reproduced, made her blood run a bit cold.

"Maybe we should take Gizmo to Mr. Hanson," Pete suggested.

Billy shook his head.

"But suppose the other ones are different?" Pete said, not without logic. "You haven't seen them reproduce, have you?"

"No."

"Well, suppose they can't do it?"

"Then it's too bad," Billy replied. "Mr. Hanson will still be able to examine the one we take him and tell us if it's a new species or not. Later, if he needs to see the water thing, maybe we'll have to take him Gizmo. But he's my favorite. I don't want to take a chance on hurting him."

With that, he gently pulled one of the other Mogwai from the somnolent mass, put it into the shoe box they had decided to use, and closed the lid firmly.

Halfway to the junior-senior high school, Billy looked at Kate, who was holding the shoe box on her lap, both hands tightly clasped over it.

"Well," he said. "Do you still think I was lying about last night?"

Smiling, she shook her head. "Even if the part about the water is made up, it's still a great story," she said.

It had been nearly three years since Billy had walked down the main hallway of his old school. Now, deserted except for a few teachers and maintenance people, it seemed smaller than he remembered. The hallways actually looked shorter, the walls closer together. Was it possible to shrink an entire school? He smiled, realizing that the mind could perform such a trick quite easily. Peeking into classrooms that should have been familiar but were not, he experienced a feeling of loss, as if all evidence of his ever having been here had been erased. They've probably even sanded down the initials I carved in every homeroom desk, he thought glumly.

They entered the science classroom, and Billy shook hands with his former teacher. A few moments later Roy Hanson looked at his watch, realized it was nearly dinnertime, and decided to answer the kids' questions as quickly but politely as possible. Although he had agreed to examine it when Pete had asked, he had not really listened to his story, which sounded off-the-wall and disjointed. He probably had a muskrat or shrew or some other animal he'd never seen around his house and, inspired by the lecture on "new" species, had visions of discovering some missing link. Still, Pete was at least interested, and it would not do to discourage or ridicule him.

"All right now," Roy said. "Let's see what we have in here."

As he started to open the box, Billy held up his hand.

"Wait, sir," he said. "There's too much light. It may even be enough to kill him in a few minutes."

Hanson turned off the overhead lights.

"How's that?" he asked.

"We'd better pull the shades, just to make sure," Billy urged.

Hanson did so, wondering if he had a monster on his hands. But it would take only a few minutes to examine the creature, probably less time than it was taking to get the proper amount of subdued illumination.

"That's fine," Billy said finally.

Hanson smiled, opened the box, and looked inside.

"Good Lord," he said slowly.

He had never seen such an animal. Touching it gently, he took its pulse, which was incredibly slow for what seemed to be a mammalian, and stroked its soft fur, which was subtly different from every other wild or domestic animal he'd encountered.

"I don't know what this thing is," he confessed.

Pete smiled broadly. "It's a new species. We'll be rich, won't we? Tell me we'll be rich."

Hanson smiled. "I can't promise that," he said. "Maybe my knowledge is incomplete. I thought I knew every type of animal on this planet, but this is certainly a new one on me." He looked at Billy. "Where did you get this?" he asked.

"My dad . . . brought it back from Chinatown."

"No papers or anything came with it?"

Billy shook his head.

"Do the thing with the water," Pete urged.

"What was that?" Hanson murmured.

"I told you," Pete said, "the thing makes another animal when you put water on it."

Roy recalled a garbled description of the creature's reproductive technique, something about a drop of water, but at the time it had seemed like more of Pete's ramblings. Now he was inclined to be more respectful.

"Just one drop, though," Billy said. "We don't want to make any more than necessary."

Hanson nodded, located an eyedropper, and loaded it from the sink. "One drop of water coming up," he said.

He paused.

"On the back," Billy said, sensing the reason for his hesitation.

Holding the Mogwai in one hand, Roy allowed a single bead of water to fall onto its back. For a long moment nothing happened. Then the crackling sound started and the creature began to shriek wildly. Kate, her hands over her face, leaped back, then slowly spread her fingers to peer out at the Mogwai's writhings. A minute later, as the frying sound reached a crescendo, a huge blister grew, abscesslike, on the Mogwai's skin, gradually broke apart, and emitted a fur ball onto the lab table.

The four watched as the sound diminished and the Mogwai's sufferings obviously subsided.

"I can't believe it," Roy murmured.

The fur ball was growing, gradually forming itself into a miniature version of its parent as it expanded.

"It's incredible," Roy breathed. "Looks like we got us our own little Christmas miracle."

Another minute passed, all of their eyes still on the growing new Mogwai.

"It'll keep growing until it's as big as the other one," Billy said. "That'll be a little while."

"Don't worry." Roy smiled. "I was all ready for dinner when you folks got here, but I don't think I'll be eating soon tonight."

"What'll we do next?" Billy asked.

"I'd like to run some blood tests. That may give me a lot of information. So why don't you take the old specimen home and leave the new one here?"

"Sure," Billy replied. "But please don't make any more of them, O.K.?"

"You can bet on that," Roy assured him. "Not until I'm darn sure what these babies are."

The three young people left then, discussing the phenomenon animatedly until they were nearly home. Then Billy grimaced and slapped his hand to his forehead.

"What is it?" Kate asked.

"I forgot to tell him not to feed them after midnight," he said, disgusted with himself.

"Don't worry," Pete said. "I'll stop by after I do my Christmas tree routine. It'll only be eight o'clock."

"You won't forget?"

Pete crossed his heart. "Word of honor," he promised. "May I turn into a Christmas tree forever if I forget."

CHAPTER ELEVEN

Pete forgot.

CHAPTER TWELVE

The greatest frustration of Gizmo's existence was that he could not communicate very well with other species. As a highly intelligent form of life, he often understood by intuition the general context of what alien beings said, but making them understand him was another matter.

Now, as Billy and the young woman returned with the shoe box, Gizmo had the feeling that things were not going very well. The only reason they could have had for taking the new Mogwai away was to study it; from that it followed that they had demonstrated how water made them reproduce; and from that it was logical to assume that one minute after the specimen Mogwai rejoined his friends, all would know. Stripe would know. And then only one piece of dangerous knowledge would separate Gizmo, Billy, and the rest of the human race from possible disaster.

Watching the moments of safety tick away as Billy approached the pile of sleeping fur balls, Gizmo wanted to cry out: "Wait! Stop!" If only he could find a way to tell

Billy that unless he segregated those four Mogwai from
each other and from water, he was in danger of becoming
one of the biggest jerks in the history of the world! But
when Gizmo opened his mouth to articulate a clear and
direct warning, nothing emerged but gibberish.

"Look, Kate." Billy smiled as he opened the shoe box.
"Gizmo must be jealous."

He reached to stroke Gizmo's head with one hand and
dropped the new Mogwai into the bunch with his other.

"There," he said. "See, Giz? They don't mean a thing
to me. You're the special one."

"He seems kind of . . . sad, doesn't he?" Kate said.

"Yeah, a little. I guess you can't blame him. There's
been a lot of excitement the past couple days."

A few minutes later they went out, leaving Gizmo to
watch the grim conspiracy unfolding before him. It began
with the four Mogwai going into a huddle, from which
constant whispering emanated punctuated by an occasional
grunt or shout of triumph from Stripe. After several minutes
they moved apart and, as one, looked directly at Gizmo.
Their expressions told him they felt they were on the verge
of a quantum power increase, that he had better stay out of
their way when it happened.

They were undoubtedly close to realizing this tremendous
power surge; yet even the pessimistic Gizmo knew it was
by no means automatic. During his own lifetime he had
seen several dozen near-explosions averted, mostly by good
fortune rather than planning, but these misses did serve
to illustrate the point that until the final mystery was solved,
containment was possible. Stripe, one of the most diabolically clever majority Mogwai Gizmo had so far encountered, knew that the last step was the most important.

Moving to the front of the group, he spoke in Mogwai.

"We've solved two problems," he said coldly. "We know

light is our enemy, so we won't be trapped into exposing ourselves to it. We know that water makes us reproduce. All that remains is to discover how we become powerful."

Gizmo looked directly into Stripe's eyes. "Well?" he asked. "Why don't you reproduce then? This family can keep you locked in the house, but it's foolish to believe they can keep you away from water."

"You'd like that, wouldn't you?" Stripe smiled wickedly. "By reproducing now, we could succeed in doing nothing but creating an army of weak creatures that could be easily eradicated. You've seen such impatience fail in the past, haven't you?"

Gizmo allowed himself to smile faintly. In fact, he always hated to see unlimited reproduction for the simple reason that it mathematically increased the chances of stumbling onto the final mystery's solution. Consistent with this, he hoped Stripe and his three cohorts would not take the step right away. The best way to discourage their doing so, of course, was by making Stripe think he favored reproduction.

And what, Gizmo mused, was the best way to delude Stripe into thinking he wanted them to reproduce now? By saying the opposite? No. (Since Stripe would automatically reject that as a ploy.) In fact, the best way to convince his enemy that he favored reproduction was to seem to favor it.

It was an elliptical line of reasoning, but with the devious Stripe, one had to be wily.

"There is an old adage," Gizmo said. "It says that the opportunity should be grasped when it arises or that moment will never occur again."

"So you think we should reproduce now?" Stripe asked through narrowed eyes.

"I am not your advisor. It just seems to me—"

"Liar!" Stripe shot back. "Do you take me for a fool? Do you really think I'll fall for such obvious psychological maneuvering?"

Gizmo, summoning all his acting ability, did his best to look innocent.

Stripe raged, smiling finally in triumph. "If you, my dear enemy, advise us to reproduce now, it can only mean one thing: that that is what *you* want. You *know* it is my inclination to believe the *opposite* of what you say. Therefore if you speak in favor of reproduction, that is really what you favor." His forehead furrowing as he followed his own convoluted reasoning, he paused, then rushed forward with the denouement. "Therefore, since you are in favor of reproduction now, we won't do it."

Gizmo looked away, rolled himself into a ball, and cherished the brief moment of victory. He realized it was a temporary thing, however, subject to the mercurial whims of Stripe's mind. But at least he had a little time to think.

Roy Hanson hadn't slept for nearly twenty-four hours, thanks to Pete Fountaine and Billy Peltzer. He'd planned for his first sane Christmas in years, and now *this*. A biological find so stunning he was afraid to stop work for a minute lest he lose his train of thought. Just analyzing the creature's blood, which ought to have been a reasonably simple matter, had been horrendously time-consuming. After extracting blood at least two dozen times (which endeared him to the Mogwai to the point where it shrieked whenever he approached), he had concluded that the blood actually changed composition in response to atmospheric, temperature, and humidity changes. This meant that the creature was theoretically capable of living in nearly every climate imaginable. It made blood testing a monumental task, though. And blood testing would be a snap compared to finding out how the animal reproduced via a single drop of water.

"Don't worry, fella," he said, staring at the hostile Mogwai. "I'm gonna solve your identity problem and then you'll love me."

It was four o'clock in the afternoon and the building was nearly deserted. Tomorrow would be the last day of classes; then Roy would have the entire Christmas holiday to study the animal.

"I was really lookin' forward to spending some time with my girlfriend," he said to the Mogwai. "But I'd better get you while you're hot."

Haunted by the idea that those kids would tell some television or newspaper reporter about the Mogwai and he would be lost in the shuffle, Roy worked compulsively and nonstop. Fortunately, he was used to such self-discipline, having worked two jobs while he was in college. He had learned to sleep on the run, think on the run, and eat on the run. Knowing that he would be spending many long hours in the lab this evening, he had sent one of his homeroom students out for some sandwiches. Munching on one, he noticed the Mogwai stare hungrily at it.

"Why not?" He smiled. "We're both in this together. Have a bite."

Pushing a morsel through the bars, he laughed as the Mogwai grabbed and downed the snack like a veteran fast-food addict.

"O.K.," he said. "Now it's time for one more jab with the needle in the interests of science."

"I know you're all caught up in this in the interests of science, but it's not helping me get my petition signed."

Kate wasn't exactly perturbed. She was concerned, however, that Billy seemed to have no time to help her contact people. While she understood that he was preoccupied with the Mogwai problem, she did not want to lose track of her main goal in life at the moment—to thwart Mrs. Deagle if there was a takeover plan in the works.

It was late afternoon, only minutes after they had gotten off work. Dorry's Pub was nearly deserted, only Murray Futterman sitting at the far end of the bar nursing a drink. Billy and Kate had said hello to him when they came in, but as he hadn't seemed inclined to socialize, they'd left him alone. Taking a table in the corner farthest away from the video games, where space invaders were being zapped by some teenagers, they ordered coffee and slowly unwound from a rough day at the bank.

"I'm sorry," Billy explained. "Really I am. It's just that I don't feel right being away from home too long. Mom may not know what to do if those Mogwai get loose or something. If it wasn't for that, I'd help you take that petition door to door—"

"Where are you keeping them, by the way?" Kate asked. "Still in your room?"

Billy nodded. "Mom lets them out every once in a while, though. Not outside the house, but downstairs. She thinks it's mean to keep them cooped up all the time."

"Aren't you afraid they'll get splashed with water?"

"Not really. There aren't any leaks or anything, and we keep the kitchen and bathrooms closed. Oh, I guess if they *knew* they could reproduce that way and wanted it, they'd find a way. But they're pretty docile. And Barney follows them around. If they get in anything he thinks they shouldn't he barks a warning."

Kate smiled. "Any more warnings from Mrs. Deagle?" she asked.

"Yeah. She mumbled something under her breath to-day—just loud enough for me to hear—saying Barney's time was almost up."

"What do you think she meant? Is she bluffing?"

"I don't know. I wouldn't put it past her to hire somebody to put a drug in his food."

They sat silently a moment, sipping their coffee. Then, without looking up, Kate murmured, "Watch it. Here he comes. With one too many."

As the shuffling figure of Mr. Futterman nearly stumbled just before reaching their table, she added quickly, "Make that two."

"Hi, kids," Futterman said, pulling up a chair. Putting his rough, scaly hand on Kate's arm, he smiled. "Now here's a new one. Most guys ask you when you get off work. But I want to know when you start."

"Not for another fifteen minutes."

"Oh."

"Why?"

"You're the best one to complain to around here," Futterman replied thickly. "Dorry's not interested. You listen. A fella can tell you his problems and you sympathize. But I can't wait fifteen more minutes."

"All right." Kate smiled. "I'm not working yet, but tell me anyway."

"It's that stupid . . . cantankerous . . . can't get her to co-operate no matter what—"

"Not your wife?" Kate interjected.

"No," he said. "It's that snowplow. Darn thing."

"But I thought you said it worked perfectly, Mr. Futterman," Billy said.

"It did. But that was before I took it in for a tune-up and they loaded 'er up with foreign parts. Every single gasket, spark plug—foreign! It's no wonder she conked out. It's like servin' chop suey at a wedding. You ever heard of anybody ever servin' chop suey at a wedding?"

Billy shook his head.

"'Course not! They serve good ol' American food. Give the guests chop suey and they'd none of 'em move for the rest of the night. Same with cars and trucks. Foreign parts are like chop suey. Boiled rice. Thick, sticky."

"I've never heard it put that way before," Kate said, humoring him, "but you may have something."

"They're payin' us back for winning the war," Futterman said in a somewhat slurred but unequivocal tone. "They're puttin' gremlins in their machinery, the same gremlins that brought down our planes in the big one."

"The big one?" Kate asked, puzzled.

"World War Two," Futterman rasped. "You know, the sequel to World War One."

Kate and Billy laughed.

"Anyway," Futterman continued, "they're shippin' their gremlins over here . . . in their cars, and stereos, and now in the spark plugs in my snowplow."

"Where's the plow now?" Kate asked.

"Around the corner. She conked out just as I pulled in a parking space. That was my only break today."

"Can I give you a lift home?" Kate offered.

"No, thanks," Futterman replied, getting shakily to his feet. "The wife's on her way. Should be outside now. Thanks for listenin' to me. I needed that."

"You're welcome," Kate answered with a smile. "Why don't you pick up some chop suey on your way home? That should make you feel better."

"Fat chance," Futterman laughed, waving as he headed for the door.

Billy leaned back and smiled.

"That was really nice," he said. "The way you handled Mr. Futterman."

"I'm used to it," Kate replied. "People are about the same all over. They just want somebody to listen to them. Especially around the holidays."

"Why's that?"

"It's because a lot of people get really depressed when they're bombarded by all this cheer."

"I always thought everybody was happy during the holidays," Billy mused.

"Most people are," Kate said. "But some aren't. While everybody else is opening presents, they're opening their wrists."

Billy winced. "A cheery thought."

"It's true. The suicide rate is always highest around the holidays."

"Stop it. Now you're making me depressed."

"Sorry. Can't have that."

The slight edge to her voice bothered him. "Do you get depressed at Christmas?" he asked.

"I don't celebrate Christmas," she replied. "As far as I'm concerned, it doesn't exist."

"Why, are you a Hindu or something?"

"No. I just don't like to . . ."

"But . . . why?"

"Do you really want to know?" she asked, looking at him in a way that was almost challenging.

"Sure . . . I guess I want to know everything about you."

She avoided his glance.

"I don't know," she murmured, her expression distant. "I don't know why Christmas is always so horrible. . . . My grandmother died on Christmas. . . . She was my favorite person. . . . I had my appendix taken out on Christmas. It burst while I was opening my presents. . . . Even my dog Snappy got run over on Christmas . . . by two big kids on a sled. . . . But the worst . . . God . . . it was horrible . . ."

"What?" Billy urged.

"It was Christmas Eve," Kate continued slowly, almost as if she were in a trance. "I was six years old. Mom and I were decorating the tree . . . singing carols, happy, excited ... waiting for Dad to come home from work." She paused, took a deep breath. "A couple of hours went by, then more. Dad wasn't home. Mom called the office ... no answer ... Then it was past the time when the stores were closed. That's when Mom and I really started to worry...."

Billy waited, dreading hearing the rest of the story, yet impatient for her to continue.

"Anyway, we stayed up all night.... He didn't come home.... Christmas Day went by like an eternity, and still nothing ... The police began a search. A week, two weeks went by. Mom was close to a nervous breakdown and neither of us could eat or sleep.... Then, one night in January it was snowing outside. The house was freezing cold so I tried to start a fire. That's when I noticed ..."

"Noticed ... what?" Billy muttered.

"The smell ... The firemen came and broke through the chimney top. Mom and I were expecting them to pull out a dead bird or a cat.... Instead they pulled out my father."

Billy, eyes wide, gulped.

"He was dressed in a Santa Claus suit," Kate continued. "He had been climbing down the chimney on Christmas Eve, his arms loaded with gifts. He was going to surprise us, but I guess he surprised himself.... He lost his footing ... slipped and broke his neck ... and must have died instantly. At least he didn't suffer long.... His body just stayed there, lodged in the chimney ... Anyway, that's how I found out there was no Santa Claus and why I don't like Christmas."

Billy's chilled expression softened as he noticed a moistness in her eyes.

"That's terrible!" said Billy. He reached out and touched her hand.

Kate sniffed, then smiled. She gave Billy's hand a squeeze. "Anyway, that's my own little Christmas carol that I tell people when they ask me why I don't like Christmas.

Actually, you're one of the few people who didn't express any doubt. Most just kind of look at you oddly and some even laugh."

Knowing he was more sensitive than the average person made Billy feel better. It gave him a thrill to find out about Kate, who was generally secretive about her personal and family life.

"I'm really sorry," he said. "I feel like the wishy-washy jerk Gerald always says I am."

Kate laughed. "No, you're not. You're just concerned about other people's feelings. If that's being a jerk, give me a jerk any day."

"One jerk, coming up," he said.

Stripe's mind was made up. After fifteen minutes of being followed around the house by the big, sad-faced dog, he had decided that drastic measures were in order. It simply would not do to have that noisy oaf in their wake if and when they decided to take some action. That was the practical aspect of the situation; the pleasant side was that it would be fun to gang up on Barney, honing their skills in the process.

Gathering the other Mogwai about him, Stripe mapped out a rough plan of action to be started immediately. The others, as he suspected they would be, were almost joyously enthusiastic.

"As soon as the woman goes next door for her afternoon coffee," Stripe ordered, "we'll gang up. Until then, we'll make individual passes with these."

So saying, he passed out some long pins he had found in Mrs. Peltzer's sewing basket. "There's also some stuff in the garbage can under the sink," he said. "Some dog food he didn't eat. You two chew that up into a soggy paste and then drop it around so it looks like he's vomited."

Lynn Peltzer started noticing Barney's unusual behavior

soon after lunch. Every once in a while he would let out a yelp for which there seemed no logical cause. The Mogwai were out but none of them appeared to be molesting Barney in any way.

The worst incident occurred about two o'clock. Barney began to cry, yipped several times, then came rushing into the living room, his snout covered with the remains of his breakfast.

"What did you do?" Lynn asked accusingly. Tracing his tracks into the hallway, she had no trouble spotting the huge splash of vomit dripping down the wallpaper. Her new wallpaper.

"What is going on?" she shouted at Barney. "Why can't you just barf on the floor like other dogs? Why am I the one with a projectile-vomiter?"

Shooing Barney away, she set to work cleaning up the mess. As she busied herself, Stripe took the opportunity to silently congratulate his cohorts and, their arms across each other's shoulders like football players in a huddle, whisper another plan to them.

Had anyone been able to observe them in action, one might have described the four Mogwai's movements as almost balletic, so well coordinated were they. While two of them distracted Barney at a discreet distance, a third leaped onto a chair and with one great swipe ripped out a section of the cake Mrs. Peltzer was icing. Then, as he moved with it toward Barney, Stripe grasped a chair and rattled it noisily against the floor. That signaled the two Mogwai on Barney's flanks to feint toward him, causing the dog to scrape his claws loudly against the tile floor.

"What's going on in there?" Lynn called out.

As Barney turned toward the sound of her voice, the Mogwai with the iced cake chunk let the dog have it full on the mouth. Chuckling silently, the four scampered out of the kitchen as fast as their little legs could carry them.

The picture was self-evident when Lynn entered the kitchen—her cake mutilated, the crumbs and icing still on Barney's chops, and not another soul in sight.

"What's come over you?" she cried.

Tossing the cake in the garbage, she banished Barney to the basement but was careful not to lock him up. Better to make him feel guilty for an hour or two and then invite him back to society. It was quite possible, after all, that his strange antics were the result of a virus or some temporary disorientation. Dogs and even Mogwai, after all, were not that different from human beings.

An hour later, while Lynn Peltzer was next door, Stripe led his troops to the gaily decorated Christmas tree in the living room. Working swiftly, three of them began unwinding several strings of lights while the fourth grabbed strands of tinsel and smaller ornaments. Then, all pushing together, they upended the tree and dragged it back and forth across the room, leaving a wake of shattered glass ornaments and broken limbs.

"Now, quickly," Stripe ordered, leading the way to the basement door, which was slightly ajar.

The four Mogwai bounded down the stairs, still carrying their strings of lights and tinsel. Barney, curled in the corner next to the oil burner, leaped to his feet, his eyes flashing. Fanning out, the Mogwai approached the snapping and snarling dog like Roman gladiators armed with net and tridents stalking their prey. Barney, hampered by fear of actually hurting them, could do little more than try to avoid them. For a brief while, spinning like a top or a mad dog chasing its tail, he was able to throw off the light cords nearly as fast as they were deposited on his back. Then a snag developed; one of the light strands got caught under his ear just as another encircled his paws. The Mogwai, meanwhile, kept up a busy barrage of jabbing needles. Soon Barney was thrashing on the floor, completely and hope-

lessly enmeshed in the light cords. By bending over the
ends and making double loops, Stripe made certain the dog
would never be able to get out without human help.

"Now let's go," Stripe cackled. "It's up to Billy's room
and to sleep."

Rand Peltzer, knocking off early that afternoon in order
to grab a few hours' sleep prior to a final pre-Christmas
selling trip, walked into the house within several seconds
of Lynn's reappearance via the back door.

She heard his scream and the basement struggles of Barney at the same time. Looking through the open doorway,
she saw the dog on the second-from-top step, his front paws
knotted together as if in prayer, the eyes wild and frenzied,
teeth bared as he tried to tear loose from the light-cord
bondage.

"What the heck happened?" Rand asked.

As Rand rushed into the kitchen, Lynn caught a glimpse
of the Christmas tree lying on its side in the living room.
Putting the grim puzzle together from opposite ends, Rand
and Lynn shook their heads simultaneously.

When they finished, Lynn helped drag the still-struggling
Barney into the kitchen and freed him from the light strands.
Rand picked random slivers of tinsel from the dog's body,
muttering to himself the while.

"How did you get this wrapped on so tight?" Lynn asked,
shaking her head.

"Must have gone crazy," Rand said.

Lynn was describing Barney's erratic behavior all that
day when Billy entered. As he heard about the yelping,
vomiting, cake stealing, and apparent kamikaze mission
against the Christmas tree, the concern in his eyes grew to
something resembling panic.

Rand, searching for a reasonable explanation, said, "He's
probably just trying to get attention away from those Mog-

wai things. Jealous, you know. As a matter of fact, I wouldn't be surprised if those little devils goaded him on."

"No," Lynn murmured. "They weren't bothering him. They've been sleeping upstairs most of the day."

"It's Mrs. Deagle then," Billy said sharply. "It's got to be her."

"Mrs. Deagle—?" Lynn said.

"She's had him drugged. She told me she would and now she's done it."

"That's crazy," Rand murmured. "Why would she want to do that?"

"Because he rubbed against her ceramic snowman and caused its head to fall off. It was loose, anyway, but that didn't matter to her. She's just looking for people and things to hate."

"Now, Billy," Lynn cautioned. "We can't point our finger at anybody. Not even Mrs. Deagle."

"But she threatened Barney. Kate heard her."

"But that's not enough proof, son," Rand said. "There aren't even any new footprints in the snow around the house."

"Doesn't matter," Billy replied. "She's got enough money to hire a real pro. I hear there are people who can be hired for that—to drug or poison pets."

Rand shrugged. "Maybe it would be a good idea if I dropped Barney off at your mother's house," he said, looking at Lynn. "It's on the way to the Millersville Mall, where I've got that sales meeting. I could leave him and bring him back for Christmas."

Billy nodded. "I'd feel a lot better if you did that, Dad."

"O.K. It's settled."

Giving Barney a pat on the head, Rand stretched and started unbuttoning his sweater. "I'll see you in a while, pooch, after I grab me some shut-eye."

As he left the kitchen, Barney padding after him, Lynn put her hand on Billy's arm. "Try not to worry," she said.

"I'm sure it's just a one-day craziness. Humans fly off the deep end once in a while and then are perfectly normal. Why shouldn't animals?"

Billy nodded. He knew she was probably right, but he couldn't help feeling better with Barney out of the house.

"Where do they come from? How did they get here?"

The small group of actors stood looking at the mysterious podlike object, their faces showing fear, disbelief, and horror in the 1956 classic movie *Invasion of the Body Snatchers*. Because it was one of Billy's favorite old-time horror films, he glanced at the screen only occasionally, usually when the sveltely gorgeous Dana Wynter was visible. Otherwise he just listened, concentrating on his artwork.

The movie, which began at eleven that night, had barely started when the four new Mogwai stirred from their long sleep and began to grumble for food. Billy tossed them a handful of chocolate candy kisses, which they proceeded to down, foil and all, in a matter of seconds. A minute later the begging sounds started up again with renewed urgency.

Billy looked at the clock. It was 11:30. There was time enough to feed them before midnight but he was too lazy to move.

"Forget it, fellas," he said. "You had a good dinner a few hours ago. Go back to sleep and we'll take care of you in the morning."

His reluctance to move caused a crescendo of group consternation, but a minute or two later they quieted down, apparently having decided their pleas were being ignored.

Roy Hanson looked at his watch and sighed. It was nearly midnight and he still could not identify several main components of the Mogwai's blood. As a result, both he and his subject were angry and exhausted—Hanson from scientific frustration, the Mogwai from the numerous irksome injections.

"No doubt about it," Hanson murmured to the creature, who glared at him from the farthest corner of his cage, "you and I are getting on each other's nerves, all right. Maybe it's time to knock off."

He studied his notes one more time, concluding that he was right in deciding that he simply did not have sophisticated enough equipment in his lab to do the proper tests. Tomorrow or the day after—or whenever the restrictions of Christmas allowed—he would take the Mogwai to a bigger lab and run more tests. For the moment, doing any more blood sampling was simply an exercise in futility.

His stomach rumbled with hunger.

"Yeah, that's another good reason to knock off," he murmured. "I'm starving."

During one stretch of four or five hours, when he had thought he was on the verge of a breakthrough, he had eaten nothing after unwrapping a large salami and cheese sandwich brought him earlier in the day. His stomach still churning, he looked at the sandwich now, half with desire and half with revulsion. The bread had already started to harden and the edge of the cheese was curling up. He lifted the top slice of bread, exposing lettuce rapidly turning limp and brown, an off-white sauce (but hadn't he ordered "no mayo"?) insinuating itself like glue between the soggy leaves and slices of soft, now quite warm, meat.

"No, thanks," he muttered, dropping the bread onto the foil wrapping. "I'd like to have some real food."

The heavy smell of food, albeit rapidly aging, sent the Mogwai into near-contortions in its cage. Whining louder and louder, it grasped the bars like an angry penitentiary inmate, hopping up and down and accompanying itself with verbal gyrations that were alternately plaintive and angry.

Hanson regarded the animal with a sympathetic glance. "Hey, I guess you are hungry at that," he said. "You're welcome to this sandwich, although I don't guarantee it."

With that, he slipped the sandwich, foil and all, through the bars of the cage.

When he left the lab, he could hear the Mogwai attacking the sandwich with undisguised gleeful gluttony.

Stripe was hungry, perhaps even hungrier than the others. While they had slept peacefully, he had lain still, his eyes closed, and planned.

With the dog gone—just an hour ago he had heard him barking as Rand put him in the car—their options were greater. If the man stayed away awhile, that reduced the odds against their eventual success even more. The problem was that he could not figure out how they would get out of the house, assuming someone did not carelessly leave a door open. Would the sheer weight of their numbers be sufficient? Stripe did not want to count on that any more than he wanted to count on a door or window being left open.

If we could just increase our size! he thought.

He knew there was a way. He did not know *why* he knew, or how the growth could be brought about. But his sense of instinct was strong. That instinct told him to wait, but not long. Perhaps two days, no more.

In the meantime, he was still hungry and infuriated that the one Gizmo called his "master" was too lazy to walk downstairs and get them something. They had tried moving him with pleas and threats, but to no avail. What other form of persuasion was there?

The young man seemed absorbed in the flickering box with the small people inside. It, like so many other things in the house, seemed to operate through a wire stuck into the wall. Stripe recalled that while studying the Christmas tree prior to making such a fool of the dog, he had pulled the cord's end from the wall, an action that had caused the lights to go out. Was it possible the entertainment box operated in the same manner?

He looked across the room, saw the black cord from the box disappear behind Billy's desk. Several feet away, near the baseboard, the same cord (or one that looked very much like it) was stuck in the wall. Stripe decided they must be one and the same. Pulling the plug from the wall would certainly get the young man's attention; if inconvenienced, he might have the sense to get them something to eat.

With that strategy in mind, Stripe detached himself from the group and slowly worked his way over to the cord. Grasping it, he cocked his ear toward the television.

"Miles!" Dana Wynter cried.

A long pause followed.

Stripe, cursing silently, waited. Had the young man turned down the sound? Or was it merely a dramatic pause in the action?

"Miles!" Dana Wynter said again, followed by more silence.

"Well, I can't wait here forever," Stripe murmured. With that, he wrested the plug from the wall and as quickly as possible snuck back to the group.

Nearly a minute passed. Then dialogue from the box told him it was still operating. Stripe gnashed his teeth, rolled over, and tried to sleep. When his rumbling stomach would not allow it, he decided to have another try at oral persuasion. Shaking his cohorts awake, he told them to really let him have it and began the whining, threatening chorus himself. Before long Billy turned his attention from his drawing and to the group.

"Boy, you guys are terrible," he said.

Remembering the times in his life when he had been really hungry, he looked at the clock next to his desk. It said 11:40.

"All right," he said, standing and shutting off the television. "But it'll have to be quick."

In no time at all he raced down to the kitchen, found a batch of leftovers, and returned to the room. The Mogwai devoured everything so quickly Billy didn't even bother looking at the clock. As he balled up the big piece of foil on which he had served it to them, he suddenly realized Gizmo had been shortchanged, but he was too tired to be a good guy anymore tonight.

"He's sleeping anyway," Billy rationalized, turning off the light and literally falling into bed.

Billy awakened, after a dreamless night, to see the first gray blush of dawn beneath the lowered shades of his room. Instinctively, he looked at the clock.

It said 11:40.

A warning alarm started to jangle in his mind.

It had a semihuman intonation, but it wasn't a person's voice.

Eleven-forty.

Ya-ta-ta, ya-ta-ta, ya-ta-ta... An old prison movie with a yard filled with men screaming ya-ta-ta, ya-ta-ta, ya-ta-ta... Now only one voice... A falsetto ya-ta-ta...

Eleven-forty.

Suddenly Billy snapped to a sitting position in bed. He put his hands over his eyes and waited for the overlapping impressions of fantasy and reality to separate. Letting out his breath slowly, he looked at the clock.

The hands were in the same position. But it couldn't be... He couldn't have overslept that long—

Even as the thought entered his slow-functioning mind, his eyes dropped, following the desk clock cord as it dis-

appeared behind the panel and down the wall to the baseboard where it . . .

The cord was out.

Ya-ta-ta, ya-ta-ta. Now the voice was more familiar—
that of an intelligent creature trying to form words, his
mouth twisting wildly, eyes wide as he gesticulated with
his short fat furry arms.

"Giz! Are you all right?"

Billy swung his feet onto the floor and looked down for
his slippers. As he did so, he caught his first glimpse of the
four unfamiliar objects in the room.

A sound was pulled out of his chest, neither a scream
nor curse nor recognizable word of any kind. Filling the
room so suddenly and profoundly, it startled Billy so much
that he felt his entire body shiver—a single massive shock
wave causing him to coil into a near-fetal position. When
it was over he realized he had both hands firmly over his
eyes.

Slowly the chattering of Gizmo penetrated his false security of blackness. Removing his hands from his eyes,
Billy prepared himself for a longer look at the strange sight
before him.

CHAPTER THIRTEEN

Usually Pete Fountaine could not think of even one reason to be happy. Being thirteen, of course, he took such things as good health and plenty of food for granted, scoffing at his parents when they offered those everyday blessings as reasons for quiet celebration. No, Pete wanted more sensational and immediate reasons to be happy, and today he had not one or two, but three.

First of all, it was the last day of school until after New Year's, which translated into no homework, no boring classes, and plenty of morning sleep. Secondly, it was his last day as a Christmas tree, a chore he had enjoyed when he was eight but now found so irksome he started dreading it in September. That meant that after this evening he had at least nine months before the aggravation started building again.

Third, and most important, he had called Mary Ann Fabrizio last night and laid the groundwork for his first major league date. True, he had not actually proposed a time and activity, but he had been on the verge several times and she seemed interested in his conversation. Strolling toward school nearly twelve hours later, he could recall entire passages of their lengthy talk. Replaying segments now, he was disappointed to note that he had passed up many excellent opportunities for jokes, suave observations, and date suggestions. But so what? All he had to do was run the sound track through his mind once again as he walked and add the appropriately wise, clever, or bold comment. And while he was at it, he could add new lines for Mary Ann, most of them expressions of amazement at how she had somehow managed to overlook this tiger of a young man for so long.

Becoming so caught up in the imaginary dialogue, Pete did not hear the footsteps behind him. Only when a new voice entered the scene did he snap back to reality.

"Hope I'm not butting into a private conversation," the voice said.

It was Mr. Hanson. His eyes were bloodshot and he walked without his usual springy step, Pete noted.

"Hi," he said.

He was, of course, doubly embarrassed. It was bad enough that Mr. Hanson had overheard him talking to himself. Now, as he fell into step with Pete, he was going to subject him to possible excoriation by his classmates for fraternizing with a teacher. Short of being impolite or breaking into a sprint, however, there was little Pete could do.

"I'm rehearsing my spiel as a Christmas tree," he explained, pleased that he had come up with something so quickly. "Every year I dress up as a Christmas tree and help my father sell them."

"Oh, yeah." Hanson smiled. "I think I've seen you, although I didn't know who it was under all those decorations. Boy, you get lit up more than the town drunk, I'll bet."

"Yessir," Pete said, forcing himself to chuckle. He wondered how many times he had heard that one since he first put on the portable lights and tinsel. (The other favorite wisecrack dealt with Pete's "needling" people.)

"Heard anything from Billy?" Hanson asked. "I guess he's curious to know what I found out about that little animal he left here."

"Yessir. Yesterday he said he was gonna call you right after Christmas."

"It might take a lot longer than that to solve this biological mystery. Those little furry things may seem simple enough, but so far they've defied classification. They look like mammals and sometimes they act like reptiles, but they aren't either. At least not in the classic sense."

"Has it grown any?" Pete asked.

"Not that I've noticed. Why not drop in a minute and see for yourself?"

Pete nodded, not sure how to say no. And he was curious to see the Mogwai again. When they entered Mr. Hanson's classroom and were free from the prying eyes of other students, Pete was somewhat relieved. Warmed by the school's steam heat, he pulled off his gloves and began unbuttoning his coat as he followed Mr. Hanson through the classroom and into the spacious lab immediately behind it.

"Good Lord!"

Pete's field of vision was suddenly obscured by the broad back and shoulders of Hanson, who, after taking a couple of steps into the lab, was propelled backward as if struck by a flying object.

"What—!" Pete heard himself call out, throwing up his hands to ward off colliding with Mr. Hanson.

Recovering his balance quickly, Hanson steadied Pete by grabbing his shoulders, then turned and ran into the lab toward a green object tucked in the far corner.

Pete followed.

From a distance the object resembled a slimy watermelon, spherical in shape rather than ovate, its skin covered and matted with a layer of sticky, veiny paste. Several strands of the wire cage—in which it had obviously been encased—were broken or bent outward by the heavy pulpy mass. A faint crackling noise, like saliva being sucked through the teeth, emanated from the general area of the object as the running sore that was its outer skin changed shape and texture even as Pete and Hanson watched.

"Wow!" Pete gasped. "Did this used to be that little animal? When did this happen?"

"Last night," Hanson murmured.

As he spoke he began searching in a nearby tool drawer, presently locating a set of wire cutters with which he snipped away the remaining wires of the cage.

"Why're you lettin' it loose?" Pete asked, looking toward the nearest way out of the lab. "I wouldn't."

"I don't want it to be destroyed or damaged by the wires," Hanson replied evenly. "There's not much danger to us now, I suspect. It's in some sort of pupal stage."

Fascinated by the hideous pod, Pete could not restrain himself from reaching out to touch it. He immediately pulled his finger back, looked a moment at the gooey substance stuck to the end of it.

"Yeccchhh," he said.

Seeing that he was about to rub his finger on his trousers, Hanson tossed Pete an old rag.

"Use this," he said.

"Thanks."

"Boy, it really sticks," Pete muttered, thankful that he had not used his pants as a receptacle for the gunk.

He watched as Mr. Hanson circled the remains of the exploded cage, studying the monstrous green gooey ball from all angles.

"What did you say this was?" he asked. "A putrid stage?"

"Pupal. Pupal stage," Hanson replied.

"Like a student in school?"

"No," Hanson said, "although it comes from the Latin *pupus*, meaning 'boy.' The pupal stage is the quiescent period in the development of an insect, following the larval and preceding the adult stage. Inside, this is going through a stage."

"Like my mother?" Pete smiled. The short period of familiarity with the object had already lessened many of his fears.

Hanson smiled slightly. "No, that's different," he explained. "This is what we call a metamorphosis. A change in form...change in appearance."

"Yeah, like my mother."

Hanson made a note on a clipboard, then suddenly dropped the pencil and snapped his fingers. "Billy," he said, his voice tinged with alarm. "Do you know his phone number?"

"Sure," Pete said. "Why?"

"Because," Hanson replied, "it just occurred to me that if we've got one of these things and it's kind of spooky, I wonder how he feels with four."

All he could remember was the line from *Invasion of the Body Snatchers*—"Where did they come from?"

Billy was still staring at the four faintly bubbling pustules, weighing whether he should try to slide quietly between them or make a mad dash for it, when the telephone rang. Almost grateful for the interruption, he grabbed the receiver so quickly the rest of the phone fell noisily to the floor. He let it lie.

"Hello."

"Billy Peltzer?"

"Yes."

"This is Roy Hanson. Something's developed here at the school lab."

"Yeah. It has here, too."

"Your four Mogwai have entered the pupal stage?"

"I don't know what it's called—"

Hanson quickly described the mass in front of him until he was satisfied Billy had four of the same.

"They must go into this metamorphosis after a certain amount of time," Hanson theorized. "That's the only explanation I can give for what's happening."

"Did you feed yours after midnight last night?" Billy asked.

"Yes, now that you mention it. Is there anything unusual about that?"

"Pete didn't tell you about feeding them?"

"No."

"Well, the Chinese boy warned us not to feed them after midnight," Billy said. "Pete was supposed to tell you that, but I guess he forgot."

"Did you feed yours?" Hanson asked.

"Yessir. It was a mistake. Somehow the cord of my electric clock got pulled out of the wall. Maybe they did it. Anyway, I thought it was only eleven-forty, so I fed them something. But I didn't feed Gizmo. Now Gizmo's the same and the other four are sitting there like they're getting ready to either explode or attack."

"I seriously doubt that'll happen," Hanson assured him. "They may be making little noises, but that's part of the hatching process. In a couple of days they'll probably turn into some life form we've never seen before."

"I can hardly wait," Billy groaned. Then he asked, "When is this likely to happen?"

"No idea."

"Is it all right for me to go to work and leave them? This is gonna be a really busy day, but I don't want to leave Mom alone if there's any danger."

"I'm sure we have some time," Hanson replied. "Anyway, show her what happened so she'll be ready to run if those cocoons produce something horrible. And keep them locked in a place where they can't get out."

Billy looked at the vegetating masses. "There's no way these things could produce anything but monsters," he said direly.

"Don't be so sure," Hanson murmured. "Remember the butterfly. Let's keep in touch the rest of the day, O.K.?"

"Yessir."

Billy hung up and finished dressing, all the while watching his new roommates. Gizmo, meanwhile, continued to chatter away, his intonation a mixture of alarm and castigation.

"Don't worry," Billy soothed, "I won't leave you alone with those things."

Lifting Gizmo from his cage and putting him in an old knapsack he found stuffed in a corner of the closet, Billy gingerly picked his way through the field of giant blisters. Arriving at the bedroom door, he remembered a disquieting fact about the locking mechanism: the knob could be locked only from the inside. True, the catch could be turned before leaving and the door closed, but then you couldn't get back in without breaking the lock.

Closing the door but not locking it, he went downstairs. His mother was in the kitchen, going about her everyday business of making his breakfast, looking for all the world as if it were just another pleasant day.

For her, of course, that was exactly the case. Billy filled her in quickly, watching her expression change from mildly alarmed to briefly amused, and finally to properly horrified.

"I'd like to see those things," she said when he was finished.

Following him upstairs, she gasped when she saw the four globs, then stood shaking her head sadly for a long time.

"The rug is ruined," she murmured.

"Is that all you can say?" Billy demanded, startled by her composure. "There's probably a monster inside every one of those pods and you're worried about the rug."

"It's a front," she said. "Of course I'm terrified that those things are in my house. But until we find out what they are, there's not much we can do but watch. That'll be my assignment for the day. You go to work."

"All right, but I think we should lock the door," Billy replied.

"Don't be silly. How will you get in then? We'd have to break the lock."

"Mom, listen," Billy said firmly. "I'm not leaving the house if that door isn't locked."

"Oh, go on. I'll be all right." Lynn couldn't help smiling, though, at his concern for her.

Billy shook his head, started to reach for the latch.

"Come on," Lynn said, grabbing his hand. "You'll be late, and jobs are hard to get these days." Then she added what she hoped was a convincing fillip. "Especially jobs where you work right next to somebody like Kate Beringer."

It didn't work. "I'm not going to the bank until that door is locked," Billy said resolutely.

"Your father won't like paying a locksmith when we have to get in again."

"But he'll like it if you're still alive," Billy countered.

Shrugging, Lynn turned the knob to the locked position and pulled the door closed. Billy tested it, nodded.

As they walked downstairs, Billy still carrying Gizmo in the knapsack, Lynn could not resist adding an infelicitous thought. "Suppose," she said, "just suppose that whatever pops out of those pressure cookers is not only a monster, but a monster with pretty fair intelligence."

Billy looked at her blankly.

"What I mean is, if they're smart," Lynn continued,

"won't they be able to figure out how to turn the latch and just walk out the door?"

Billy sighed. What she'd said had some merit, of course, but he really didn't want to think about it.

"If they're that smart, Mom," he said, "I figure there's nothing the human race can do but learn how to surrender."

CHAPTER FOURTEEN

It was Friday, the day before Christmas Eve, and throughout Kingston Falls the holiday buildup reached a crest, causing a lethargy in some and hyperactivity in others. In school, youngsters squirmed in their seats, as resistant to instruction as a cat to sarcasm; workers not under siege by last-minute shoppers went about their jobs in a desultory manner, like dieters approaching a plate of steamed carrots. In the shopping areas it was a different matter, however, as the lazy or super-efficient or guilt-ridden began their final sorties on the gift shops and department stores. Watching them carefully during the holiday season, one might have noticed a marked change in their attitude as the days clicked off before Christmas. Friendly, even jovial and outgoing at the beginning, now, as the final shopping days approached, they resembled fierce, dedicated soldiers or, in some cases, zombies programmed to perform a specific task regardless of the obstacles. Driven by desperation/determination to ferret out those last few presents, their eyes focused only on their goal. Like a plane or ship moving through dense fog or dead of night, each was an isolated pulse of life surrounded by a vacuum; the only beacon ahead or to the side was the gift—that special something that would bring a smile of delight to the person who had everything, convince Herbie the kid who started looking forward to Christmas in February that he need never fear disappointment again, or, best of all, provide the equalizing element so that no one would feel cheated.

A cold wind, the harbinger of more snow, whipped through Kingston Falls, knocking askew and then loose an "S" on the marquee of the Colony Theatre, which then proclaimed as its main attraction, NOW WHITE AND THE SEVEN DWARFS. No one noticed, or if they did, they couldn't bother with a second glance. It was, after all, a time for important decision making. In the town square, Pete Fountaine, Sr., seller of Christmas trees, trembled in the cold as he realized that once again he was nearing the point of no return. How much longer could he keep the tree prices sky-high? It depended, of course, on how many desperate people there still were, people who had waited this long and were afraid to wait longer. From this point on in the day, both sides knew it was a battle of wills to see who would weaken first. As often as he had played the game, Pete Senior never could predict how it would turn out. Three years ago, he had kept prices high to the end and been rewarded with a rash of late albeit angry buyers; two years ago, he had kept the prices high and been stuck with hundreds of trees; last year, he had lowered the prices early and still gotten stuck.

Pumping his arms to warm himself, he watched Father Bartlett stop at the corner mailbox and carefully drop in several stacks of greeting cards. Did he actually expect them to be delivered in time for Christmas? Of course not, Pete

Senior chuckled. He knew that the cards, one and all, were addressed to those left off Father Bartlett's mailing list who had surprised him with cards.

Pete Senior wished he could be as busy as the bank across the way. A constant flow of people went in and out of that building, for if Christmas was the very life of the holiday season, the bank was the heart. Nearby, in their warm patrol car, Sheriff Reilly and Deputy Brent, guardians of the town square, sat and watched to make sure no one's holiday was marred by a bank heist, a fistfight over a present, or a fender battle over a parking space.

Inside the mercantile chamber, which pumped signatures on paper one way and cash the other, Billy and three other tellers worked as fast as they could. Nevertheless, the population of Kingston Falls had never seemed so large or single-minded; from the first minute after opening, a steady stream of customers, which snaked through a line marked by velvet cords, had been backed up nearly to the doorway.

Billy didn't mind the work. In fact, he preferred having something to occupy his mind instead of worrying about those pods in his home. Only the fact that his mother was a very sensible, strong person who had promised to leave at the first hint of trouble kept his nervousness to a minimum. During several very brief breaks in the banking action he had attempted to tell Kate what had happened, but he had probably sounded incoherent. Having Gerald Hopkins standing nearby, watching for the first error he made, didn't help his composure.

Nor did the appearance of Mrs. Deagle.

Watching her pause a moment after entering the bank, Billy knew she was going to head straight for his window. And for a few seconds it appeared that was her destination. Then, veering away from him, she caused him to exhale with relief as she pushed her way past the next customer heading for Kate's window.

"Help you, Mrs. Deagle?" he heard Kate ask, ostensibly friendly but cold underneath.

"Yes, dearie," Mrs. Deagle crooned. "I understand you've been circulating a petition trying to prevent me from closing that saloon you work in."

"If this is a personal matter, it might be better to discuss it after business hours," Kate replied.

"This is a personal business matter," Mrs. Deagle shot back. "I always mix business with pleasure. And now it gives me a great deal of pleasure to tell you that your petition is useless. As soon as the holidays are over, I'm selling a hundred and four properties to the Hitox Chemical Corporation."

"Just as I suspected." Kate smiled.

"Just as you suspected, but are powerless to prevent.. As you no doubt realize as a result of your snooping, your own home is one of those properties and so is that saloon. After the first of the year, I'll sign the deal and all of you will have ninety days to get out. What do you think of that?"

"I guess there's nothing I can say," Kate murmured. "It's just the kind of a Christmas present I can see you giving."

"I'll thank you not to be impertinent, young lady."

Kate opened her mouth as if to respond but in a split second changed her mind. Instead, she spoke gently. "Mrs. Deagle, you're going to hurt a lot of good people. My folks can afford to move, but some of the people you're forcing out just don't have the money to buy a new place. Isn't there any way we can prevail upon you to change your mind?"

"You have two chances," Mrs. Deagle said, smiling wickedly. "None and less than none. And now if you'll deposit this check, I'll be on my way home."

Billy looked at Kate. For one of the few times since he had met her, she seemed truly hurt and at a loss for words. His next act was impulsive and certainly reckless. Spotting a broom tucked beneath the counter, he grabbed it and pushed it through the opening in front of him toward Mrs. Deagle.

"What's that?" she mumbled huffily, drawing back as if he meant to strike her.

"It's a broom," Billy answered.

"What do you want me to do with it?"

"I thought you might need a ride home," he said.

Mrs. Deagle's eyes widened as several customers in the near vicinity began to chuckle.

Leaving her holding the broom, Billy took the deposit slip in front of him and began to work on it, all the while sneaking a glance at both Mrs. Deagle and Kate.

The old woman was furious and seemed ready to explode. Kate, on the other hand, could not suppress a smile. Billy was not sure what was going to happen next, but he was certain that, whatever the outcome, brightening Kate's day made it worth it.

Preoccupied with the object in his laboratory and exhausted from his long hours of research, Roy Hanson was as anxious to get through the day as his students, who were already restless to get into the new snow. Despairing of getting their attention with unusual teaching methods or subject matter, too stubborn to just let them sit and study or talk, he had decided to review their study of the brain in the hope a little material would stick with someone. Before him on his desk was a colorful, electronic model of the human brain with various sections that flashed on and off. Weighing close to a hundred pounds, it was a splendid instructional tool—and a shame to waste on such a lost cause of a day. Hanson had little choice, however, so he plunged ahead.

"Anybody know what we call this?" he asked, pointing to the lit portion of the brain.

No one answered.

"Chuckie?" Hanson said, nodding toward a chubby, oversized youth with prominent teeth.

"Ah, the crouton?" Chuckie murmured.

"The crouton," Hanson repeated, rolling his eyes. "Get them in my Caesar salad all the time. Any other guesses?"

Samantha Weaver, the smartest student in the class, caught his eye. "Thalamus," she said confidently.

"Close, but I'll get another doctor to do my brain surgery," he replied. "It's the medulla oblongata." Then, his irritation beginning to show, he said, "What is it with you kids? I mean, look at this thing. When I was your age, I was learning this stuff from old books. You people have something outa "Star Trek" and you still can't learn it."

He glared at them. They in turn avoided his glance. And in the grim silence that followed, a wet pop, like a piece of ripe fruit splitting, could be heard very distinctly. It came from the lab.

Hanson decided to ignore it, but when it happened again, he knew he would have to investigate.

"Open your books to page one-thirty-seven and study the brain glossary. I want everybody to know it."

As he stood up to go to the lab, his gaze met that of Pete Fountaine.

That's right, Pete, he thought, I believe its time has come.

Looking nervously at his watch, he strode smartly out of the classroom, breathing a silent prayer his chastised students would not hear their tough teacher scream for help a moment later.

Gizmo put his ear against the bedroom door and listened carefully for the tenth time since he had left the knapsack's safety in favor of keeping watch. Too bad Billy's mother didn't share his concern, he thought. Oh, she made periodic trips into the hallway to see if anything dramatic had happened, but otherwise she seemed to go about her business as usual, answering the telephone and chatting in a completely normal way. If she was worried, she managed to hide it quite well, clucking good-naturedly at Gizmo as he crouched near the flower stand just outside Billy's room.

There was no way she could have known what was likely to happen in a matter of minutes or hours; nevertheless, it maddened Gizmo to see how these Earthlings had adapted to living in the shadow of disaster. Blast Mogturmen! If he had made them able to communicate as well as most other animals, Gizmo would have been able to tell them that their best course of action was to burn the Peltzer house. Yes! It sounded terrible, but it was the only way. Bright fire, paralyzing with visual pain even as it destroyed. Otherwise . . .

"Oh, no . . ."

The sound of her voice, low and plaintive, interrupted Gizmo's fatalistic chain of thought. Yet the sadness in Lynn's tone gave him hope that she had come to the realization that drastic action must be taken.

Hurrying back downstairs, he moved through the dining room and stopped just at the edge of the kitchen, where she was talking on the phone. Listening to her was really not eavesdropping in the strictest sense, as he did not understand every word these people said; rather, he usually got a sense of what they were talking about, and now he knew immediately she was involved in a personal matter, distressing but not life threatening.

"But Rand, honey," she said, sighing, "we're expecting you tonight."

At the other end of the line, standing in the middle of a frenzied convention room, Rand Peltzer tried not to be distracted by the parade of robots, bizarre mechanical toys, and noisy salespeople who moved back and forth. "I know, honey," he said. "But they've closed most of the roads, at least the main ones. And the ones that are open . . . they're so treacherous . . . But I promise if it clears a little, I'll try to drive home."

"O.K.," Lynn murmured. "Just be careful. . . . I mean, we've never spent a Christmas apart."

"Yeah. How's everything there?"

Lynn hesitated, but only briefly, deciding in a split second that it would do no good to tell him about the things that were upstairs. He was a terrible driver on snow and ice, and if he were in a hurry . . .

"Fine," she replied. "Billy went to work and I'm sitting here with Gizmo."

"See you soon, then."

"Bye, honey," Lynn said, and hung up.

"Bye."

"Hello," Billy said.

Getting an "urgent" telephone call at work, especially on this day and under his present circumstances, made Billy nervous for several reasons. He was, first of all, concerned that his mother was in some kind of danger; nor was he made comfortable by Gerald Hopkins's hanging around after he gave him the receiver (expecting, no doubt, at least a death in the family for the call to be legitimate); finally, the dust from the battle with Mrs. Deagle had barely settled and he was still the center of attention of most eyes in the bank. Under the magnifying glass, he found it difficult to compose himself and his hand shook when he lifted the receiver to his mouth.

"It hatched," the voice at the other end said, startling him with its succinctness.

"What?"

"I said it just hatched," Roy Hanson said at the other end of the line.

"What . . . what is it?" Billy stammered.

"Hard to say right now. Why don't you come by and have a look? It's almost time for you to quit, isn't it?"

"Yes," Billy replied. "But . . . listen, I'll have to call home first and find out what's happened there."

"Sure. I'll be here."

"Listen, Mr. Hanson, you don't think it's dangerous, do you?" Billy asked, aware that several sets of eyes were on him.

"Well, it's no butterfly," Hanson replied. "I can tell you that."

"I'm gonna call home first," Billy said. "And if everything's all right there, I'll drop by."

"Good. See you in a while then, I hope."

Billy hung up, dialed his home phone number. When his mother answered, he spoke quickly and decisively. "Listen carefully," he said. "Mr. Hanson at the school just called to tell me the Mogwai came out of its pod. So ours probably aren't far behind. Can you go upstairs and see what's happened with them?"

"How can I?" Lynn demanded. "You made me lock the door from the inside."

Billy had forgotten that.

"Then go up and put your ear to the door. You'll be able to hear if anything's moving around."

"All right. Shall I call you back?"

"I'll wait," Billy said. Hopkins and Mr. Corben were staring at him, not to mention Mrs. Deagle, but he was too agitated about the latest Mogwai development to care. A minute later his mother picked up the receiver.

"All quiet," she said.

"Good. I'll be home soon. I'm leaving now, but I thought

I'd make a pass by school first. Maybe Mr. Hanson will know more by then or be able to give me some advice on how to deal with these new critters."

"O.K. I'll be careful."

"When's Dad coming home?"

"Not until later. He's been held up by the snow."

"Oh . . . well, bye."

Billy hung up, then went to close his window, and reached for his jacket.

"Sorry, Mr. Corben," he said to his boss, who watched him with a quizzical expression. "There's a small emergency at home and I've got to take care of it."

"Wait just a moment," Mrs. Deagle said, emerging from the background to assert herself. "This man was impertinent and I demand you fire him."

"Mr. Corben can fire me later," Billy said.

"And he will," the voice of Gerald Hopkins called after him as he raced for the front door.

Stripe thought at first, as consciousness started to return, that while sleeping he had slipped his head beneath one of the heavy rugs in Billy's room. But he soon realized that it wasn't just his head that was immobilized in some foreign environment; his entire being seemed to be in a state of suspended animation. Try as he might, he could see nothing but a filamentous curtain, as if he were packed past his eyes in heavy soup or grease. Nor could he hear much beyond a murky burble every time he moved what, with his blunted senses, he judged was his head.

His first emotion was curiosity; the second—panic— followed quickly. It came with the sudden surety that he and his cohorts had been drugged and packed in crates or some other strong containers and were now awaiting destruction. We waited too long, he thought angrily; we knew how to multiply but didn't. I, their leader, was tricked by that mealymouthed, smooth-talking minority Mogwai into delaying reproduction until the secret of greater size and strength was revealed. Now, too late, Stripe saw the fiendish logic of his adversary's strategy. With only four majority Mogwai, they were not only manageable but could be trapped at some opportune moment and eliminated. But how could Gizmo and his human allies have drugged and imprisoned dozens, scores, perhaps hundreds of them? It would have been impossible. In waiting for greater power, as opposed to numbers, Stripe had failed. Nearly deaf and blind, immobile, physically and mentally helpless, his main emotion was self-loathing at what his stupidity had cost them.

As the shock waves generated by his thoughts coursed through him, Stripe thought for a moment that his physical presence shifted. Was there not a soft white, out-of-focus area ahead of him where only gray had been before? Struggling to move toward it but being unable to do so, he experienced new pulsations of frustration and anger. If only he could be free a minute! Just a single minute of time so that he could place one claw on the lower jaw of the creature called Gizmo, another on his upper, pause to enjoy the look of anguish and panic, and then pull, tear, and twist downward.

The mental image brought Stripe pleasure, but it was nothing compared to the joy he experienced a moment later. That was generated by the flash of knowledge that *he could kill Gizmo*. . . . Countless times before, he had tried to envision doing violence to him, but something inside his brain had invariably denied him even the pleasure of imaginary retribution. It was as if that thought was automatically short-circuited out of existence before it could be implemented. Now he remembered. Mogturmen, that bungling do-gooder, had programmed his precious Mogwai creations so that they could not kill one another, or, for that matter, even think seriously of it.

Why then could Stripe now not only picture himself killing Gizmo, but know deep down that what he saw would not be just a mental image but a certainty if they met again? There was only one answer. *He was no longer a Mogwai!*

If he could have leaped for joy, Stripe would have done so at that moment of recognition.

Now his thoughts and intuitions were crystallizing even as new developments were taking place in the physical realm. The white area he could see ahead was definitely closer and brighter. Stripe became more conscious of having a body as opposed to being a helpless blob suspended in liquid Styrofoam. If he concentrated very hard, it seemed a possibility for him to actually propel himself toward the mouth of the cave—toward the light. Though its intensity tortured him, he knew this was the painful portal through which he must pass—he was moving more perceptibly now, definitely moving—through which he must pass—a rushing sound grew so rapidly it was deafening, competing with the growing light to control his agony—must pass to be—

Reborn!

Suddenly, through a thick haze at first and then with startling clarity, Stripe saw the room again. The bed . . . drawing table . . . drawn window shades . . . all the familiar things.

And some unfamiliar ones. Notably three huge pods surrounding him. Staring at them curiously, it took Stripe nearly a minute to realize that he himself was projecting from the top of a fourth huge wad. With the realization came a new rush of panic. Could the four objects be carnivorous plants of some sort, plants that even now were in the process of devouring him? Could it be that his "rebirth" was nothing more than a momentary escape from the jaws of this hungry plant?

Struggling fiercely, he pulled his arms upward, twisting

Rand Peltzer (right) shops for a special Christmas gift for his son.

Billy Peltzer (left) introduces Gizmo to his friend, Pete Fountaine.

Billy and his father test Mr. Peltzer's latest invention, the Bathroom Buddy.

Five Mogwai
sleep peacefully
next to
Billy's bed.

Kate Beringer (left) and Billy uncover Mrs. Deagle's
plans for the development of the town.

Roy Hanson
runs some
experiments
on the Mogwai.

Billy and Mrs. Peltzer find five strange pods in Billy's room.

Lynn Peltzer defends her kitchen against a Gremlin attack.

Billy trails Stripe to the YMCA building.

Before Billy's eyes, the swimming pool hisses, boils, and explodes.

Mr. Futterman crouches, horrified, as the snowplow comes to life.

Mrs. Deagle, about to meet her untimely end.

Kate tries to maintain order in Dorry's Pub...

...but chaos reigns.

Kate and Billy run for cover as…

…the theatre, filled with Gremlins, blows up.

Billy tracks down Stripe
in the department store.

"Bye, Billy."

his shoulders like a cork being screwed out of a wine bottle, pounding rhythmically with his fists, sideways and down, up and sideways, until—

Splat.

Stripe's right arm shot like a rocket through the pulpy mass, rose high into his field of vision in a dripping wet salute of triumph.

But what an arm! Surely it wasn't his. And yet it was. It moved, rotated, pointed according to the dictates of his mind. Looking at it, like a person slowly returning to complete consciousness after a long sleep, Stripe knew. The final piece of the puzzle was in place. The power and strength had come.

He took a moment to survey the imposing appendage raised above him. No longer ending in a soft furry paw, the arm was nearly two feet long, rippling with muscles beneath a scaly skin ringed with white, green, and brown stripes. His arm seemed more an instrument of destruction than a commonplace tool for lifting and manipulating objects. A combination maul and trident, the heavily boned fist ended in three giant claws, each sharpened to a glistening point.

I am no longer a Mogwai, Stripe thought.

I am a Gremlin.

He had no idea how he knew the word, just as he had no knowledge how or why the physical metamorphosis had occurred. Those details were not important at the moment. What mattered now was the feeling of power about to be fulfilled. Worming free of the pod, he stood next to it momentarily, looking down at the rest of his new body. Bouncing lightly on the tips of his enormous clawed feet, he savored the realization that finally, freed from the puny Mogwai body, he would be able to satisfy the urges that had tormented him so long.

Best of all, he had not only been reborn, but in the process had redeemed himself and his strategy. Shaking with anticipation, he looked intensely at the other pods.

"Hurry, hurry, hurry!" he hissed gleefully at them. "We've got work to do, great fun to enjoy!"

A green mist was hanging gently over the broken pod, as if someone had sprayed a wintergreen aerosol there. No one actually had, but it could have used it, in Roy Hanson's opinion. Whatever it was that had just come into the world had brought an unpleasant smell with it, acrid, hot, faintly redolent of material scorched by an iron.

He stood at the doorway to the lab, returning after having made certain no students remained in or near his classroom. At least no immediate explanation was needed and now there was privacy to study what had been produced.

Looking across the lab at the green glow, he hesitated. In the tub directly below the cloud of fallout material was the new product and the remains of its pod. He had taken only a few seconds to look at it before calling Billy; that was all he'd needed to realize this was indeed no butterfly but a potentially dangerous animal. The flash of teeth— fangs was a better description—had told him that. He could still see them in his mind's eye—two rows of widely spaced, finely sharpened teeth framing the entrance to a huge, wide, bloodred mouth, the same color as the malevolent eyes that had flashed at him during his brief look at the beast.

It was getting ready to make its first foray into the world. Bits of the pod were already on the floor and were being joined by others as the creature—whatever it was—churned restlessly in the smooth metal tub. The basin wouldn't hold it very long, Hanson knew, suddenly realizing he had no idea how to handle the animal or protect himself.

Standing still, he looked around the room. The shades, which he had drawn in order to keep the Mogwai from crying out in pain, gave him an idea. If the creature was afraid of light, Hanson would use this aversion as a means of protecting himself. At the moment the lab was quite dark. If it got free, the animal would be at ease regardless of where it went.

"Which is not a good idea," Hanson said.

He went to the light panel and one by one flipped on the lights of the room's perimeter. When the outer rim was illuminated, he added lights to the adjacent interior areas until he had created an island of relative darkness in the very middle of the lab. Surveying the scene, he felt more at ease. The safety of bright lights was less than ten feet away in every direction.

"Maybe I'm gettin' chicken in my old age," Hanson muttered to himself. "But it's better to be safe than sorry."

He had already decided that he needed a blood sample to compare with the others he had taken of the parent creature, so he wheeled the cart containing his equipment to the edge of the light. In the case was a sterile container with dozens of samples and already-sterilized hypodermic needles. After checking to make sure he had a pair of heavy gloves, Hanson paused again.

"This baby won't be so easy to handle," he said. "Maybe I better get a bribe."

Walking briskly out of the lab, through his classroom, and into the hall outside the canteen, he bought a Snickers bar from one of the vending machines and started unwrapping it as he returned to the lab.

Then, pausing once again at the rim of darkness, he smiled. "Hey, man," he said. "Let's go. What are you, scared or something?"

Pushing the cart to the tub, he looked inside.

The animal was lying on its side, obviously still cleaning itself of debris from the pod before exploring further. When it spotted Roy, it fixed him with a cold stare.

"Hello, boy." Hanson smiled. "How was your trip to Pupa-land?"

The animal regarded him with neither friendliness nor open hostility.

"I figured you might be hungry after all you've been through," Hanson continued, "so I got you a candy bar."

He held out the bar but the animal didn't reach for it.

As he waited for it to make up its mind, Hanson studied the creature closely. He estimated that it was about two and a half feet tall, a biped with incredibly long arms. The brown soft fur of the Mogwai had been replaced by dark, rippled armor plating that looked rock-hard. Its paws and feet were now three-toed claws and along its back ran a ridge of armor, not unlike that of a prehistoric reptile. The only feature that remained in any way similar to the old Mogwai was its nose, which remained pug and cute in the midst of a face that was notable for its malevolence.

"C'mon, boy," Hanson urged, moving the candy bar closer to its mouth, "there's nothin' to be afraid of."

Well into the darkened area, Hanson continued his line of patter, perhaps as much for his own benefit as the animal's.

"See the candy bar?" he crooned. "Doesn't it look good? C'mon, you better eat something, fella."

Putting his hand on the edge of the tub, Roy noticed a bit of movement at the base of the animal's nose. It had obviously gotten its first good sniff of the candy bar and was interested. Moving the bar forward, Roy released it barely a split second before a giant paw reached out to grab the delicacy.

"Good," Roy laughed, partly in relief that he had escaped with his hand intact. "You'll like it."

Slurping noisily, the Gremlin began devouring the bar in a bite and a half. Hanson wished he had bought several more to keep it busy while he tried to get a blood sample.

"I think you trust me now, so we'll trade. Candy for blood, O.K.?"

Reaching gingerly into the cart, he slowly brought out a hypodermic needle and took a couple of more steps closer to the animal. It continued to munch happily, and soon Roy was in a position to reach out and get his sample.

Lifting the needle from where he had hidden it alongside his leg, he made a quick movement forward.

Fast as Roy was, the Gremlin was quicker. At first sight of the syringe, its eyes narrowed and the pupils glowed a fierce purple.

My God, Hanson thought. It remembers.

He did not have time to think further. With a loud snarl, the Gremlin hurled itself out of the tub in Roy's direction. One set of claws dug into the man's shoulder while the other reached clear around his torso to enter his chest like giant staples.

As he fell screaming to the floor, Roy Hanson saw that he was a good five feet from the lighted area.

Gizmo's temperature rose every minute Lynn was on the telephone. Didn't she realize he needed to communicate with her? To tell her that the creatures upstairs must be destroyed? It was a terrible thing to consider, their destruction, but once a Mogwai entered the pod stage, Gizmo's loyalty to it—and its to him—ended abruptly.

He had seen it happen before, as had the three other minority Mogwai on this planet, and the results were nearly always disastrous. The most recent episode, not caused by a spawn of Gizmo, had occurred late in 1983, when a single Mogwai somehow got aboard an American space shuttle craft, *Columbia*. Because of strict government secrecy, details were never published concerning exactly how the Mogwai was allowed to reproduce, feed after midnight, and turn into a Gremlin. In any event, the Gremlin eluded capture by the six-man crew long enough to shut down the computer handling the craft's guidance and navigation systems. When the scientists switched to the number two computer, the Gremlin found a way to cause an overload. It then got into the system that senses the ship's acceleration, position, and angle of attack. Over the Indian Ocean, *Columbia* actually started falling out of orbit and was out of contact with Mission Control for forty-five minutes. During that hectic time the pilots and scientists managed to pursue the Gremlin into a storage compartment and kill it. Returning to earth eight hours late as a result of the Gremlin's meddling, the crewmen were debriefed by government officials, who warned them not to describe what had actually happened on the mission.

Before that...a montage of Gremlin-created or -influenced events, some major and some trivial, rushed through Gizmo's mind....There was...the Memphis runaway escalators of 1972...the 1969 Super Bowl...the East Coast power failure of November 1965...a lesser-known power failure a month later in Texas, New Mexico, and Juarez, Mexico...the closing in 1963 of the New York *Mirror*, a newspaper that simply could not get the Gremlins out of its machinery...the 1962 collision of a runaway train, jet plane, and seagoing tanker at Danzig, Poland, the largest sea-air-land disaster in history...the Bay of Pigs paramilitary fiasco of 1961...the hilarious but potentially dangerous three-day episode at the Onawa, Iowa, buttonhole factory in 1957...the myriad antics of World War II all the way back to the complete disappearance of Vansk, until 1936 the largest city in Siberia...

Now it was Kingston Falls's turn. Or so it seemed. But it did not have to be—yet. If Gizmo could somehow convince the Peltzers that locked doors and careful listening were not enough to—

He heard a click...then a sliding sound, which seemed to come from Billy's bedroom upstairs. Crouched at the foot of the foyer stairway, he listened intently for nearly a minute, but except for Lynn's chattering on the telephone, the house was quiet. He had just about convinced himself his imagination was playing tricks when a popping sound came from upstairs.

Scurrying into the kitchen, Gizmo was forced to pull up short, spinning like a top on one paw, when he reached the counter. He looked around nervously. Lynn had hung up the phone and was no longer in the kitchen. Nor was she in the pantry, basement, or anywhere else on the first floor. Was it possible she had gone upstairs without Gizmo seeing her?

Climbing onto the kitchen counter, he looked out the back window, shading his eyes carefully. He spotted her then, at the far end of the yard throwing bits of old bread to the birds. She was in the habit of doing this, especially when the ground was covered with snow, but didn't she realize leaving the house today simply was not a good idea?

There's not much I can do but wait, Gizmo thought, watching the ballet of stark black pecking forms against the white backdrop.

A moment later another sound came from upstairs, much louder than the first ones.

"Hurry, hurry," Gizmo called to Lynn in Mogwai words. "We need you back here."

Performing her task with infuriating slowness, Lynn showed no sign of coming back soon.

Gizmo gnashed his teeth, pounded on the window with his tiny paws. The light from outside caused him intense pain, even though it was late afternoon on a cloudy day, but he forced himself to continue rapping.

Sklurk. Wump.

More sounds from upstairs.

With a final angry glance at Lynn, Gizmo hopped down from the counter. Something had to be done. What, he knew not, but at the very least he had to know if the Gremlins had come out of the bedroom or were still in the post-metamorphosis stage. Moving quickly to the base of the stairs, he looked up into the hallway outside Billy's bedroom. Was the door open a crack? Or was that just the way a shadow fell?

He waited, one ear cocked in the direction of upstairs, the other toward the kitchen so that he would not miss Lynn's return.

The long silence continued.

As he waited, Gizmo considered methods of thwarting or at least delaying the Gremlins once they began their offensive of mischievous destruction, as experience told him they soon would. The key, in his estimate of the situation, was the bedroom door. Until it became very dark outside, the Gremlins would not attempt to escape via the windows. That left only the door, which, although locked, was by itself a slim reed against the storm. But if another obstacle could be placed outside the door . . . an obstacle such as . . .

Fire. Of course. But how could he make it happen? Gizmo's brow furrowed as he thought furiously, trying to conjure up memories of how—And then he had it. Wasn't there a container of something in the father's workshop—?

Thinking no further, he headed for the basement, several times spinning at corners as his whirling paws slid on the kitchen tile floor. Momentarily, as he sat recovering from a nasty slide in the kitchen, he considered taking another look outside for Lynn, but he soon decided that could wait. The important thing at this moment was to locate the container and, as he recalled, something with which to ignite the liquid. If Lynn came in by the time he found what was needed, Gizmo would make her see what he had in mind.

If she remained outside, he would tackle the dangerous but necessary job alone.

Determined now and buttressed by a certain fatalism, he negotiated the basement stairs two at a time until he was five from the bottom, at which point he fell headfirst the rest of the way. Shaking himself, he got up, raced into the workroom, climbed onto Rand's bench, and studied the array of cans, jars, and bottles stacked on the shelf above it.

Straining to remember the configuration of foreign letters and colors on the can, he finally found it and, without too much difficulty, got it down. It read: LIGHTER FLUID. The words meant nothing to him except the important fact that instant fire was produced when a match touched the liquid.

Easily locating a pack of matches, Gizmo began the ticklish task of trundling up the basement stairs with his cargo. Arriving at the kitchen counter, he dropped his load, climbed a stool, and peered outside once again. He did not see Lynn at first, which caused hope to rise in him that she was already at or near the door. A moment later, however, he spotted her, farther away than ever, talking with a neighbor.

Shaking his head angrily, Gizmo hopped off the stool, grabbed his weapons, and began the ascent to the upstairs hallway.

Two steps from the top of the stairs he paused, listened, and once again studied the door from this much more advantageous perspective. It did seem to be open a crack. Was it always that way in the locked position? Or—

Dismissing the thought from his mind lest it deter him from continuing his mission, Gizmo crawled onto the landing with his gear. Fortunately, the heavily carpeted stairs and hallway deadened any sounds he might have made under less favorable circumstances.

Carefully unscrewing its top, Gizmo lay the lighter fluid

can on its side, aimed the opening at the floor just below the door, and pushed. The wall of the container yielded to his weight, propelling a thin stream of liquid into the general vicinity he hoped to saturate. But immediately after, in flexing back to its original shape, the can made a hideously loud snapping noise.

His mouth agape, Gizmo stood frozen to the spot, his paws as unmovable as lead ingots.

Even when he heard heavy footsteps on the other side of the door coming toward him, he could not move.

And then the door opened, revealing a leering Gremlin face topped with a mane of coarse white fur and a gigantic three-taloned hand, which quickly and roughly encircled his tiny body.

CHAPTER FIFTEEN

Billy roared up to the school, amazed at how few students he had passed on the way but relieved that he would not have to deal with the traffic bottleneck at the entrance circle. Pulling as close to the front entrance as possible, he got out of the car and trotted to the door.

It was locked.

Inside, past the cross-hatching of wired glass, he could see that the main hallway was in almost total darkness. The Christmas exodus seemed to be more complete this year than ever. There was a solitary figure in the hallway, however, so Billy pounded on the door with one hand and rapped his key against the glass with the other. Reluctantly the figure—who turned out to be veteran maintenance man Waldo Sodlaw—ambled up to the door and yelled the obvious thing.

"Closed," he said.

"It's an emergency," Billy replied. "Please let me in, Mr. Sodlaw."

Perhaps knowing the old gentleman's name helped. In any event he grimaced one time, sighed, and finally opened the door.

"Thanks," Billy said.

"What's the emergency?"

"I've got to see Mr. Hanson."

"He's gone."

"Are you sure? Did you see him leave?"

"No, but I made a pass through his class. He wasn't there. Left the lights on in his lab, so I turned 'em off."

"Well, I'd better check," Billy said, starting to move down the hall.

Sodlaw followed. "I told you," he said. "He's gone. Now let me close up and get my work done so I can go home."

"I'll only be a minute," Billy yelled over his shoulder.

Breaking into a trot, he left Sodlaw far behind but could hear his footsteps echoing through the deserted halls when he turned into Hanson's lab and stopped.

The lights were off, shades drawn, and no one seemed to be about, but Billy felt a presence. For one thing, the room had a strange smell, completely unlike any of the dissecting smells he remembered from his days in biology lab. When he heard a sharp intake of air, he jumped, looked around, but could see no one. He stood, listening. Behind him, far down the hallway, Mr. Sodlaw was carrying on a semihysterical conversation with someone else outside the building, something about a book left behind. Billy tried to separate those voices from a new sound closer to him— much closer—which reminded him of young girls trying to suppress a giggle. But where was it coming from?

Billy had taken a step toward the light switch when he saw something that sent a chill up his spine.

A shoe, with the foot inside it turned at an odd, uncomfortable angle, as if . . .

Walking slowly toward it, he saw the rest of the body

lying behind the lab table, the twisted form of Roy Hanson.

"Mr. Hanson!" Billy cried out. A wave of panic threatened to make him run from the lab, but he resisted. If the man was only injured or even in critical condition, Billy could do much more good by staying than rushing out. Breathing a silent prayer that Hanson was still conscious, he forced himself to move toward him.

One quick glance at the body told him that Hanson was indeed dead. The same glance indicated that the death was not of natural causes. With mounting horror, Billy gasped at the sight before him.

Three dozen hypodermic needles had been inserted into various parts of Mr. Hanson's torso, making the unfortunate man into a grisly pincushion. In addition, there was a major gash, as if he had been knifed or clawed.

A high-pitched scream reverberated through the lab.

It was not uttered by Billy. Hearing the first echoes of it, he whirled to look into the shrieking jaws of what seemed to be something out of the dinosaur age. High in the air, at Billy's eye level, the dark green, armor-plated thing had hurled itself toward the young man from its hiding spot on the top of the nearby cabinet. The combination scream-giggle ended just as the Gremlin struck Billy's chest, knocking him backward and sideways. Tripping over Hanson's body, Billy cringed away from the massive claws as they passed less than an inch from his face.

In an instant he regained his feet but so had the green demon, which immediately hopped onto the lab table and started another bombing attack. Billy ducked, causing the Gremlin to clatter noisily against the wooden cabinets near the floor. It quickly regained its feet, sprung forward, and with one huge claw gouged a section of corduroy and flesh from Billy's leg.

"Holy—"

The epithet died aborning as a second lunge by the Gremlin brought the two together in a clinch, one of the creature's claws bearing down heavily on Billy's eyes. Turning quickly away, he lashed out with his forearm, striking the Gremlin across the side of its face. It seemed more surprised than hurt by the blow, but Billy was able to slide out of its hot, greasy embrace.

"Mr. Sodlaw!" he yelled.

Simultaneously, he made a break for the door. Though smaller, the Gremlin made up the distance between them quickly, hurling itself against the wall in a kind of carom shot that closed the door and brought it face-to-face with its adversary.

Billy looked around. There was no other way out. His wound, which he had been able to ignore during the heat of battle, now began to throb with pain as he faced the leering creature blocking his way out of the lab.

Then, with frightening speed, the Gremlin launched itself once again, a savage missile speeding directly toward Billy's chest.

In all his centuries of life Gizmo had never been in such a perilous situation.

He was actually in the clawed fist of a Gremlin, vulnerable to mutilation or death by a variety of means. How had it happened? And why? Only a few days before he had been happily snoozing away his peaceful life in the old Chinese man's shop—and now this! Like mortal beings on every galaxy, he suddenly felt terribly unprepared as the moment of death approached.

The cackling face before him, identified by the coarse white fur, could belong only to Stripe, he thought.

"So, minority Mogwai," its different but still recognizable voice grated. "We meet again."

Gizmo nodded sadly.

"We're almost ready now," Stripe laughed.

Gizmo looked around the room at the remains of the four pods and three new inhabitants, who waited impatiently for Stripe to complete his business. Only slightly smaller than he, none of them had the distinctive Stripe mane, but Gizmo was certain they were every bit as evil.

"Let's get going," one of them said. "There's no action here. It's boring."

"We'll go," Stripe yelled back. "How about a game of Gizmoball first, though?"

With that, he flipped Gizmo toward one of the others, giving his body a heavy spin so that objects whirled by crazily during the brief but frightening trip. The second Gremlin hurled him all the way across the room in much the same manner, but the third Gremlin conveniently allowed Gizmo to bounce off his claw tips before landing on the floor.

The unfortunate Mogwai could not help crying out as, his side cut and bleeding, he landed with a thump on his back.

Stripe went into a fit of hysterical laughter.

"Pick him up!" he yelled. "Throw him again!"

His partner obeyed. Five or six more times Gizmo made the horrifying, increasingly nauseating flight from one set of clumsy claws to the next. Then, caught by Stripe, he suddenly felt himself held aloft and turned head down so that he was looking directly into the fierce red eyes.

"One more throw," Stripe giggled. "Then, the next time I get you back, I'm going to rip you to pieces."

Going into a grand windup, he finally released Gizmo, sending him spinning toward the Gremlin awaiting him across the room.

Billy's mind must have decided that, death being close at hand, it would slow down the final moments of his existence so that he might savor the very act of breathing. In any event, as the Gremlin flew toward him, Billy suddenly felt as if everything were moving in slow motion. Scant microseconds passed, but during that interval he scanned every section of the lab within his field of vision—into the cabinets filled with beakers and Bunsen burners (but no weapons); the counters, with their microscopes and slide dishes (but no weapons); to the walls, with framed pictures—

And a fire extinguisher.

A sudden rush of hope caused his body to perform a marvelously reflexive movement: as if he had had his legs shot from under him, Billy dropped downward like a rock, causing the Gremlin to fly over him, its claws flailing frantically in an effort to catch a piece of anything. Even before the falling motion was completed, Billy seemed to twist in midair, his body arching sideways and upward toward the hanging extinguisher. Like a third baseman knocked to the dirt by a hard drive to the chest, he was on his feet in one motion and at the wall.

Tearing the extinguisher loose, he got it in front of him just as the Gremlin sprang again. As it became a blur rushing toward him, he managed to hit the ON switch.

The velocity of the Gremlin's flight caused it to become an instant casualty. Shrieking wildly, its head flew into the funnel of the extinguisher with such force it tore the instrument from Billy's hands. As both the extinguisher and Gremlin struck the wall opposite, a terrible clatter was heard, followed by the rushing noise of the foam and the scream of the creature, which was unable to remove itself from the red tube. Thrashing wildly about the floor as it was force-fed the noxious foam, it kicked, jerked, and clawed great slices out of the wall before it died.

Billy lay on the floor, still stunned, until he heard nothing but Mr. Sodlaw's continuing conversation far down the hallway. Getting slowly and painfully to his feet, he looked about him, just to make sure it wasn't all a dream. But Roy Hanson was still there and so was the extinguished Gremlin.

Any exhilaration he might have felt at being spared had a very brief existence.

"Mom!" he called out, suddenly remembering that there might be four more of the same type monsters at home.

Rushing into Hanson's classroom, he picked up the phone and dialed his home number. He was relieved when his mother answered after only two rings.

"You O.K.?" he asked.

"I think so," Lynn replied. "I couldn't get out of listening to Mrs. Haynie, who just finished psychoanalyzing me."

"Is everything all right at home?"

"Yes. To my knowledge."

"Listen," Billy continued. "Get out of the house."

"Why?"

"Those Mogwai turn into terrible things. Killers."

"Really—"

"Mr. Hanson's dead," Billy interrupted her. "The biology teacher who was studying one of them. It killed him, Mom. I saw it. And then it attacked me."

"Are you all right?"

"Yes. I'm cut up a little—"

"Can you make it to Dr. Molinaro?"

"Forget me, Mom," he said impatiently. "I'm telling you to leave the house. And take Gizmo."

"But we've nowhere to go. And maybe those things won't—"

"Mom, I'm telling you—"

"Just a minute," she interrupted. "I think I heard something. A noise. Like a thump."

"Leave. Just leave!"

"I will. First I'll check upstairs one more time, and then I'll grab Gizmo and go. O.K.?"

"Yeah. Hurry. I'll stay on the line. Give me a shout just

as you go out the door so my mind will be at ease."

"All right," she said, placing the receiver on the counter and starting out of the kitchen.

The flight that was scheduled to be Gizmo's next-to-last turned out to be his last, thanks to an errant throw by the overenthusiastic Stripe.

Careening wildly toward the Gremlin across the room, Gizmo realized—even in his disoriented situation—that he was not going to hit the intended target. Rising higher and higher, he passed above the gleaming claws and headed for Billy's trophy shelf. As the objects raced closer to him, Gizmo tried to curl into a ball to protect himself.

Fortunately, he hit the set of yearbooks first, comparatively soft objects, spun down the length of the shelf in a whirlwind of papers and metal trophies, and finally dropped off the end—next to Billy's laundry chute. For a split second Gizmo looked dumbly at the square opening before suddenly realizing that, wherever it led, it was his highway to freedom. Hurling himself upright as the Gremlins approached, their fangs bared and claws glistening, he hit the wooden door like a fullback sacrificing his body to get a first down. A moment later, his ears ringing and head throbbing from the impact, he plunged downward into the black void that smelled vaguely like his friend Billy.

"Hurry up, hurry up," Billy nearly shouted into the receiver. It had been at least three minutes since his mother had promised him she would grab Gizmo and return with a final word before leaving the house. What could have taken so long? Was she in trouble? Was Gizmo in some godforsaken hiding place?

He looked anxiously at his watch, weighing the benefits of staying on the line—which was basically for his own peace of mind—versus hanging up and getting home as soon as possible.

"I'll give her thirty more seconds," he murmured, watching the digital numbers flash by.

As so often happens when an ultimatum is delivered to either a person, a nation, or fate itself, the response was less than the deliverer hoped—in this case, nothing.

"All right then," Billy said decisively. "That's it. I can't wait any longer."

Hanging up the receiver, he took off toward the front door, his mind filled with conflicting emotions. His sense of responsibility told him he ought to find Mr. Sodlaw so that the body of Roy Hanson would be taken care of; another voice warned him that the scene back in the lab, coupled with his running out of the building, could get the police after him in a hurry; but he was too anxious about the safety of his mother and Gizmo to do the "right" but very time-consuming things. Ignoring Mr. Sodlaw, who appeared out of a side corridor a moment later and began shouting questions after him, Billy slammed against the front door with his shoulder, spun around from the force of the impact, and raced toward the car.

Ten feet from the vehicle, in trying to save a few seconds, he reached in his coat pocket for his keys and, in separating the VW key from the others, took his eyes off the snow-covered ground ahead. A moment later, having missed the curb, he was lying facedown in a snowdrift.

The key was somewhere else.

Lynn was barely out of the kitchen when she heard the series of bumps and scrapes that told her where to investigate. The first sound came from above and proceeded vertically downward into the basement after a brief pause at the first-floor level. She recalled that the laundry chute had a wooden lip there on which clothes occasionally got hung up. She had asked Rand to repair it many times, but as he always managed to have an excuse, Lynn had been dealing with the situation by keeping a long pole in the basement next to the washer-dryer and chute. Playing the sounds through in her mind, she had no doubt at all that a small animal had fallen—or been thrown—down the chute, managed to cling briefly at the lip, and then continued into the basement. Because of the midpoint delay, it was likely the animal, whatever it was, was still alive and well.

Before descending into the basement, she paused.

"If . . ." she said. "Maybe I'd better . . . Just in case . . ."

Going to the kitchen cabinet, she got out the large sushi knife Rand had bought just after he'd discovered this Oriental delicacy (and become interested in developing a machine that would replace those talented people who put the dishes together right before your eyes). Moving down the steps cautiously, she went to the laundry chute and gently opened the door. Holding the knife in front of her, she looked inside.

A pair of glazed eyes stared back at her. Swathed in a jumble of undershirts and socks, the object blinked once but made no other movement.

Was it Gizmo? One of the others? Lynn couldn't tell. The dim lighting and chaotic layer of dirty clothing prevented her from making a visual identification and she was not about to reach in and touch the creature.

While she hesitated, a series of other sounds from the first floor quickly convinced her that what was happening immediately above her was more pressing than getting this animal, whatever it was, out of the laundry chute. As a matter of fact, she thought with a flash of decisiveness, it might not be a bad idea to keep this baby prisoner for the time being.

Reaching into Rand's tool chest, she grabbed a hammer

and three-penny nail. A few seconds later the chute was nailed firmly shut.

Picking up her knife once again, she started quickly up the basement stairs, slowing down only when she reached the top step. Opening the door, she looked into the kitchen and took a step into the room.

A moment later one of her antique china dinner plates shattered against the wall behind and above her, sharp pieces and powder raining onto her head and down the back of her dress.

Lynn screamed. The sound was soon mixed with a high-pitched hysterical giggle.

Regaining his feet but not his composure, Billy looked about for the lost keys. Had they disappeared in the snow-drift along with him? Or been thrown clear?

He stood perfectly still so as not to disturb the snow or possibly bury the keys beneath his weight. Searching with his eyes from a squatting distance, he saw nothing. Meanwhile, Mr. Sodlaw was rapidly approaching, muttering inaudible imprecations.

"Hey, boy," he shouted when he was a dozen feet away. "You're supposed to check in with me before you leave. How do I know you ain't got a microscope or something else stuck in your coat?"

"Hold it," Billy said evenly, and then shouted back when Sodlaw continued charging forward. "Hold it, I said!"

Shocked into immobility, Sodlaw glared at the upstart, his wide mouth moving nervously as if working up to a good string of threats and rejoinders.

"I dropped my keys in the snow," Billy explained. "Please don't mess up anything."

Sodlaw stood his ground while Billy looked, but he continued talking.

"Listen," he said. "I let you in when I wasn't supposed

to, and then you run out on me. If somethin's gone, I could lose my job."

"Nothing's gone, Mr. Sodlaw," Billy replied.

"How do I know that? What was you doin' in there?"

Billy spotted a gleam of something shiny in the snowdrift. Reaching down, he pulled out his keys.

"Gotta go now," he said. "Do you want to pat me down? It's O.K., but be quick."

He unbuttoned his coat and held his arms out straight, the better to facilitate Sodlaw's frisking him.

The old man took a step forward, then shrugged. "Never mind," he muttered. "I guess you're all right. It's just that you ran out so quick, like somethin' awful happened or you stole somethin'."

Billy was already in his car and grinding the engine to life. For a second he considered telling Sodlaw what had happened before speeding off; he rejected the notion instantly.

"Merry Christmas," he said instead, roaring off as quickly as his fishtailing rear-engine car would allow.

After Lynn finished dodging the first barrage of expensive dishes, she had a brief respite in which to look at her attackers. One stood near the china cabinet in the dining room, giggling and searching about for new objects to throw. It eventually decided on a heavy punch bowl, tipping it off the shelf and roaring gleefully when it broke neatly in two.

The second Gremlin was busily going through Lynn's pots and pans, tossing them underhanded and backward as it dug through the drawers. A third was in the pantry, systematically emptying the contents of every box and jar onto the floor. It took only a moment for Lynn to assimilate everything she needed to know about them—that they were powerful, ugly, destructive, and, most important, dangerous. Common sense indicated that she should run screaming

from the house and summon help. Overriding that was a
fierce anger that they were vandalizing *her kitchen*. An
equally fierce determination to defend this precious, hard-
won home prevented her from doing what was both safe
and wise.

"Get out of my house!" she yelled.

She did not expect them to either understand or obey the
order. What she was doing was serving notice, giving them
one last opportunity to cease their depredations before *she*
attacked *them*. It was, in effect, a declaration of war.

A chorus of glee, mixed with shattering dishes and crumpled boxes, was their answer.

"All right," Lynn murmured, grasping the knife tighter
and moving into the middle of the room.

It was not a good move in that she was vulnerable from
bombardment from three sides instead of just one. Objects
flew at her head, a plastic coffee mug striking her temple
along with a cloud of pancake flour. Angered to the point
of blind fury, Lynn lashed out at the Gremlin closest to her,
which stood on the counter she had used only a few hours
ago to make cookies. The blow struck home, the sushi
knife's diamond-sharp blade gouging a sizable portion from
the Gremlin's thigh. It roared furiously at Lynn, found another knife in the cabinet just above its head, and prepared
to throw it.

Lynn let fly the coffee cup, causing the Gremlin to recoil
and stumble backward. In so doing, it caught its clawed fist
in the top of Rand's patented orange juice maker.

Seeing that the animal was momentarily hung up in the
machine, Lynn lurched forward and flipped the START switch.
With a loud whirr, the device started, its powerful engine
drawing the arm of the Gremlin in even farther. With a
scream of agony it began to spin round and round, the arm
disappearing up to the shoulder as a stream of greenish mush
spewed out of the juice spout. Fascinated and horrified,

Lynn watched as the entire Gremlin was sucked into the machine and regurgitated as pulp.

A barrage of bottles and cardboard startled her from her temporary paralysis. Timing their throws craftily so that a steady stream of debris fell on her, the two Gremlins left in the kitchen renewed their attack with even greater fury. Now they concentrated on heavy and sharp objects, a paring knife striking Lynn's cheek and drawing blood. Terrified and furious, she lunged toward the closest Gremlin but in doing so slipped on the glop covering the kitchen floor.

Lying helplessly, she saw both of them crouch prior to leaping.

Billy had gone through several traffic lights, but at Granger Street a moving van backed out directly in front of him, causing him to jam on the brakes. The sudden action caused the car to do what he prayed it wouldn't—stall.

Billy yelled, took a deep breath, and turned the ignition key. For a minute the grinding sounds, which gradually became weaker, told him the familiar story he had been plagued with so long. The carburetor was flooded.

Getting out, he shoved the VW as far off the road as he could and started running.

"Merry Christmas," a few passersby shouted at him.

Even as she reached for the aerosol can of Raid lying inches from her face, Lynn wondered how long her luck was going to hold. A moment later she squirmed sideways to avoid one of the leaping Gremlins and let the other one, still airborne, have a heavy squirt of the vile-smelling chemical directly in its eyes. Temporarily blinded and infuriated, it crashed into the first Gremlin and, slashing wildly with its claws, tore several big chunks of flesh from its brother's body.

Forgotten in the confusion, Lynn scrambled to her feet, still holding the aerosol can.

Backing toward the counter, she suddenly became aware of another presence in the kitchen. Whirling, she saw a third green monster poised to strike. Because it was standing on the counter, its horrible red eyes were on the same level as hers, a pair of mesmerizingly penetrating orbs that seemed to generate their own evil light from within rather than reflect outside illumination. Aiming the insect spray at it, she succeeded in forcing it to back into the corner just in front of the microwave oven. Then with a quick, almost spasmodic leap, she managed to push the Gremlin backward through the open door and into the oven.

Closing the door quickly, she set the temperature to maximum, turned the oven on, and leaned against the door so the thrashing beast could not get out. With the other hand she held the aerosol can in front of her to ward off the angrily circling Gremlins planning their next attack.

A minute later, as she heard popping, disintegrating sounds from the oven, an errant thought crossed Lynn's mind. Thank God I listened to Rand for once, she thought, because he talked me into getting the oven with the big door.

Looking back and down through the glass into the oven, she could see that the Gremlin had been baked into a huge oozy green omelet, the evil red eyes now decorating the bottom portion of the lump like twin spurts of catsup.

No sense worrying about that one, she thought, making a sudden rush for the kitchen door and living room. Her quick lunge carried her past the Gremlins but they caught her near the Christmas tree, one tripping her low while the other landed on her back. Lynn screamed as the animal's knifelike claws tore into her shoulder. Struggling wildly but futilely, she knew that it would be impossible for her to

handle two of them. All she could do was make it as difficult
for them as possible.

With that desperate strategy in mind, with one Gremlin
clinging to her leg and another to her back, she closed her
eyes and hurled herself into the twinkling Christmas tree.

As he broke from a fast trot into a desperate sprint, Billy
wondered if anyone on earth had ever been forced to see
what he had just seen.

Approaching his own home, he was impressed with how
cheerful and peaceful it looked, the warm lights of the
interior offering pleasant contrast to the snow-covered land-
scape outside. The centerpiece of the idyllic home scene
was the large Christmas tree aglow with twinkling lights, a
never-changing symbol of the holiday spirit, an emblem of
peace and contentment.

Then, just as the image had finished registering on Billy's
mind, the tree fell completely out of sight.

"Holy—" he gasped as he began to sprint. "Please . . .
don't let it be too late . . ."

Running on the snow-covered street with its alternating
layers of ice, soft snow, and car-created ruts was not easy;
several times he fell, scraping his hands as he threw them
forward to protect himself, but he never took his eyes from
the picture window of the house. The silhouette he wanted
to see, that of his mother, refused to appear and bring him
a quick answer to the question that haunted him.

Stumbling up the front porch steps, Billy slammed into
the house, reaching out automatically to grasp the wall sword
he knew would be heading toward the floor momentarily.
It did, almost providentially settling into the hand awaiting
it just as Billy saw that Lynn was still alive but bleeding,
her neck protected from the claws of one Gremlin by a
tangle of Christmas tree limbs and ornaments.

Leaping forward, Billy swung the sword, missed, and swung again.

One of the Gremlins, the one with a mane of white fur, ducked the blows, but the second took the full force of Billy's swing just above the shoulder. The edge of the sword dug into the armor plating, then gathered momentum as it reached the soft subcutaneous tissue, neatly severing the body from the Gremlin's head, which rolled into the fireplace. Its expression, caught in a terrified leer, slowly melted to a grotesque frown as the head burned to a crisp.

As Lynn struggled to get to her feet, she and Billy heard a giggle from across the room. It was Stripe, his eyes aflame with anger and defiance.

For a moment Billy seemed about to go after him; then he turned his attention to his mother.

"Are you all right?" he asked, putting the sword down so he could assist her.

"I think so," Lynn murmured. Ever practical, she added, "I think that's the last one. Maybe you'd better get it."

Billy picked up the heavy weapon and started after Stripe, but the Gremlin, now having realized that he was at a disadvantage, looked for a way to escape. Leaping onto a windowsill, he managed to avoid Billy's first swing, which imbedded the sword in the molding. By the time Billy wrestled it free, Stripe had rolled himself into a ball and hurtled himself at the window, shattering the glass. He landed on the snow and scurried off into the night.

"Oh no!" Billy muttered.

He and Lynn took a moment to examine each other's wounds, which were colorfully bloody but not severe.

"Where's Gizmo?" Billy asked.

"In the basement. I think he must have jumped down the laundry chute when all this started."

"Good."

Lynn smiled, brushed a sweaty lock of hair from her forehead. "I nailed the door shut," she said. "That was before I knew who was who."

Picking his way through the kitchen debris, Billy paused a moment to look at the two Gremlins, one baked and the other blended, which his mother had dispatched.

"Boy," he said, shaking his head. "You really are a tiger, aren't you?"

"Let's put it this way," Lynn replied. "I'm not one to be leaned on."

Descending into the basement, Billy found a claw hammer and pulled out the nail in the door of the clothes chute. He opened the door, looked inside.

"Gizmo," he said. "You in there, pal?"

A rustle of material was followed by the gradual emergence of the two long triangular ears and soft furry head of Gizmo. Blinking nervously at the light, he soon broke into his familiar falsetto hum. When Billy reached out, he moved quickly into his hands to be lifted from the jumble of clothing.

"Hey, are you all right?" Billy asked.

Putting Gizmo on the top of the washer-dryer, he examined him for broken bones, noting where he had been cut in several places.

"Let's go put some tape on those cuts," he said, carrying Gizmo upstairs.

Lynn, beginning to straighten up the kitchen, stopped to pet Gizmo and compliment him on still being among the living. "I thought they'd killed you," she said.

"Hey, Mom, look," Billy said suddenly.

Gizmo's eyes were wide as he stared at the remains of the two Gremlins in the kitchen. His expression seemed pleased but somewhat restless, his head swiveling nervously from side to side and off toward the living room.

Lynn looked at Billy blankly.

"Don't you get it?" Billy said. "He's wondering what happened to the other guys. He knows that two are down and wants to know about numbers three and four."

Taking Gizmo into the living room, he showed him the Gremlin head in the fireplace and the ghastly looking body on the hearth. Gizmo grinned and then frowned.

"Yeah," Billy said. "You're right. One got away."

Gizmo started to make anguished noises.

"What's the matter?" Lynn asked.

"We have to get the last one, Mom," Billy replied. "It's no good unless they're all caught or destroyed."

"Well, there's time enough for that," she said. "We can call Sheriff Reilly and let him track it down."

"You don't understand. We don't have much time. If that last one reproduces, it'll start all over again."

"You've got some bad cuts," Lynn protested. "I'd rather you go see Dr. Molinaro."

"Mine aren't as bad as yours."

"All right. We'll both go."

"Tomorrow."

"After they become infected, you mean."

Billy knew his mother was being logical, but he also felt that logic dictated a prompt hunt for Stripe. Although he usually obeyed his mother for the simple reason that she was often right, Billy shook his head. "I'm going now," he said. "While his tracks are still fresh and before he has a chance to multiply."

"All right then."

He located Gizmo's knapsack and put him inside. Hurrying upstairs, he pulled on a sweater for extra warmth. He ran back down to the hallway, and as he shrugged into his coat, he felt a cold metal object in his pocket.

Lynn watched as he pulled it out. It was a can of Raid.

"It's my secret weapon," she said. "You may be able to use it. And don't forget your sword."

Grabbing a flashlight and strapping Gizmo and the knapsack onto his shoulder, he kissed his mother and went out into the snowy night.

CHAPTER SIXTEEN

Few people needed or wanted to visit the formidable Mrs. Ruby Deagle at her home, and fewer still dared try bearding the lioness in her den. That was just the way Mrs. Deagle wanted it, of course. The fewer visitors, the better. Even her late husband, Donald, though a wealthy real estate dealer, had been a burden to her during his last few years. It wasn't because he had a lingering illness; she just didn't like having him around. He had served his purpose, after all, creating a financial empire that would enable her to live very well, so when he shuffled off it was more a relief to Ruby Deagle than a tragedy.

Alone now with her nine cats, she began her typical evening by pouring food in their bowls but not placing the bowls on the floor until the cats had purred and meowed and curled themselves around her ankles for at least five minutes. That was their payment for the free food—obeisance, adoration, and humbling acknowledgment of her ultimate power.

Laughing, she placed the bowls on the floor and watched them fall over each other in their eagerness to eat.

"Cats," she said to herself. "They're so much nicer than people. And they don't have money problems to whine about."

When they had finished eating, Mrs. Deagle would relax before the television, watching her favorite game shows. She especially loved the ones that forced the contestants to utterly degrade themselves in exchange for prizes or money. "I wonder what fools are going to expose themselves tonight," she said aloud, clutching her satin housedress closer around her neck.

The big old house was chilly, but Mrs. Deagle refused to turn the heat up higher than fifty-five degrees even when ice formed at the edges of the windows. "Why should I make the oil companies any richer?" she demanded, whenever her nephew Weldon dropped by with some legal papers and complained about the cold.

She also did not enrich the furniture companies, having kept the original pieces bought just after her and Donald's wedding; those musty chairs and tables had been augmented over the years by furniture taken hostage from families unable to make mortgage or rent payments on time. As a result, the huge rooms—kept dark for economy reasons and piled high with assorted junk—resembled a warehouse containing the contents of unclaimed-freight auctions. If others didn't like it, Mrs. Deagle rationalized, it was just too bad. She was comfortable in these somewhat Gothic surroundings, and that was all that mattered.

Her one concession to modern technology—for even the television was an old black-and-white model—was a device appended to her stairway. Basically a wheelchair attached to a motor and pulley, it had been recommended by Mrs. Deagle's physician so that she would not strain her weak heart by climbing stairs. Although the reason she had the chair was serious, Mrs. Deagle still got something of a thrill when she sat in it, pushed the appropriate button, and automatically ascended to the second floor. Although she would never have admitted it, she often manufactured reasons for going up and down the stairs so that she could enjoy the ride.

She had already seated herself in the device and was about to flip the switch to UP when the doorbell rang.

"Blast!" she rasped. "Who can that be at this hour? Don't people have any regard for others' feelings?"

She walked slowly to the front door, opened it, and peered outside.

It was Mrs. Harris, bundled in an old coat, shivering as she held an envelope in her gloved hands.

Mrs. Deagle did not invite her inside.

"Yes?" she asked coldly.

"I got last month's mortgage payment for you," she said, a bit proudly. "We sold a few personal items and—"

"I'm not interested in that," Mrs. Deagle shot back. "I have a bank that handles my business, you know."

"Yes, ma'am, but it's just that I didn't get the money until after closing and since you said—"

"If I recall, I said I'd like to have everything that's due me, not everything that was due a month ago."

"Sorry, ma'am."

"Is that it?"

"Yes'm."

Mrs. Deagle reached out, snatched up the envelope, and smiled archly. "You probably won't have to worry about dealing with me much longer," she said, "since it's my intention to sell a good deal of my properties to Hitox Chemical. Your place is one. Good evening."

Leaving Mrs. Harris standing with a decidedly confused and unhappy expression on her face, Mrs. Deagle slammed the door.

Returning to the kitchen, where a fight had broken out among the cats, Mrs. Deagle cleaned up around the cats' dishes, made herself a cup of instant soup to enjoy with her television, and ambled into the dank cavern of worn velvet she called her living room.

She was barely settled in her overstuffed rocker when the doorbell rang.

"Again!" she shouted. "This is disgusting. The loser probably stood there for ten minutes, screwing up her courage, and now she wants to plead with me to change my mind. Donald was right. All those little people out there are lazy, mindless slugs who are good for only two things—cheap labor and food consumption..."

As she started toward the door, she made an addendum of her own. "And the creation of garbage," she added fiercely. "He forgot about that."

Opening the door, she was greeted by the sound of carolers, a trifle off-key but enthusiastic.

"Joy to the world..."

Mrs. Deagle threw her hands in the air, a gesture accompanied not with a loud hosanna but a wail of misery.

"Stop!" she shrieked. "Stop emptying your cesspool into my ears!"

The young carolers, shaken but determined to win over Mrs. Deagle, continued:

"The Lord is come.
Let earth receive her King..."

"Go away! I hate carolers!" Mrs. Deagle shouted. "Get off my front lawn! Take your whiny voices somewhere else! To the sanitary landfill! Go-o-o!"

Her shrillness caused the carolers to lose their concentration and place in the music. The melody began to disintegrate in an untidy fugato of overlapping sounds.

"That's better," Mrs. Deagle declared, smiling at the silent group. "If you just stand in the snow and keep your mouths shut, it's much more enjoyable."

She wheeled around and the door slammed behind her.

Confused and hurt, the youngsters looked at one another for comfort. No one said anything for a long moment.

"Let's try the houses in that new development," one of them finally offered. "They're young people, real nice, not like this old . . ."

"Woman," another added charitably.

As the group trudged across the field, they one by one became aware of a member who had not started out with them. Much shorter than the others, he or she was hidden by stature and what seemed to be a heavy scarf at first, and then each assumed the new member was one or another caroler's younger sister or brother who had dressed up in a Halloween outfit and become part of the group. Eventually, when it joined in the caroling, the newcomer's voice generated more attention than its size, shape, or color. Rather like someone singing with the teeth firmly clenched, the words came out blurred and high-pitched, somewhere between the twang of a Jew's harp and the indistinct falsetto of a chipmunk who didn't know the words.

"Maybe," one of the carolers now suggested, "it's that kid who's causing the problem."

"Nah," another replied. "It's just Mrs. Deagle. She hates everything."

"But have you heard how he sings?"

"Sure, but so what? We're not supposed to be the church choir. This is just to make people feel good."

"Yeah. I guess you're right."

Despite agreement that the new kid was not to be criticized because of his—or its—singing, one young man decided he wanted to at least find out who their free-lance caroler was. Walking closer to the newcomer, he was surprised when it moved quickly away from him.

"Hey," the boy said. "Don't you want to talk? I just wanted to find out who you are."

The small person didn't answer.

"That's a neat costume you got, but it's the wrong holiday. This is Christmas, not Halloween."

Still no reply.

"I'll bet I know who you are—Eric Wallman. Right?"

The little person didn't answer.

A list of approximately a dozen names of area girls and boys produced a similar lack of reaction.

"Hey, come here. I want to talk to you."

The interloper did not advance, so the young man took off after it. Although the costumed kid moved with surprising speed and agility through the snow, the longer strides of the older pursuer eventually brought them within inches of each other. As the young man reached out to grab the mysterious visitor, he was suddenly met with an unseasonably hostile snarl, and a sharp pain slashed into his arm.

"Ow!" he cried out.

Looking down, he saw blood seeping through the slashed sleeve of his jacket. More angry than hurt, he cupped his hands to yell after the departing delinquent.

"You're a lousy singer anyway! We don't need you! Your voice stinks!"

They had walked for nearly an hour, going from one clear trail of tri-pronged Gremlin footprints to a jumbled patch and then—usually via luck rather than skill—onto a clear trail again. To keep both their spirits up and his mind active, Billy continued to talk aloud to Gizmo and himself, planning their next move as they trudged along together.

"Giz, I just thought of something," Billy said. "Water

makes you guys reproduce, right? And snow is just frozen water. But snow must not have had any effect on Stripe. Otherwise, this whole area would be crawling with those things. What are they called, anyway? They're sure not Mogwai. They're more like those things Mr. Futterman told me about. What did he call them? Grebblies? Gremlins? Yeah, that's it. And to think, I thought he was crazy. Anyway, for water to make you reproduce it must have to be a warmer temperature. Stripe won't find any water outside like that, so luck is with us."

Billy knew he was rambling on as a means of bolstering his confidence, but presenting his thoughts out loud, even to Gizmo, helped him get them in better order.

He remembered once in high school when he had written a report on Sherlock Holmes and been quite impressed with the legendary detective's ratiocinative powers. For the most part—at least in those adventures Billy recalled most vividly—Holmes was able to predict his villain's next move by the simple process of putting himself in his opponent's place. This Billy now proceeded to do with reference to Stripe.

"Let's see now, Giz," he said. "Where would we go if we were Stripe?"

Considering the rather narrow parameters within which Stripe could operate, the question was not really a very difficult one.

"Outside, it's dark and he's free to move about as he pleases, but apparently the snow is too cold to use for reproduction," Billy reasoned. "Inside, there's the thing he's probably looking for—warmer water. But most of these houses are brightly lit now. Then there's the problem of getting in. How can he do that? Well, he could curl into a ball and throw himself through a glass window, the way he did back home. But that would attract a lot of attention and he could get caught. . . . Unless he picked a house with nobody home. . . . Or . . . he could try to sneak in, say, when somebody else went inside a house . . . or if the door was left open a minute . . ."

He had been subliminally aware of the carolers' singing in the distance for perhaps a quarter hour before it struck him that there might be a connection.

Breaking into a faster pace, he headed toward the sound of the voices. "This may be a long shot," he said to Gizmo, "but if we were Stripe, I think we'd try hanging around those carolers. At the worst, they'd help hide our tracks. And if somebody left a door open while the group was singing, maybe there'd be a chance to slip inside . . . Anyway, it won't hurt to ask. Maybe they've seen him during their travels."

Having convinced himself that he had an excellent case, Billy pulled the knapsack cover down tighter to shield Gizmo from the cold and started to run at a brisk pace. A quarter mile down the road he caught up with the singers.

"Hi," he said. "I'm looking for a little fella about this high."

He held his palm about two and a half feet off the ground.

The response was immediate.

"Yeah," one of the carolers said. "We saw him. Is he your kid brother or something?"

"Not exactly. Why?"

"Because he's a creep. Neil tried to find out his name and he ran away. Then when Neil caught up to him, he pulled a knife on him."

Billy looked around.

"Is Neil here?" he asked.

"No," another fellow said. "He went home when he saw how bad his coat was ripped. His arm was bleedin', too."

"Why you looking for the creepy midget?" another caroler asked.

"Because he's supposed to be home now," Billy replied.

He saw no reason to alarm them by telling the truth. "Which way did he go, anyway?"

Several pointed toward a darkened building, which loomed as a heavy shadow between two smaller, brightly illuminated homes. It was the YMCA.

"Don't know why he went that way," one of the carolers said. "It's closed tighter'n a clam."

"Maybe he was just afraid," another offered.

"Thanks," Billy said. "And tell Neil I'm sorry if the little guy hurt him."

As he started to move off, three or four of the young people simultaneously spotted Gizmo peeking out from beneath the knapsack cover and trotted after him.

"Hey," one of them asked. "What kind of animal is that? He's cute."

"It's a Mogwai," Billy replied.

"Where do they come from?"

"Nowhere around here. Look, I gotta go. Thanks a lot for your help."

Waving a quick goodbye, he trotted toward the darkened building, picking up the familiar tri-pronged trail of Stripe less than a minute later. Running faster, he followed the fresh tracks nearly all the way around the building until they ended.

Directly below a broken window.

"This must be the place, Giz," Billy said, his voice a blend of anticipation and anxiety.

As he picked the remaining shards of glass from the ledge so that he could boost himself through the broken window, Billy recalled the uproar of a few months ago, when a typewriter had been stolen from the YMCA office. Some aroused citizens, perhaps overreacting, had proposed that every public building in the entire town be wired with the best antiburglary devices and patrolled around the clock by armed guards. Others, proud of Kingston Falls's reputation as a safe place to live, took the view that until the theft proved to be more than a solitary aberration, a continuation of normal prudence should suffice. Several invitingly weak locks at the high school and YMCA were replaced, as were broken windows on the ground levels. Now, as Billy pushed himself through the opening, he remembered one highlight of last summer's great security debate among Kingston Falls's town leaders.

"I'm all for spending the money to provide the office areas of these buildings with burglar devices," one councilman had said, "but I don't see why we should waste money making the ground floor of the YMCA burglarproof. The only things there are a bunch of nailed-down metal lockers, a basketball court, and other nonportable facilities. What are they gonna steal? Anyway, the cops patrol that area closely and the neighbors watch the place."

Now, as he balanced himself precariously on the ledge, Billy wondered if, despite the weather and poor visibility, someone had already spotted him. If so, he knew it wouldn't be long before he heard sirens, for the people of Kingston Falls prided themselves on their respect for law and order and were not inclined to look the other way when confronted with criminal activity. Criminal activity, he thought, is that what I'm involved in? He knew such was not the case, but he had to admit that to an outsider his actions certainly appeared illegal. What would he say if the authorities caught him inside? No excuse being logical under the circumstances, he would be arrested for breaking and entering—it was as simple as that. He wondered if he would be allowed to receive his Christmas presents in jail.

"So back out, then," he said aloud. "It's last call for chickens..."

Accepting his own challenge, he gave himself a strong push into the building. Landing on his side in the darkness,

he quickly located the flashlight, which had rolled out of
his pocket, and started to get to his feet. As he did so, an
unearthly treble giggle reverberated through the lower floor
area. It sounded close by, but because the hall was so spacious and empty, Billy knew Stripe could be fifty or a
hundred feet away.

Pausing, he decided to give his eyes a chance to adjust
to the darkness before moving ahead. A minute passed. No
sound could be heard except the floppy chains of a car
passing near the center. Another minute crawled by. Billy
could feel Gizmo's warm breath on the back of his neck,
hear the slight rustle of material as his arm shifted position
against his side. Other than that, nothing . . . No clawed feet
clattering over metal lockers, no more giggling, nothing.

Finally a sound shattered the ghostly silence. Not a soft
or subtle betrayal of its maker's whereabouts, but a definite
and distinct sound one would expect to hear in a facility
such as this.

A dribbling basketball.

Blep . . . Blep . . . Blep-blep-blep . . .

Not a basketball being dribbled, Billy amended, but a
basketball that had been dropped or fallen and was even
now coming to rest.

Orienting himself, he moved as quickly as the darkness
permitted in the direction of the equipment cage, a part of
the ground floor the councilman had forgotten when he'd
claimed there was nothing worth stealing here. But the cage
was always locked, Billy recalled, and not with some hang-
on job that could be sawed or broken off. Arriving at the
door, he reached out to touch the bronze square lock, which
had always reminded him of the type one sees in prison
movies. He pushed gently, then with more force. The door
was still locked.

Then how, he began to ask himself—

A hard object striking him on the head provided the answer. It was followed immediately by a hysterical giggle, very loud and directly above him.

Swinging the flashlight upward, Billy heard the giggle segue to a shriek of pain and then something that sounded very much like an extended curse in Mogwai language. For a moment he saw the flashlight beam striking Stripe's red eyes, and as the Gremlin's head jerked convulsively backward, he could see that there was a six- or eight-inch space between the ceiling and the top bar of the cage. Too narrow for a human to slide through, it had obviously been an easy maneuver for Stripe.

Now that he had broken the darkness, Billy decided to keep the flashlight beam trained on the Gremlin, for if it got away again—

He had little time to think about the consequences of another mistake. A shower of debris made up of every small object in the cage rained down on him. It consisted, as nearly as he could tell while dodging the pieces, of base-balls, nails, screwdrivers, a wrench, an old sneaker, hunks of wood, and everything metallic Stripe could handle. Avoiding the objects as best he could while shielding his head and Gizmo from the barrage, Billy somehow managed to keep the flashlight on Stripe throughout the angry shower. He had no strategy other than to see if he could flush the creature out of the cage and attack it with his sword, a strategy that depended largely on how long the flashlight batteries—

Suddenly the light was gone, a sharp object having struck Billy's hand, causing him to drop it. As the flashlight hit the floor, the plastic front flew off, sending the batteries and bulb assembly clattering in different directions.

Billy's groan blended with Stripe's giggle in the abrupt and total darkness.

Falling to his knees, Billy spread his palms and began

feeling for the component parts of the flashlight. He located
the batteries quickly, then the bulb assembly, and finally
the top. While he tried putting the thing together in the black
void, he could hear Stripe making his escape down the side
of the cage, the clawed feet landing with a metallic thump
only a yard or two away. Had he not been busy with the
flashlight, Billy would have started swinging the sword
blindly, so close did he feel to the Gremlin. A moment later,
with the flashlight operating again, he swung it down the
hallway just in time to see Stripe turn the corner.

He was headed across the basketball court, his sharp
claws scratching noisily on the smooth wooden surface,
toward a corner with some small utility rooms and the door
leading to the large room containing—

"Oh, no!" Billy breathed as he broke into a run. "The
swimming pool! We gotta beat him to that door!"

Racing at full speed, the light bouncing ahead of him,
he noted with a grunt of satisfaction that Stripe had veered
off in the direction of the utility rooms. Good, Billy thought,
now we've got a chance at least.

Having reached the swimming pool doorway first, they
could now prevent Stripe from making it to the pool—until
their batteries gave out. But in the meantime Billy could
try to locate the main switches.

"Here," he said, as he shrugged off the knapsack. He
put the flashlight in Gizmo's paws so that it shone away
from his face but directly outward from the door. "You hold
it just like this. Don't move, O.K.?"

Gizmo held the light firmly in his paws, gulping thickly
as Billy disappeared into the darkness.

As he stumbled off, Billy worried what Gizmo would
do if and when the main lights were located. The pain would
hurt him as much as Stripe, possibly kill him as it had the
Mogwai that died on the back porch in the sunlight. He
hesitated briefly, debating whether to go back or not. Then

he plunged ahead. If the lights go on, he reasoned, Gizmo will be able to fall back into the knapsack and avoid the pain. Stripe will be immobilized with pain and I'll be able to finish him off.

Sword in hand, he groped his way along the wall, wondering which he would encounter first—Stripe or the light switches. A minute later, after encountering nothing but smooth cold squares of tile with his groping fingers, he began to think the search for either or both was endless.

"Where are the light switches?" he murmured helplessly, looking back over his shoulder to make sure the flashlight was still guarding the door. Although the batteries had waned visibly, Billy reckoned they had a few more minutes' worth of life. Realizing that and despairing of locating the switches—if they existed—in this corner of the gymnasium, he started for the opposite wall.

He had gone perhaps fifty feet when, looking back toward the pool door to see how much weaker his batteries had gotten, he saw the last act of Stripe's clever strategy. Obviously having figured out that Gizmo was holding the light while Billy tried to outflank him or locate the overhead switches, Stripe had hugged the wall near Gizmo, creeping slowly toward him while shielding himself from the direct rays of the light. Now, too late, Billy saw the Gremlin's unmistakable form, black except for the chiaroscuro outline created by the light. In diabolically slow motion the figure rose high in the air next to Gizmo, a cobra ready to strike its prey.

"Look out!" Billy shouted across the court. "Look out, Gizmo! He's—"

The flashlight fell noisily to the floor and rolled away as a series of growls and tiny yelps echoed through the gymnasium. Heading toward the dim outline of the pool door, Billy literally threw himself into the tangle of bodies. Two simultaneous bolts of pain struck him in the shoulder and side. Swinging his fist in a wild backhanded arc, Billy felt it strike a solid object, heard Stripe whine.

Lashing out again in the direction of the sound, he landed another blow, causing Stripe to disengage himself and scamper into the pool room.

"No!" Billy heard himself shout futilely.

As the sound of Stripe's scratchy claws moving across tile grew weaker, Billy hastily retrieved the flashlight and started into the pool room. At the door he turned off the flashlight, though he could barely see without it. Even in his present state of near-panic, he knew that the light must be used judiciously—not only because it was getting weaker, but because a sudden movement by Stripe in the wrong direction now...

A protracted and especially evil giggle told Billy that the worst had already happened. Stripe had discovered the swimming pool and its power of illimitable reproduction.

He was standing at the far end, hopping up and down lightly, his nose inhaling the heady aromatic mist rising from the surface, his arms making wide joyous arcs above his head in the manner of an athlete who has just scored the winning points of a game. Each time he hit the tile floor during his victory dance the giggle increased slightly in volume, so that he sounded rather like a human bagpipe hopelessly hooked on a single hysterical chord.

"No..." Billy breathed. "Please, *no!*"

The gentle touch of fur against his hand told him that Gizmo was all right, a bit of good news as he stood helplessly watching Stripe lean forward into the water.

Turning on the flashlight, Billy raced to the far end and pointed it into the water. Stripe had sunk gently to the bottom of the pool and was lying facedown, his arms relaxed at his sides. For a long moment Billy dared to hope—

A gentle rumbling destroyed the hope. Stripe's back was aflame with tiny pods erupting to life and spreading across the surface of the pool. Like a giant rolling fungus, they divided and redivided, churning the water into a green froth. The gentle rumbling soon became a roar, a deafening wail of a hundred inhuman voices crying out in pain.

Billy watched, fascinated, but for only a moment. Then, grabbing Gizmo, he half ran, half stumbled out of the building.

CHAPTER SEVENTEEN

Collapsing on a gentle slope fifty yards from the YMCA building, Billy found himself a spectator of a grim show that was largely his creation. At first there was little to watch or hear but a greenish glow emanating from the swimming pool area and a faraway giggling chorus. Then there was movement inside the building and a marked increase in the chorus's volume. Soon Billy could see one form and then dozens moving past the windows—each a fully grown Gremlin!

"Oh no! When they multiply as Gremlins, they don't lose a beat, do they?"

Gizmo blinked back a tear. He could have told them of the dangers and all this could have been avoided...if he had been able to communicate better...if these humans had taken his advice...If, if, if...

Now there were no more ifs. To Billy's way of thinking, his last hope was now gone. As he and Gizmo scrambled up the slope only minutes before, he had entertained the

notion of calling the fire department so that they could set
fire to the pods while they were waiting to hatch. But there
were no pods, no intermediate stage even momentarily vulnerable to destruction or movement to a place where they
could do less harm.

Billy sighed. "What can we do now, Giz?" he asked
wearily. "Just give up, go home, and wait? There's nothing
else we can do, is there?"

That was the sensible course of action, but he knew he
couldn't surrender now. Having helped unleash these devilish creatures on Kingston Falls—and perhaps the world!—
he owed it to himself and everyone else to do everything
possible to rectify his mistake. That was the major, most
moral, consideration. He also knew that merely sitting still
would drive him crazy.

"I guess," he said slowly, "this means we'll have to go
to the police."

He did not relish explaining what had happened to Sheriff
Reilly and Deputy Brent, who were as hardheaded a pair
as were ever born. Even describing a normal problem to
them was often difficult, so hung up were they on the idea
that everyone else in the human race was devious, dumb,
or both. Added to this was the perfectly reasonable resis-
tance anyone would have to a story dealing with Gremlins
or other alien creatures. A dedicated movie buff, Billy already had visions of the scenario that would be acted out
at the police station. As in so many horror movies, he would
explain what had happened. The police would be skeptical,
to say the least. Then, to convince them of his story's
validity, he would suggest they go to the high school in
order to see both Roy Hanson's body and the remains of a
dead Gremlin. After much prodding they would accompany
him there—and, of course, both bodies would be missing.
Either that, or the Gremlin would be gone and the police

would have no choice but to arrest Billy on suspicion of murder.

Faced with explaining his story to these men, Billy hesitated. But not long, for the inside of the YMCA was obviously swarming with bodies. Passing by the windows, they made the building look like a dimly lit concert hall or theatre a minute after the night's entertainment had ended.

"Let's go, Giz," Billy said finally. "I guess if we're gonna stop those guys from taking over the whole town, we'd better tell the cops."

A quarter hour later, at the tiny Kingston Falls Police Department station, Billy told his story as simply and unemotionally as possible, avoiding as best he could the hysterical-sounding descriptions used by movie characters.

The reaction of the police was somewhat different than in films or TV, although Sheriff Reilly and Deputy Brent did wear the typical "let's-humor-him-and-maybe-he'll-go-quietly" attitude of law enforcement officers in similar situations. Seated at their wooden desks, drinking egg nog from Styrofoam cups, they were perhaps more informal and a bit friendlier than one might expect, especially at the outset. When it became obvious that Billy was serious, they allowed him to proceed well into his narrative before interrupting.

"Gremlins," Reilly said at that point. "Like little monsters, you say?"

"Right."

"Green, of course," the sheriff continued, casting an almost imperceptible wink at Brent. "Little monsters are always green, you know."

"Yes, they're green," Billy admitted, wishing they had been some other color.

"With sharp pointy fangs and long claws?"

"Yessir."

"Thousands of 'em, huh?"

"I didn't count," Billy replied. "I couldn't. It looked like a couple hundred, anyway."

"Well, a couple hundred little green monsters with fangs and claws is enough, if you ask me." Deputy Brent smiled. "Now where did these Gremlins come from?"

"My father. He gave me one as an early Christmas present a few days ago."

"A present . . ." Reilly grunted. "Your father usually give you vicious monsters for presents?"

"No, no," Billy replied, a bit more nervous now. "You see, they aren't vicious at first."

"'Course not." Brent nodded, his condescension now becoming quite evident.

"Matter of fact, they aren't even Gremlins when they start out," Billy continued. "Could you dim the lights in here?"

"Why, they hurt your eyes?"

"No, sir. I've got a Mogwai—that's what the Gremlin comes from—in this knapsack, but bright light can hurt him, maybe kill him."

Brent shot Sheriff Reilly a "this-is-going-to-be-good" look and stifled a yawn.

Hoping that a look at Gizmo would convince them that they indeed had alien creatures on their hands, Billy waited, trying not to appear manic. After a moment Brent took a couple of steps toward the wall switch and killed the overhead lights.

Billy opened the knapsack, pulled out Gizmo. The two policemen studied him carefully but with a lack of the affection and delight expressed by other people.

"This is what a Mogwai looks like before he becomes a Gremlin," Billy explained.

"Yeah." Brent nodded. "I've seen those before. They

come from some South Pacific island. Think they're called a weepee or kepplee or something."

"No, sir," Billy corrected. "This is not an ordinary animal that lives on Earth."

Brent shook his head. "Maybe that's what the guy in the pet store told your pop, but I seen 'em on television. One of those wildlife shows."

Knowing it was futile to argue with Brent, Billy swallowed his protest.

"So this becomes a Gremlin, huh?" the deputy said.

"Yessir. He *can*, but he doesn't have to." Knowing he was beginning to sound a bit like the typically incoherent, frustrated, and generally discredited movie character, Billy plunged on anyway. "You see, they become Gremlins if they . . . eat after midnight . . ."

Deputy Brent's cheeks exploded outward as he choked on a slug of his drink. Twin trickles of saffron liquid started to dribble from either end of his mouth. Wiping his lips on his coat sleeve, he turned away, coughing.

"Eat after midnight," Sheriff Reilly murmured, taking up the line of questioning where Brent had left off before becoming convulsed. "I don't get it."

"Maybe he means sundown on Fridays," Brent interrupted, still gagging slightly. "Jewish Gremlins."

"Let's be serious," Reilly said. "I'd really like to get to the bottom of this. Now he turns into a Gremlin if he eats after midnight. Midnight in what time zone? You mean I can take this little critter to the state line where the time zones change, and if he eats on one side of the line it's O.K., but if he eats on the other side he turns into a monster?"

"I guess so . . ." Billy stammered. "I've never thought of it that way."

"And is it the act of his mouth chewin' the food or the stomach digestin' it?" Brent added quickly, having gotten his esophagal problem settled. "You know that food lays around in your stomach awhile."

Dismissing him with a wave of his hand, Reilly asked, "How much food? One mouthful after midnight? Is that enough to make him crazy?"

"I . . . guess . . ."

"Suppose he eats at ten o'clock and gets something stuck between his teeth, something that comes loose after midnight?" Brent interjected. "Does that count as food after midnight if he swallows it?"

"Is water food?" Reilly added.

"Nah," Brent replied. "Water's got no calories. If he eats something with calories, that's what does it."

"How about diet drinks?" Reilly asked, deadpan. "They got only a couple of calories."

"That's all you need," Brent replied. "One calorie and it's food."

"My wife told me about some foods that have minus calories," Reilly said. "Like your body uses more energy chewin' 'em up than you get from the food. Things like celery and lettuce and raw carrots . . ."

Realizing he was getting nowhere fast, Billy took a step toward the door.

Sheriff Reilly held up his hand. "Wait a minute," he said. "Where you goin'?"

"I'm leaving, I guess," Billy said. "I know it sounds crazy, but I didn't make up the rules—"

"We're just tryin' to find out what's goin' on," Reilly replied evenly, his face betraying very little overt sarcasm. "Like, suppose you dropped dead or left that little critter here. If you said he'd grow into a hundred Gremlins if we fed him after midnight, I'd like to know more. Like, if it's not O.K. after midnight, when does O.K. begin again? Six o'clock? Sunup?"

"Another thing," Brent added, not waiting for Billy to

reply. "How's he do this multiplication act? Does he need a female or what?"

Billy sighed, did not answer. He had decided not to tell these men any more about Gizmo; nor would he tell them about the incident at the high school. Let them think he was a lunatic if that was their pleasure. At least they couldn't lock him up for that.

"Listen, I'm sorry I bothered you," Billy said. "I guess I just didn't tell my story right, so I don't blame you if you think I'm crazy. I just dropped in to tell you that you may be getting some reports tonight about vandalism, or people being attacked or frightened by little green monsters. Maybe you'll believe those people aren't crazy because of me. At least I hope so. And if nothing happens, that's all right, too."

Closing the knapsack cover on Gizmo, he started for the door. As he closed it behind him and walked into the dark cold night, he heard the two policemen's voices break first into a smothered chuckle and then uproarious laughter.

"Well, Giz," Billy asked sardonically, "how'd I do?"

The series of bizarre and tragic events that convulsed Kingston Falls began a few minutes later.

The first episode, a seemingly isolated mishap, was reported by WKF radio newsman Harman Ellis at 7:57 P.M. as a local item to fill out the second hour of his evening talk show. Little did he realize at the time that it was but the tip of a catastrophic iceberg that would keep him and his listeners in a frenzy for the rest of the night.

I have here a warning for motorists in the Kingston Falls area. All four traffic signals at the intersection of Randolph Road and Route 46 have become jammed with green showing in both directions. Two cars and a tractor trailer collided there about a half hour ago, all three drivers assuming they had a clear road ahead. Both cars were heavily dam-

aged but no one was seriously injured. Motorists are advised to avoid this intersection—Randolph Road at Route 46—until maintenance crews can repair the sticking signals. Stay tuned to this station and we'll let you know when traffic is moving smoothly again. . . .

Remembering that his VW was parked just a couple of blocks from the police station, Billy decided to see if he had gotten a ticket or the car had been towed away during the three hours since he had been forced to abandon it.

"I won't be surprised," he muttered to Gizmo. "No matter what's happened, it won't shock me, the way this day's turned out."

Turning the corner, he received the ultimate shock under the circumstances. Not only was the car where he had left it, there was no ticket on the windshield. And when he got in and turned the ignition key, the motor started with the gentlest, most obliging purr within his memory.

"It's a trick," he murmured. "It must be."

Making a U-turn, he was soon back on Main Street and heading home, but he had no idea what he should do next or whom to contact. All he could do was hope the Gremlins somehow got sidetracked before they could do too much damage.

. . . back again with another announcement—actually three announcements—that sort of makes me think Kingston Falls is being used as a testing area for pranksters. We now have a traffic signal that is showing red in all four directions and traffic is backed up for half a mile there. It's at Mountain Road and Rolling Vista Highway. Police are on the way to direct traffic there, so if you're listening to this in a car on one of those thoroughfares, sit back, calm yourself down, and hang on. Just be thankful you're not on Delta Drive near Carmody Street, which is where pedestrians and motorists alike were attacked by about fifty runaway tires. Somehow they'd gotten loose from a nearby Tire Warehouse

outlet store and started rolling down Carmody in one mass.
Several cars were dented and one woman suffered abrasions
when she jumped out of the way of one tire into a utility
pole. That's not all. It's been reported tonight by a non-
drinking source that customers entering the Governor's Mall
Shopping Plaza were struck by a rain of brooms from the
roof of that facility—no less than three dozen at a clip.
Security guards at the mall were unable to apprehend the
throwers. Anyway, think we're on a Gremlin hit list? Prob-
ably not. It's more than likely just some last bits of craziness
before Christmas. Stay tuned and we'll keep you posted.

At the corner near his church, Billy suddenly hit the
brakes, sliding sideways and nearly into a snowdrift before
coming to a halt. Slamming the car into reverse, he backed
up a hundred feet so as to be near the familiar figure coming
out of the church's side entrance.

"Father Bartlett!" Billy called out through the partially
rolled-down window.

The hunched figure paused, edged its way across the icy
sidewalk toward the car.

"It's me, Billy Peltzer."

"Merry Christmas, Billy—"

"Father, please, go back to the church," Billy warned.
"It's not safe out here."

The elderly man smiled. "I'm just mailing off a last-
minute Christmas card, Billy," he said, pulling it from his
pocket. Then almost to himself, he added, "I sure didn't
think they would send me one."

"Can't it wait, Father?"

"I suppose it can, but it's only a block. What seems to
be the problem—you think I'll slip on the ice?"

"No, Father, it's a lot worse than that. Will you take my
word that it's not safe out here, mail your letter, and come
right back?"

"Why, I certainly will. And Merry Christmas to you."

"Thank you, Father. Same to you."

Billy put the car in gear and puttered off. Father Bartlett watched him go, shrugged, and continued his trip to the corner mailbox. As he walked, his eyes darted from side to side and even back over his shoulder once or twice, but no one seemed to be lurking in the shadows or following him. From his work with various youth groups, Father Bartlett knew that young people of today were a lot more serious and susceptible to anxiety problems than their parents or grandparents. It was the world we lived in, and one could hardly blame Billy Peltzer for having a sudden attack of nervousness, even during the holiday season.

Arriving at the mailbox, Bartlett pulled down the door and dropped the letter inside.

A second later the card flew back at him, striking the front of his coat and falling to the snow.

Blinking, Father Bartlett reached down and grabbed the letter. Slowly he opened the mailbox door, peered into the blackness, shrugged, and redeposited the envelope.

Again it flew back.

"Guess this must be a joke of some kind," he murmured, forcing a good-natured tone to his voice just in case he was being taped. Retrieving the card, he stood silently, surveying the scene about him with nervous eyes. He had seen shows on television, of course, in which the average person was the butt of a joke played by hidden cameramen, but surely in this poor light—

On the other hand, modern technology could accomplish just about anything.

He decided to have one more try. Even if he was being taped, he reasoned, he hadn't embarrassed himself. As a matter of fact, his attitude had been quite good—a mixture of genial surprise and amusement; parishioners seeing such a tape could accuse him of being neither a bad sport nor a dullard. Just in case this was a hidden camera prank—and

he certainly couldn't lose anything by assuming it was—
he decided to add a cute touch of his own.

Pulling down the door once more, he moved his face
close to the opening and said in a slightly louder voice,
"One more try, and that's it. Then I'm taking my business
to another mailbox."

The words were no sooner out of his mouth than he felt
his hand gripped by a cold object. As he started to pull
away, another claw or hand slipped around his neck and
started to pull his head into the mailbox.

"This has gone far enough!" he shouted, managing a
laugh that was more hysterical than hearty.

Now, having lost his hat, his bare head was being forced
painfully against the icy cold rim of the mailbox. Twisting
and turning, the normally implacable Father Bartlett began
to scream for help.

*What we're gonna do now, considering all these reports,
is dispense with our regular format and open our telephone
lines so you can call in and discuss this...phenomenon
with me between announcements. Now, we don't want to
spread panic, but we would be remiss if we didn't report
what's going on and warn all of our listeners to stay inside
if possible. Get that last-minute Christmas shopping done
after the holidays. Your loved ones will understand. Anyway...we've had numerous calls from people who have
seen very small animals or humans darting in and out of
the shadows. These...beings are approximately the size of
three-year-olds, but they handle themselves like Olympic
athletes. Frankly, we don't know what they are, and the
problem is made worse by all these people or things wearing
costumes.*

*About eight-fifteen, these things were seen in the vicinity
of the Governor's Mall Shopping Plaza, about the time
shoppers began getting caught in the sliding glass doors.
According to nine people who received minor cuts and*

bruises, the doors seemed to open invitingly early for patrons and then snap shut with terrifying speed. Maintenance crews at the mall say the problem is under control now, although most customers are using the nonautomatic doors.

In another section of Kingston Falls an incident occurred that may or may not be related. Patrons at Simone's, a first-class French restaurant on Winslow Pike, reported that a food fight started there about eight-thirty. According to one source, portions of food flew from one table to another, although no one saw who threw the food. Several waiters carrying heavy trays were apparently tripped and the tablecloths whisked from beneath the eyes of diners, carrying bowls and dishes into the aisles. Eventually the scene became so chaotic, a riot with French food broke out. One woman is being treated for béarnaise sauce inhalation.

"You had to go makin' fun of the kid, didn't you?" Sheriff Reilly muttered as he and Deputy Brent raced once again for their cruiser. The past hour, after what had started out as a slow night, had been frenetic and inexplicable.

"Me?" Brent replied defensively. "You were the one who started it. Anyway, I still don't think it's his little green monsters. I think it's kids gone crazy 'cause they got nothin' to do. And that radio station that keeps sendin' out reports every ten minutes ain't helpin'. Crazy people hear stuff like that and they start thinkin' of things they can do to top it."

"All right, never mind." Reilly shrugged. "Where are Dudley and Warren?"

"At Governor's Mall."

"O.K. You and me got a choice—the troubles at the TV station or the people bein' attacked by Christmas trees. Which do you want?"

Brent shrugged. "I'd just as soon leave the media alone. Let 'em solve their own problems. Probably a normal screwup anyway."

"Then we'll do the trees."

Swinging left on Washington Avenue, Sheriff Reilly headed the cruiser back toward the center of town. The streets were fairly deserted considering it was so close to Christmas, giving Kingston Falls a ghost town atmosphere, but at least that made it easier to get from place to place. Moving rapidly to the end of the block, he turned again at Waterton, the cruiser's wheels spinning slightly as he—

"What—" was all Reilly was able to say before the police cruiser hit the first of a solid wall of upright objects.

After grinding and bumping to a halt, the bottom of the car sounding like the hull of a ship struck by a torpedo, the two policemen hopped from the cruiser and surveyed the damage in the glare of the headlights.

"Now who did this?" Brent muttered.

Ahead of them, extending for the entire block, were nothing but cinder blocks, placed upright on their ends like tiny grave markers, their square forms lined up one by one as far as the eye could see.

—just in from the Kingston Falls Police Department. Motorists are advised to avoid using Waterton Avenue between Washington and Adams. Police say that unknown persons have blockaded the street with concrete cinder blocks apparently taken from Williamson's Building Supply yard nearby.

Another bizarre development occurred just a block away from St. Francis of Assisi Church, where Father Edmund Bartlett was mailing a letter. While doing so, he was pulled into the mailbox past his shoulders by a pair of unseen hands or claws, suffering cuts and bruises in the process. Meanwhile, a neighbor who spotted Father Bartlett trapped in the mailbox called for help and he was pulled out. When the helpers got a look inside the box, however, they fled.

Unfortunately, that's not the last item in this latest list

*of unusual events taking place this evening. A basketball
game between the Tigers and Whales of the Presbyterian
Intermediate League had to be canceled this evening when
it was discovered that all of the basketballs had been filled
with peanut butter. The contest has been rescheduled for
January eighth.*

*Finally—for the moment—we have received word from
Channel Ten to the effect that the trouble is not in your set.
That station's interference has been caused by unknown
problems with the equipment.*

*Did I say Gremlins earlier? It certainly looks that way.
Stay tuned.*

"Man on the radio said it was Gremlins, Murray," Mrs.
Futterman said, coming back into the living room with a
cup of coffee for her husband.

"Maybe he said it as a joke," Futterman growled, re-
sisting the temptation to kick his television set. "They always say it as a joke, but nobody believes it."

When fiddling with the dials some more failed to improve
his fuzzy TV picture, he leaned back wearily. "Not again,"
he muttered. "Just when Perry Como was comin' on."

"Him singing 'Ave Maria' again?" Mrs. Futterman asked,
and then continued, "I'd think you'd be sick of that by now.
They play it every Christmas."

"That's part of Christmas. What did the radio say about
the television?"

"Gremlins," Mrs. Futterman repeated. "Nobody knows."

"They probably got a bunch of foreign components, if
you ask me," Futterman growled. "Same with this darn
Sony. I knew we shoulda got a Zenith."

Flipping the dial, he encountered terrible grainy interference on every channel, his cheeks getting redder with
every turn. Slamming his fist against the side of the set, he
beamed with delight momentarily as several stations re-

turned in beautiful color, and then banged it again as the cross-hatching reappeared.

"That's not just the one channel," he snarled. "It's either the set or the antenna."

"Well, let's not worry about it now," Mrs. Futterman said with a soft smile.

" 'Course I'll worry about it now," he shot back. "My favorite Christmas shows are on. Why should I sit here and look at snow inside and snow outside?"

Suddenly he was on his feet and striding toward the hall closet. His wife merely watched as he started bundling himself up, knowing it was futile to argue against it.

"Where are you going?" she finally asked meekly.

"I'm gonna check the antenna," he said. "Maybe it blew over."

Pulling a woolen hat over his head, he went outside to the end of his walkway and looked back toward the roof.

The antenna was still intact but Mr. Futterman hardly noticed. What he noticed much more was that it was surrounded by a trio of small, long-armed figures that brought back a rush of memories from World War II.

For a long moment he simply stood, slack-jawed, staring at the three playing with his antenna. Then, remembering the rifle he kept loaded in a locked closet downstairs, he walked back toward the house, his eyes never leaving the roof until he reached the front porch.

—nother warning for motorists in the Kingston Falls area. We have reports that a series of detour signs have been placed on the downtown bypass road in such a way that drivers have been circling the reservoir for several hours. Some drivers, in their frustration at not being able to find their way out of this cul-de-sac, have stopped their cars and created huge bottlenecks, not to mention several collisions. All we can tell you about that situation is that

several local garages have volunteered to send trucks to lead motorists out of the area. These trucks will have large yellow signs identifying them.

Shoppers are advised not to use Kingbank's automatic teller at all three locations and West Kelvin Bank's Fast-Cash machines. These are issuing shredded bills and returning ID cards bent in half. Officials of both banks have issued statements saying this is not the work of the so-called Gremlins, but is part of normal problems both banks have been experiencing.

It took a while for Sheriff Reilly and Deputy Brent to calm down the trio of women who had been attacked by the vending machines at the Green Bend rest area; having survived what was apparently a very harrowing situation, all three wanted to talk about it.

"We were standing between the two rows of machines," the tall woman with bluish hair began. "Alice was trying to decide whether or not to get some cheese crackers when all of a sudden the soda cans just started coming straight out. Not dropping down, mind you, like when you put money in for them, but they were *hurled* out. One hit me right there, on my bad shoulder, and another got Maude on the chin. She's still woozy."

Brent nodded and made a note on his pad, not because he needed or wanted it, but because he knew they expected it.

"Look at this," the one called Alice said, displaying a mean-looking cut at the base of her nose. "You wouldn't think this could come from a pack of chewing gum, would you?"

"No, ma'am," Sheriff Reilly replied.

"They were just whizzing out of there," the third woman sighed. "I thought it was the end of the world."

"You know, we're not very agile," the second one said.

"When they started shooting that stuff at us, we just couldn't get out of the way."

The two officers nodded, made a few sympathetic remarks, and returned to their cruiser.

As they drove back to Kingston Falls, Sheriff Reilly finally stopped muttering to himself long enough to say, "Well, I guess we better talk more with the kid."

"The kid?"

"Yeah. The one with the funny little animal that turns into Gremlins if you feed it after midnight. You got his name, didn't you?"

"I thought he gave it to you, sheriff."

"You had the complaint sheet, and I saw you write something down after he came in."

"Oh, that was just a note to remind myself to call home."

"Great."

"I think I know who he is, though. He works in the bank. We can find out."

"All right. I think maybe we better find out what he knows before we do anything else."

—lines are still open. That's 922–7400, and be prepared to hang on awhile because our switchboard, very appropriate for this time of year, is lit up like a Christmas tree. O.K. Here's our next caller. Go ahead, sir, you're on the air.

Oh. Yes. My name's Willkie Smith and I've just come from a Howard Johnson's restaurant that spit this terrible stuff in my face . . .

The restaurant spit at you?

No. One of them machines in the men's room that you use to dry your hands and face. The hot air machines . . .

Yes. Go on.

Well, I turned it on to do my face and suddenly I was covered with this awful-smelling orange stuff.

A liquid? Are you at liberty to say what it was?

I don't know. It smelled like it come out of a toilet, except it was older, like with mold and—

Well, maybe that's a bit too graphic. Where was the restaurant, sir?

Commerce and Lawndale. You know what I think? I think this is part of God's plan. Now it says in the New Testament—

The look on her husband's face told Mrs. Futterman that he was about to embark on a holy crusade. Although a generally volatile man, he never got that steely-eyed, twitching-nerve-in-the-cheek expression except when somewhat crazed or messianic. She had seen it when someone stole the radio from his car, and another time when his favorite football team lost the divisional championship on a bad call by the officials. When he emerged from the basement with his rifle, she knew she had read him correctly.

"Murray," she said, taking his arm. "What is it?"

"Gremlins," he replied. "On the roof."

"What kind of Gremlins?"

"No time to explain now. You just stay inside—"

"But if you go out in the street and fire off that rifle, you'll be reported for sure," she protested.

"Let go of my arm, Jessie," he ordered.

She did so and he continued on his heavy-footed mission.

Outside, he was halfway to the street and had the first Gremlin in his sights when he realized that Jessie was right. Firing off a rifle from his front lawn was pretty foolhardy, especially when there was a window in the back of the garage which would provide an even better vantage point. Moving quietly into the garage, he groped his way past the snowplow, which took up all but six inches on either side, and pushed the window open. He smiled, for the view of his rooftop was perfect, and from here the sound of his rifle would be partially muffled.

Lining up one of the Gremlins, he squeezed off his first shot. The little green demon proved it was neither imaginary nor immortal by falling in a heap and sliding off the roof. Futterman laughed out loud. It felt good to fire the rifle again, to be locked in combat with the enemy—

A low chattering sound interrupted his excited train of thought. Where was it coming from? The rooftop? Somewhere nearby? There was no time to think about it. If the two other troublemakers near his antenna were to be dealt with . . .

He threw the rifle to his shoulder and fired again. Another Gremlin dropped.

In his excitement and eagerness to bag his third enemy soldier, Futterman hardly heard the snowplow's engine roar to life.

The third Gremlin started to slide off the roof.

"Oh, no, you don't!" Futterman yelled, moving the rifle to follow him. In a split second he had the little target in his sights.

Now the snowplow seemed almost to lean forward, its wheels ready to burst from their positions like sprinters from starting blocks. The engine roar became deafening as—

Bam! Bam!

"Hot darn!" Futterman cried out. "I got you, you little son of a—"

He never completed the phrase. With a mammoth lurch forward, the snowplow tore through the back wall of the garage, taking Futterman with it in a shower of timber and bricks.

—*know all of you are interested in what the weather's going to be for the next few days, but you won't be able to find out by calling for the weather. No one's sure why, but calls to the telephone company's weather number are going directly to Carl's Sub Shoppe on West Monticello Drive. But you can't get the weather by dialing Carl's Sub Shoppe*

*because calls for Carl are somehow going directly to the
Gamblers Anonymous hot line. A few minutes ago an official
with the phone company informed us that the Kingston Falls
relay station was broken into earlier this evening and that
everything is in a state of chaos. So stay off the phone unless
it's an absolute emergency.*

*Meanwhile, three more cases of people being trapped in
pay phone booths turned up in—*

"Well, what do you think, Kate?" Dorry smiled, leaning
forward onto the bar. "Think it's Gremlins, Commies, the
end of the world, or just ordinary screw-ups?"

The pub was nearly deserted, thanks largely to the rash
of strange and frightening incidents taking place in and
around Kingston Falls. At first the early evening customers
tended to regard the bizarre events with satirical amusement,
but when reports were heard of electrical malfunctions causing fires, a man being electrocuted by his Christmas tree,
and other life-threatening situations, even the most hardened
scoffer began to think about protecting his loved ones. An
even greater exodus from Dorry's Pub followed reports that
in another bar across town, lye, ammonia, aqua regia, and
other deadly chemicals had turned up in cocktails. The result
was an evening so slow that Dorry was seriously considering
closing the bar and going home before midnight.

"It's probably Gremlins," Kate replied.

"That's really what you think?" Dorry asked, wide-eyed.
He had always regarded Kate as a particularly down-to-
earth person, incapable of believing in Santa Claus, evil
spirits, or other supernatural beings.

"That's what the guy on the radio thinks it is," she said
simply.

Dorry wondered exactly what had won her over. True,
the radio had described incidents involving apparently
driverless cars, and more than a few callers had mentioned
seeing the little green monsters in the Kingston Falls area.

But wasn't it possible that mass hysteria, fed by the constant radio reports, was taking over? Didn't anyone remember Orson Welles's famous "War of the Worlds" episode before World War II? Dorry didn't actually remember it himself, not having been born yet, but he had read about the panic that had gripped the nation then. Now, hearing Kate's profession of belief in Gremlins, he better understood America's abject fear of 1938; if a reasonable young woman such as Kate Beringer could be convinced that little green monsters existed, anyone could.

He was about to pursue the topic further with her when he noticed the vanguard of their battalion standing near the front door. Although Dorry did not realize it, his pub, with its very subdued indirect lighting, was a magnet for the Gremlins, an ideal spot for them to relax after their early-evening knaveries. Darting out of the shadows bordering the main square, they gravitated naturally to this wondrous arena of free food, drink, games, and music.

A person's jaw dropping—even several jaws dropping in concert—is not generally considered a measurable sound. Tonight, as Dorry and his few customers one by one noticed the collection of forms moving slowly through the foyer toward them, their jaws dropping seemed to generate a negative force so powerful and complete, not unlike a black hole in space, that it could be felt and heard as clearly as any explosion.

The brief moment of paralysis and terrifying silence was immediately followed by a detonation of people, Dorry included, toward the side and rear exits. Chairs fell, drinks were dropped or spilled, and bodies stumbled as the Gremlins took over the bar as rapidly and thoroughly as if an opening night theatre next door had just discharged its patrons. Chattering to each other in broken Mogwai, hopping excitedly as they spotted the game machines and pool table, the Gremlins inundated Dorry's Pub in less than a minute.

Dorry was the last person to escape via the rear entrance. Looking back over his shoulder, he saw a confused and surrounded Kate hesitate and then retreat behind the bar as the sea of green cackling faces spread in unearthly agitated waves from one corner of his establishment to the other.

—a state of emergency at the Governor's Mall Shopping Plaza ever since the electronic doors jammed, trapping some hundred and fifty people inside the complex. The telephones are still working, however, although one by one the lines are being taken out of service by the same unseen forces that have been terrorizing Kingston Falls since shortly before eight o'clock this evening.

At last reports, eyewitnesses stated that chaos broke out in the mall when the escalators started moving at terrific speeds, perhaps as fast as seventy or eighty miles an hour. Passengers were spun off like tops and hurled through plate glass windows or into each other. This was followed by all the lights being turned off and the background music being turned up to a deafening volume. We'll keep you posted on the situation at Governor's Mall, as we know many of you in our listening audience have loved ones or friends in that facility. We repeat that so far there have been no fatalities although many have been injured.

Elsewhere in the area, two more people have been attacked by Christmas trees—

Swallowing the last morsel of her Dinty Moore Beef Stew—one large can of which lasted her three days—Mrs. Deagle sat back to await the start of her favorite nighttime soap opera on television, the one with so many despicable characters, whom she found singularly attractive.

Once again the doorbell's ringing disrupted her pleasure. Even more aggravating was the persistence of the callers, one of whom kept his finger against the button so that the chimes continued to sound endlessly.

"Fools!" Mrs. Deagle hissed, struggling to her feet. "I'll have them arrested."

Flinging the door open, she nearly choked on the angry words she had prepared for the unwanted callers. She gasped. For how could one even begin to preach responsibility and common sense to a group outfitted such as this one? Were they a joke cooked up by the angry carolers?

"What is this?" she finally managed to growl. "A late Halloween prank? Well, I'll thank you to get off my porch and lawn this minute or I'm calling the police!"

The group, apparently oblivious to her attitude, began a singsong mumbo jumbo that was totally incomprehensible to Mrs. Deagle.

"Get out of here!" she shouted. "I don't want to hear you and I don't want to see you. Those costumes are terrible, anyway. Very cheap and tacky and unconvincing."

The giggly dirge continued. Leaving the front door open, Mrs. Deagle went inside and looked around for something to throw. As she did so, two of the creatures padded into the house and faded into the darkness.

A moment later Mrs. Deagle returned holding a broom. While inside she had considered dousing them with a bucket of water, but her arms weren't strong enough to lift a full bucket much less throw it.

"All right," she grated, moving toward the unwanted visitors, "now scram or else."

When the Gremlins continued singing, she lifted the broom and began thrashing left and right. More surprised than hurt, the creatures tumbled off the porch onto the snow, quickly hopping to their feet to snarl defiantly at her.

The exertion had caused Mrs. Deagle's heart to start pounding, and the night air was cold. An urge to return to the comparative warmth of her living room gripped her, but she took one final moment to glare them down before turning away.

"And don't come back," she snarled, going back inside.

The chill had worked on her bladder and she felt an urge to go upstairs to the bathroom.

"Miserable little creeps," she muttered, seating herself on the electric stairs climber and turning the switch to UP. As she was in the process of doing this, one of the Gremlins watched with increasing fascination; meanwhile, in the kitchen, its partner took the opportunity to grab a late snack by stealing some of the cats' food. A huge tabby, not liking this, hissed and took a swipe at the Gremlin's leg. He received a quick kick that sent him half sailing, half sliding across the kitchen floor.

"What's that commotion?" Mrs. Deagle whined. Putting the machine in neutral, she climbed down and started for the kitchen, grumbling as she stumbled along. Arriving at the swinging door of the room, she pushed it open to see a half dozen cats standing with tails upraised and fur as straight as a poker, their wide eyes fixed on the door leading into the dining room.

"What is it?" Mrs. Deagle demanded. "I swear, sometimes you stupid animals are more trouble than you're worth."

It took her a while to clean up the spilled food, calm down the cats with some milk, and make a perfunctory search of the dining room for them. She saw nothing. While she did these things, the Gremlin at the stairway had a wonderful time with the old woman's elevator chair, twisting wires and changing leads almost as if it were a born electronics expert.

Finally, the troubles apparently over, Mrs. Deagle sighed wearily and returned to her original problem, that of going to the bathroom.

"At last," she wheezed, "a chance to relax."

As she spoke, she disengaged the chair from neutral and pushed the switch back to UP.

—*body was identified by his wife as that of Murray*

Futterman, a professional handyman and mechanic who was born in Kingston Falls and lived here all his life except for a brief stint in World War Two. How Mr. Futterman was literally pushed through the wall of his garage by the snowplow is not known. The machine was still running when his body was discovered beneath it.

Another unusual accident occurred not far away at the home of Mrs. Ruby Deagle, wife of the late real estate millionaire Donald Deagle. Mrs. Deagle, who used a stair-climbing device because of a bad heart, was found dead in that chair only minutes ago. The unusual thing was that the chair and Mrs. Deagle were not in her home but in a vacant lot a tenth of a mile north of her Decatur Drive residence. The police officer who examined the circumstances of the case said that the chair apparently had gone completely haywire, carrying the woman up the stairs, through a window in the hallway, and onto the vacant lot. To have achieved such a trajectory and distance, the officer estimated that the chair must have been going at least two hundred miles an hour.

This just in—a report that the green monsters have taken over an entire bar for the evening. Because of the demands placed on the Kingston Falls Police Department by the events of the past few hours, the owner of the bar known as Dorry's Pub could not get in touch with the police, so he called this station to warn everyone to stay out of Dorry's Pub. That's Dorry's Pub, 460 West Main. The owner said that all of the customers got out safely when the little people entered except one waitress.

Meanwhile, two more people fell into open manholes—

"Kate!" Billy shouted, hitting the brakes so quickly the car spun completely around in the road.

He was nearly home, but now he would have to go all the way back to town.

"Darn," he muttered, "this is all my fault—"

Yes. My name's Damian Phillips and I have a theory about all this. I have a brother who recently retired from the CIA and he says the Russians developed a robot that—

"Shut up," Billy snapped, reaching forward to turn the car radio off. Accelerating as much as he dared to on the icy streets, he peered through the small square of clearness generously given him by the VW's antiquated defrosting system. Like most citizens of Kingston Falls, he had been amused initially at some of the pranks committed by the Gremlins, partly because he had experienced a secret longing to see what might happen if every traffic light showed green. But that and pulling a man into a mailbox and rolling tires down a hill were far cries from the most recent mishaps engineered by the Gremlins.

"Mr. Futterman is dead," Billy whispered. "The poor guy. I can't believe it."

He did believe it, though, and the corollary was painfully self-evident. If these creatures could kill Mr. Futterman and Mrs. Deagle and perhaps others, they could also kill Kate without a second thought.

His engine roaring as the wheels spun beneath him, Billy breathed a silent prayer he would make it in time.

CHAPTER EIGHTEEN

Dummy, she thought, you had an opportunity to get out of this place but you blew it. It wasn't that long a chance and making it would have involved a little shoving, but you had to act civilized and cool and sophisticated.

So now you're a civilized, cool, and sophisticated prisoner, she mused, not going easy on the self-recriminations.

"It's even worse than that," she muttered under her breath as she poured another round of drinks. "It's a new definition of perpetual motion. I'm the only waitress for the thirstiest, meanest, sloppiest bunch of drunks in the world. What a living nightmare!"

Trapped behind the long rectangular bar at Dorry's when the torrent of green demons poured through the door and enveloped her like a snag in a stream, Kate had initially diverted the Gremlins' attention by mixing and pouring drinks as fast as she could and passing them around. It had worked, or at least kept the unruly mob from murdering her or, as they used to say in cheap fiction, subjecting her to a fate worse than death. The problem was that there was no time

225

to even think, much less plan a hasty and safe exit. As soon as she filled one batch of glasses, another batch of empties was plunked down in front of her by a leering, giggling, slimy-fanged customer. One consoling factor emerged as she carried out her arm-wearying ordeal: they weren't particular. At first, Kate had mixed real cocktails—Manhattans, martinis, whiskey sours—but soon it became obvious they would drink anything. So when a bottle of bourbon ran out, she added rum or tequila or whatever was handy to the drink. One Gremlin sitting at the end of the bar even developed a taste for bitters, throwing a tantrum when Kate finally ran out.

Now, though not much more than a half hour had passed since the Gremlins had arrived, Kate was exhausted and Dorry's Pub looked like a cross between party headquarters on election night and Omaha Beach the morning after D day. The air, smelly and sticky, was filled with flying objects—bottles, glasses, cue sticks, billiard balls, chairs, whatever was not nailed down. A raucous babble of foreign sounds, squeals, and high-pitched giggling kept the tension level dangerously high. Amid the noise, a few passed-out bodies lay on the floor, which oozed with spilled drinks, bits of food, and crushed popcorn. Kate fought back increasingly powerful urges to scream and make a sudden rush for the door, acts which she knew would call attention to her and perhaps seal her fate forever.

"Just keep calm," she murmured over and over again. "Sooner or later there'll be a chance to make a break. Or help will come. Or they'll all pass out at once."

She wasn't sure she believed it, but it made sense to continue serving them. At least she was invisible, or visible only when they needed a drink.

As more Gremlins drifted into the pub and supplies began to run low, however, the devilish creatures became more onerous and overbearing. Although she could not understand their language, Kate noted that the typical Gremlin drunk and his human counterpart displayed the same impatience when service didn't keep up with their needs.

Faces leered openly, no longer bothering to feign coolness. Some seemed to delight in holding her up, shouting in her ears, deliberately spilling drinks, anything to keep her from doing her job.

"Where is everybody?" she hissed between clenched teeth. "Aren't there any cops in this town?"

Suddenly a cigar-sucking Gremlin popped up in front of her, waiting to be served. Kate poured him a drink. Screeching angrily, he threw the glass and its contents into the crowd near the pool table, clawed the counter, and seemed about to leap at Kate.

"What?" she yelled.

The creature gestured to the dead cigar.

"Why didn't you say so?" Kate muttered.

She located the butane lighter and moved it quickly toward the Gremlin's face, snapping it on. A jet of flame six inches high shot from the lighter, causing the Gremlin to squint, grunt in pain, and stumble backward.

"Sorry," Kate murmured.

As she adjusted the flame to a lower level, a plan was forming in her mind. Those rules Billy mentioned when he turned the Mogwai over to Mr. Hanson—wasn't one of them something about avoiding bright direct light? Of course, Kate reassured herself, that's why the Gremlin with the cigar didn't care much for the high flame when it came close to his eyes.

Kate looked around. If direct light was her ally, she was mired deep in enemy territory. Why couldn't she have been trapped in the bank or an office building? Then her only problem would have been getting to the switches in order to turn on the overhead lights and escape in the pain and confusion.

Dorry's Pub was a completely different situation. Dimly lit, there was not an overhead light throughout the entire lounge area. They called it romantic, old-fashioned, cozy, but for Kate it was a trap. Unless Dorry kept a flashlight or two behind the bar, she had no way of using light as a secret weapon. He's got to have a flashlight, she thought, flinging open doors and panels, all the while continuing her duties as waitress, punching bag, and slave to the green masses at the bar.

Probably having gotten bored with pool, video games, food, and drink, she noted that they were becoming more and more obnoxious. Kate was gradually losing her patience, too, her annoyance and fear rising as she went through one drawer filled with useless junk after another.

"I can't believe it," she whispered angrily, "there's nothing. Absolutely nothing. How can a bar not have a flashlight behind the counter?"

There were several packs of matches, she noted, all gaily decorated in green and white with the outline of a four-leaf clover, a shillelagh, and the telephone number and address of Dorry's Pub. For a moment she toyed with the idea of setting them on fire one pack at a time and holding them before her, forcing the Gremlins to retreat like Dracula from a crucifix. Lots of luck, she thought. Such a strategy might irritate the closest Gremlins, but there was so little shock value in a pack of slowly burning matches, she had no faith in the plan.

"Still," she mused, "if it's the only game in town..."

A claw reached about her waist as a second, not belonging to the same owner, grabbed at her arm. Twisting away, Kate walked quickly to the middle of the bar, trying not to appear frightened or intimidated.

The two Gremlins followed, elbowing their way through

the double and triple layers of fellow carousers packed along the rail of the bar.

Clutched in her left hand, which she carefully but casually tucked beneath her apron, were the packs of matches, Kate's only slim hope. If she could get them all in a single ashtray and light the whole thing at once, maybe, just maybe—

Two more Gremlins seated at center bar reached out for her, the more aggressive one lying flat on his belly in order to grab Kate's thigh. As he did so, a roar of approbation burst from the other Gremlins near the scene. Reacting instinctively, Kate picked up the nearest bottle and slammed it alongside the Gremlin's head, not pulling her punch in the slightest degree. A heavy liquid thunk, like a cantaloupe hitting the floor, told her the blow was a solid one. As the creature nose-dived onto the bar, its eyes rolling up into the top of its head and the smile collapsing into a confusion of flaccid drooling lips, Kate felt the first surge of relief since her ordinary evening of waitressing had turned into a torture test.

Following her knockout blow, Kate noted grimly that the reaction of the other Gremlins was not exactly what she had expected. Humans—even construction workers, Kate thought ironically—would have laughed at the comeuppance rendered on their buddy, partly because an innate sense of justice would have told even the vilest drunk that the grabber got what he deserved. Apparently the Gremlins didn't look at it that way, instead regarding Kate's act of self-defense as an attack on all of them. In a moment the quasi-happy jabbering changed to an ominous rumble as the Gremlins angrily debated what to do with this evil person.

Oh-oh, Kate thought, quickly picking up the drift of their muttering. Unless I miss my guess, they're talking about me. Looks like it's match time.

She hastily began tearing the matches from the books

and putting them in an ashtray, shielding her actions by leaning against the cash register. It was while fumblingly doing this that she saw the camera.

It was Dorry's Instamatic, carefully stashed out of sight behind the register. And it had a flashcube. A perfect offensive weapon that could open a pathway out of captivity. She grabbed it with a quick compulsive gesture that was not lost on the Gremlins at the bar.

There was no time to plan the best way out or gain a head start before using the flashcube. In fact, the hordes were already pouring over the counter so fast Kate barely had time to get the camera in position, find the button, and push. Her mind wasn't even allowed a moment for the dubious luxury of agonizing over the possibility the device wouldn't work.

Psheee—ick.

The sudden burst of light from the flashbulb created an immediate vacuum at the bar, Gremlins tumbling backward and over each other in their reaction to the pain. Kate used the precious seconds of chaos to race to her right and fling herself around the right side of the counter. There she ran into a new group of angry Gremlins.

A second explosion of light gouged a six-foot wedge of empty floor space ahead of her. She plunged forward, trying not to notice the clutching claws immediately behind her. Now the green creatures were mobilized by fury, their screeching chorus swirling around Kate like vaporized hatred. As she advanced spastically toward the front door, she realized they had no intention of taking prisoners in this small but bitter conflict.

Blocked once more by a new curtain of green-brown bodies and vengeful eyes but now within sight of the exit, she pushed the button again.

Psheee—ick.

Thank God, she thought, it worked.

Struggling forward into the temporary no-man's-land, she stumbled into the foyer. A split second later Gremlins were all about her, screaming and clawing. She could feel pinpricks of pain all over her body as they fought to get a good claw's grip on her. One hand against the wall to keep from falling, she brought the camera forward again. Let it work one more time, she prayed, just once.

The camera clicked, but this time there was no detonation of brightness, no howl of pain and rage from the enemy, no recoiling in terror away from her. Instead they surged forward around their target like waves breaking over a rock.

Kate let go of the camera, heard herself scream, could not help falling forward into the turgid green sea with its clawed wavelets reaching for her.

Even as she fell, Kate saw a huge flash of light against the foyer wall. Their giggles of vengeful glee turning to shrieks of pain, the Gremlins scattered to the shadows, leaving Kate alone on the floor, her torn clothes and body bathed in a trapezoidal pattern of illumination shaped by the front windows.

For a moment Kate's numbed mind worked sluggishly. Had the fall somehow triggered the flashcube? Then, as she freed herself from the shock of the past few moments, she realized the lights came from outside, that the headlights of a car were pointed directly into the building. Not knowing how long these saving beams would last, she scrambled to her feet as quickly as she could and raced for the door.

Outside, a figure that had just gotten out of the car called her name in a familiar voice.

"Billy!" Kate shouted back.

"Are you all right?" he asked, folding his arms about her when she ran to him.

"I . . . I think so. But those things . . . How many are there?"

"I don't know," Billy replied. "They're everywhere. I thought they'd gotten you, too."

"Me too? Who else?"

"We don't have time to stand here talking about it," Billy said. "We gotta get help. I don't know wh—"

As he spoke, the idling VW started to miss, its rhythm punctuated by heavy lurches and a slamming sound from the rear. Leaping into the car, Billy stabbed at the gas pedal, but in his haste gave the engine too much fuel. With a single gag, it died.

"Not now!" Billy swore.

Kate got in beside him.

"Is it all right?" she asked. "I'd like to get away from here soon."

"It's temperamental," Billy replied, turning the key. When the engine failed to start immediately, he turned off the lights and sat back.

"What are you doing?" Kate whispered. "Giving up?"

"No. It's just that it may be flooded, so it's best to wait a minute or two."

"But the lights—"

"Leaving them on will wear down the batter—"

A beer bottle slammed against the windshield, creating a spider web of broken glass and frightening Kate and Billy nearly out of their wits.

"That's why I asked about the lights," Kate murmured. "It's the only thing keeping them away."

Another heavy object smashed into the windshield.

"Maybe we'd better run," Kate suggested.

"Just a second," Billy said.

Turning the ignition key once again, he ground away for nearly a minute without success. Meanwhile a hail of ashtrays, bottles, and pool table accessories bounced off the hood or clunked against the side of the car.

"Yeah," Billy said finally. "You're right."

Reaching into the back of the car, he grabbed the knapsack with such a jerk that Gizmo nearly fell completely out, his fall being broken only by his feet getting tangled in the strap. Grumbling in Mogwai, he ducked back inside and then reemerged, only the tip of his nose and eyes showing.

Not recognizing Gizmo in the darkness, Kate recoiled, thinking the car had been infiltrated by Gremlins.

"It's O.K.," Billy said. "It's only Giz. Let's go."

Getting out of the car, they dashed through the barrage of objects flying from the tavern, pausing only when they had crossed the street. They looked at each other and smiled, both realizing at the same time that they were just outside the bank, the door of which was open.

"Can you beat that?" Billy said. "They even found a way to get in the bank after closing hours."

"Maybe we'd better check and see if everything's all right," Kate suggested.

Billy nodded. They went inside and turned on the lights, which caused a scurrying of feet out the back door. In the harsh glow of the overhead incandescent lights the vandalized bank looked as if a typhoon had recently passed through. All of the tellers' windows were broken, pieces of furniture lay on their sides, cash drawers were open and money of all denominations was everywhere.

"I guess they figured it was just useless paper to them," Billy said.

"And to make sure it would be useless to everybody else, they tore all the bills in pieces," Kate pointed out, picking up several mutilated dollars and then letting them fall back to the littered floor. "Boy, I think I'll quit this job," she added, looking around at the monetary mess. "We'll never get this to tally."

"Yeah . . ."

A soft moan echoed through the bank, causing them to exchange chilled expressions.

"Who's there?" a distant voice asked. "I can hear someone. May I be of assistance?"

"Sounds like Ger," Billy remarked.

Kate nodded.

"We're not open for business yet, but it's all right to come in and chat," Gerald Hopkins's voice said in an uncharacteristically agreeable tone.

"He must be in the vault," Kate said.

Billy took her hand and together they walked past the executive offices to the room at the end of the corridor. Its door was ajar.

"Is somebody out there?" Gerald's voice asked. He sounded distracted, singsongy, almost drugged.

Billy pushed the door open and gingerly they entered the room.

Kate gasped.

The vault and anteroom were in total disarray, but that was the least terrifying element they saw. On the floor lay the inert body of Roland Corben, his features relaxed as if he were enjoying an afternoon nap. Kate and Billy knew immediately that he was not sleeping, however.

"Poor Mr. Corben," Kate breathed.

Their eyes rising from the floor at the same time, they saw Gerald Hopkins in the background, apparently locked in the securities room of the vault. Gripping the steel bars like a penitentiary inmate, he smiled out at them, speaking in a deferential but firm tone of voice.

"I'm so sorry," he said. "You're both too big to use this bank."

"What?" Billy responded, puzzled.

"This bank is for little people only," Gerald explained. He held his palm approximately waist-high and then continued in the same strange voice. "We're going to redecorate this entire bank, lower the tellers' windows, make the furniture smaller—everything so that little people will feel more at home here."

He gestured grandly but in a sort of slow motion, as if he were in a trance or dreaming. "This is going to be the first bank just for little people," he said softly. "Think of it. And I'm the president."

Kate and Billy stole sidelong glances at each other.

"If you ask me, I think his buttons are in the wrong buttonholes," Kate whispered.

"Could be," Billy replied.

"The world has needed a facility for little people for a long time," Gerald intoned. "And now, with me as their leader, they're going to get it."

"Little people," Billy said. "Do you mean the Gremlins?"

"I don't know what they're called. All I know is they talk very fast and so funny Mr. Corben didn't understand them. That's why they—"

He broke off then, frowning.

"Yes?" Billy urged. "Go on."

"Never mind, it's too unpleasant. All I can say is that Mr. Corben didn't want to go along with the little people. Of course, he's quite old and set in his ways. That's why he didn't understand their needs. But I did. So they established me as first president of their bank."

"Just as I thought," Kate whispered. "He's as soft as a nickel cantaloupe."

Gerald Hopkins fixed Billy with a gaze that was somehow both intense and vacant. "You can be my head teller if you promise to be respectful to the little people," he said. "Your name escapes me, but I remember your face." With that, he threw his head back and giggled in a way that was eerily close to that of the Gremlins. "Yes, but I'll let you work for me. . . . Minimum wage, naturally."

"I can't believe this," Kate breathed, shaking her head. "I told you terrible things always happen at Christmas time."

"It's not the holiday's fault," Billy murmured.

"Now if you'll pardon me, I have a lot of work to do," Gerald said in a more formal tone. "People who will be investing in the new bank are coming soon, so I have to be ready."

"Would you like us to see if we can get the door open?" Billy asked.

"No, it's perfectly all right. Good day."

He smiled blandly but with a certain finality and returned to the inside of the vault. Taking a seat at the small desk inside, he began writing with an instrument that if not imaginary was invisible to Kate and Billy.

"When the Gremlins raided this place and attacked Mr. Corben, I guess it was just too much for him," Billy said. "His mind must have gone. At first I thought he was putting on an act for us, but now . . . Poor guy."

"Well"—Kate shrugged—"at least he's got his own bank now. That seems to have made him happy."

As Gerald continued working at the desk, Kate and Billy quietly left the room.

"What next?" Kate asked.

"I don't know."

A moment later they stood at the entrance of the bank, staring out at the deserted streets of Kingston Falls.

"Where do you suppose everybody is?" Kate murmured.

The town seemed like an old movie set, no sign of life intruding on its eerie serenity. A few small lights glowed in houses but that was all.

"Everybody must be hiding in their basements or attics until help comes," Billy suggested. "Either that or they got in their cars and left."

He looked at his watch. It was four o'clock. "Not very long until daybreak," he added. "I wonder what the Gremlins will do when the sun comes out."

"Probably find a dark place and hang out until night again," Kate said.

"Yeah."

"I think we should find a radio and see what's going on.

If they haven't destroyed the station, we might find out
something."

"Good idea," Billy seconded. "Suppose we were the only
ones left in town because the government decided to nuke
the whole place. Wouldn't that be funny?"

"Hilarious."

"I think there's a radio in Mr. Corben's office."

"Yes."

They went back into the bank and rooted through the
debris. Mr. Corben's desk radio had been smashed and its
cord chewed to a frazzle, but in one drawer they found some
small transistor radios the bank used as gifts for new ac-
counts. One of them still worked.

*—peat, stay in your homes until the official all clear is
given. Lieutenant General David Greene of the United States
Marine barracks at Phoenix is here now and has agreed to
take a valuable minute of his time in order to explain what
his troops, who are already standing by near Kingston Falls,
are going to do. General Greene . . .*

*Thank you, Harman. First of all, we're urging everyone
to stay indoors. That will make our job a whole lot easier.
You see, we don't really know what these small creatures
are, having only just arrived and having nothing but reports
to go on. Now, they could be masqueraders or a new form
of life from an alien galaxy. That's a long shot but we like
to be flexible. That's why we're not coming into your town
with flamethrowers and machine guns and rocket launchers.
We don't want to destroy property or endanger lives and
we do want to take these animals or people alive.*

*That sounds like a good juggling act, General Greene.
How do you plan to do that, sir?*

*Well, we hope to literally flush these invaders or trouble-
makers into the open. You see, rather than rely on weap-
onry, we've procured and brought with us several huge
portable pumps and fire hoses. What we'll begin doing in*

*about thirty minutes, as soon as our pumps are loaded, is
go from building to building looking for these . . . things.
When we find them, instead of firing on them or taking a
chance on having them injure our men, we intend to turn
the hoses on and round them up that way. You know, there's
a lot you can do with a heavy stream of water directed the
right way.*

That sounds like a terrific plan, General Greene. . . .

"Terrific!" Billy exploded. "It's terrible! If they come
here with hoses and spray a lot of water around, we'll have
millions of Gremlins instead of a few hundred."

"Then we've got to head off those soldiers," Kate said
calmly. "Talk them out of it."

"Have you ever tried to talk a general out of a plan he's
devised?"

"No. Have you?"

"No. But in the movies it never works."

"Maybe this time it will be different. After all, Billy,
you know more than they do."

"Yeah, I know," Billy said. "It *is* my fault. I'm to blame
for this whole mess."

"There's no time to worry about blame now. If you're
going to talk these troops out of using water, maybe you
should have a better plan for how to round up the Gremlins."

Billy sighed, nodded.

They were at the entrance of the bank again. Billy looked
both ways on Main Street, scratched his head thoughtfully.

"Wait a minute," he said finally. "Where are the Gremlins, anyway?"

"The same as before, I suppose," Kate replied. "Going
from building to building."

"But there's nothing moving. I don't see or hear anything, do you?"

"No, now that you mention it."

Billy hopped off the sidewalk and began walking quickly in the direction of Dorry's Pub. Kate followed.

"Where are you going?" she asked when she caught up with him. "Not back in the pub, I hope."

"Yeah."

"Why?"

"Just a hunch."

Her features reflecting her anxiety, Kate trailed behind him. She had no desire to return to Dorry's if those creatures were still inside. On the other hand, if he had an idea how to get rid of the greenies and needed her help, she had no alternative but to go along with him. And despite the perils she had been through, there was still something in her that rose to the challenge when her courage was tested.

"Do you have a flashlight in your car?" she asked.

"Good idea," Billy said.

The battered VW was still there at curbside, looking worse than ever as the centerpiece of the garbage shower hurled at it from the pub. Billy reached inside the car and found the flashlight on the seat, which glowed yellowishly.

"I'd estimate we have less than a minute's life left in that thing," Kate predicted.

"That may be just enough," he said.

Billy in the lead, they edged their way into the foyer of the pub. Every second Kate expected to be engulfed by either a new barrage of missiles or by the Gremlins themselves, their claws flashing. She doubted that the flashlight would be much help in deterring a Gremlin attack, its weak beam projecting only a few feet into the darkness. When no assault came, she began to feel better, especially when they turned the corner and moved into the main lounge area. There, by the subdued indirect lighting of that room, they saw wreckage and destruction of monumental proportions, but there wasn't a single Gremlin in sight.

Billy looked around, whistled softly as his eyes took in the wall-to-wall panorama of vandalism.

"Poor Dorry," he said sadly.

"What do you mean, 'Poor Dorry'?" Kate protested with a bit of a laugh. "It was almost 'Poor me.' But for the grace of God, I could be one of those piles of trash." Squeezing his arm, she added quickly, "And thanks to you, of course."

Billy's expression was a mixture of pleasure and mild embarrassment.

They stood silently for a moment. Finally Billy said, "Well, where do you suppose they all went?"

"Beats me." Kate shrugged.

They walked back outside, stood on the sidewalk, and continued their puzzled surveillance of Kingston Falls's forsaken town square area.

Billy wondered how long it would be before the marines showed up with their fire hoses. Perhaps they were already inspecting homes and buildings at the far end of town. Still hoping to first locate the Gremlins and then find a way of dealing with them, he closed his eyes, straining his mind to think, think, think.

"Where would I go if I were a Gremlin?" he said aloud.

"A Gremlin who's afraid of bright light, with sunrise on the way," Kate added.

"Good," he said. "That's important. I guess, putting myself in their place, I'd try to find a building, a big building with no windows so I could hide ... You know, they tend to stick together. I'll bet if we can find one of them, that's where all of them will be."

"So how many buildings can there be without windows?" Kate asked.

"Just two. And they're both at the end of the next block."

Billy started to run, then spun and hopped into the VW, giving the key a turn just on the off chance the engine would turn over.

It did. Kate hopped in beside him.

A minute later he slowed the car as they moved through the intersection of Main and Garfield. On one corner was the Colony movie theatre, its marquee still advertising NOW WHITE AND THE SEVEN DWARFS. On the adjacent corner was the Montgomery Ward department store. One of the entrance doors to Montgomery Ward hung open as evidence of the fact that sometime during the night some Gremlins had found a way inside.

Billy parked the car and got out. He was frankly undecided as to which building to try first, until he noticed that Gizmo's head was completely out of the knapsack, his nose twitching nervously.

"Which one, Giz?" Billy asked.

Gizmo peered anxiously but meaningfully at the movie theatre.

"Then let's go," Billy said.

It soon became evident that Gizmo's nose was working well, for as they neared the theatre they saw countless Gremlin clawprints in front. Other evidence of the devilish creatures' presence could be seen in the numerous bits of vandalism—broken glass, a door hanging askew from a single hinge, three-pronged scratches along the walls.

"I guess this is the place, all right," Kate said, surveying the damage.

Gizmo waved his arms, put one paw over his mouth, and cocked an ear.

From inside the theatre auditorium emanated a continuous rush of sound made up of giggles, yelps, and conversational jabber, in more or less equal parts.

"Sounds loud enough to be all of them," Billy said hopefully.

"Well, now that we've found them, what do we do about it?" Kate asked.

"I'm thinking."

Negotiating their way between bits of glass and over-
turned lobby furniture and ashtrays, they moved quietly into
the deserted lobby, the floor of which was littered with
crumpled wads of popcorn and torn candy wrappers.

"They sure are sloppy eaters," Kate observed. "Of course,
it must be hard to eat popcorn with fangs like theirs that
are so far apart. It keeps falling out the spaces. Another
thing I noticed about them—"

As Kate's voice grew in volume, Billy looked at her a
bit sharply.

"I'm sorry," she whispered. "I guess I'm rambling on
because I'm nervous. Just the thought of those guys coming
at me again gives me the creeps."

Billy nodded. "I understand."

"I'll be quiet," she promised.

Huddled near the back of the lobby, the three listened
to the babble of Gremlin voices for a long moment. Kate
wondered if they were involved in a heated discussion of
some issue or just conversing idly. From her previous experience with them she knew they were intelligent creatures,
diabolically so. Did they know now that they faced a crisis
with the approach of dawn? If so, were they working up a
plan of action in the event they should be discovered and
attacked? At that moment Kate would gladly have given a
month's pay to understand what they were saying, but that
was impossible, of course.

"Couldn't we just bolt the doors or nail them shut?" she
finally whispered to Billy. "That would keep them inside
until help came."

"It's an idea, but I don't think it'll work," he replied.
"Some doors are off the hinges; the glass is cracked or
broken. If we tried to fix that, we'd be discovered before
we finished. But there is one possibility—"

Grabbing her suddenly by the arm, Billy pulled Kate

around the corner of a vending machine and put his finger
to his lips.

Clawed feet could be heard scratching on the tile floor
of the lobby. But it was only one set, Billy noted thankfully,
hoping the thump of his beating heart didn't carry across
the room.

A moment later, when the sound of the footsteps stopped,
Billy and Kate peeked around the edge of the machine. The
Gremlin with the flowing white mane was scooping up the
last of the popcorn from the front and corners of the glass
display case, slurping noisily as he shoveled pieces into his
mouth. After a gigantic belch, he shuffled back into the
auditorium.

"That was Stripe," Billy said. "He's the smartest of the
bunch and probably their leader, unless I miss my guess."

"Now what was the other possibility?" Kate asked.

"Blowing them up," Billy replied.

"With what? Do you happen to have a few sticks of
dynamite in the car?"

Billy shook his head. "Maybe something better. I used
to work in this theatre just after high school. If it still has
the same boiler problems, we may be in business."

"I don't get you."

"The boiler kept building up pressure," Billy explained.
"But the fella who owned the place was too cheap to install
a new one. Instead, he put on this release valve that we had
to check at least three times a day to make sure it was still
working. He kept saying that if anything happened to that
valve, we'd all be blown to kingdom come."

"Suppose the valve's disconnected or turned off?" Kate
asked.

"Like the man said, I guess," Billy murmured. "Poof!"

"O.K., but will it be seconds, minutes, hours, or days
before the explosion?"

"He didn't say."

"That's too bad, because it's important, don't you think? If it's a matter of seconds, we'll check out with the Gremlins."

Billy nodded. "Yeah. I think there'll be time, though, at least a couple minutes. But that's my problem, not yours."

"What do you mean?"

"I mean there's no reason all of us should go down to the boiler room. As a matter of fact, two bodies will make twice as much noise—"

"But you may need help."

"What kind of help?"

"Somebody to hold the flashlight while you work. It's not much light, but it may be the difference between getting the job done quickly and fumbling around in the dark."

"Yeah," Billy admitted. "But—"

"No more debate, O.K.?" Kate interrupted. "Now let's go before I lose my nerve."

"All right. You take Gizmo."

Handing the knapsack to Kate, he led her across the lobby to the maintenance room door.

It was locked.

"Does this mean our demolition derby's off?" Kate asked, disappointment and hope mingling in her voice.

"No. There's another way to get to the basement, but we'll have to cross the back of the balcony."

"Oh-oh."

"I couldn't have said it better myself. You ready?"

"As I'll ever be."

Staying close to the wall, Billy led the way up the balcony stairs. At the top, he put his hand on Kate's arm, indicating that she would have to keep her head down while crossing the back of the balcony.

The seats were not as high as he remembered them to be, nor was the rear aisleway as wide. Thus they were forced to move with heads nearly between their knees, a torturous duck waddle through the darkness. Above and in front of them the Gremlin chatter continued. Occasionally a piece of popcorn or a crumpled cardboard box landed on their shoulders or caromed off the rear wall. But they finally arrived at the opposite side of the balcony and the red door with the black stenciling that read EMPLOYEES ONLY.

Stretched out nearly prone, Billy eased the door ajar and held it open so that Kate could enter. He then followed, breathing a deep sigh of relief now that they had some space between themselves and the Gremlins.

A narrow spiral staircase whirlpooled downward into the darkness of the basement. Kate and Billy half slid, half fell down the musty metal steps, using the flashlight sparingly in order to save the weak batteries. When they reached the bottom, Billy took the lead again, groping his way into the boiler room.

"Turn on the light," he whispered. "I think the valve should be about here."

The pale light moving back and forth across the ceiling revealed a tangle of electrical cables, joists, pipes, decomposing insulation, and, finally, the release valve Billy remembered so well.

"It's still there," he said, grinning. Moving a few feet away to the boiler itself, he smiled broadly when he saw the pressure gauge. "And it's really high," he added. "Even with the release valve working."

"Great," Kate said sardonically. "Maybe it'll blow so fast we won't even be able to make it back across the balcony."

"We won't have to do that," he said. "There's a small door out of the basement that works only from the inside. We'll be able to use that."

Grabbing a wrench from the top of the boiler, he returned to the release valve.

"We had to make sure this stayed open," he explained as he began working. "But it couldn't be too far open or steam would escape into the basement and theatre. Now let's see what happens when she's closed all the way."

Working the wrench quickly and efficiently as Kate held the light, he twisted the valve until it refused to turn another fraction of an inch.

"Now let's get outa here," he said.

Kate, needing no urging, followed, rapping her head and elbows several times as they rushed precipitously across the low-ceilinged room jammed with crates and boxes. Above them, a steady rumble, punctuated by occasional loud raps, indicated that the restless Gremlins were still twisting, turn-ing, and jabbering in their seats.

Ahead of them, a recess in the corner of the room held a narrow metal door, rusty at the corners. Billy reached it first, gave it a strong push.

"No," he cried out. "No!"

"It's not locked?" Kate whispered, horrified.

"It can't be," he said.

He slammed his shoulder against the door again but it refused to open.

"I guess . . . it's just stuck . . ." he said, attacking it once more. "It . . . hasn't . . . been used . . . for a long time. . . ."

"Are you sure it opens out?" Kate asked. In the darkness it was difficult to see how the door was mounted.

"Yeah," he replied. "I . . . used it once."

Searching about for something, anything, to help him with, Kate's hand fell on a cold metal object.

"Try this," she said.

Billy took the crowbar with a little smile of thanks, wedged the end of it near the upper corner, and pushed with all his might. The door moved outward grudgingly, a crack of perhaps a half inch appearing. Encouraged but rapidly be-coming exhausted, Billy moved the crowbar down and pushed

again. Finally, after a half dozen solid thrusts, the door
sprang open with a rusty yawning sound.

Outside it was considerably lighter than when they had
entered the theatre, most of the stars having vanished in the
first glow of dawn.

"This way. Hurry!" Billy said, grabbing Kate's hand and
leading her to the right. Still holding the crowbar, he paused
to insert it through the handles of the theatre's rear exit
doors, then raced toward a small alleyway across the street.

"Suppose it doesn't—" Kate began.

Her question was choked off by a muffled crash, then a
grinding noise so loud it seemed as if all the machinery in
the world were breaking down at once. A split second later
a huge flash of flame arced from the basement level to the
roof in one upside-down lightning stroke, sending smaller
crimson explosions leaping outward. Three blasts followed
in quick succession, forcing the theatre's side outward and
then shattering it like an oil tanker being torpedoed. In
hardly more than a minute the structure was converted to a
vast brazier of fire rapidly becoming obscured under an
impenetrable pall of smoke and dust.

"It worked," Billy said.

Kate, smiling slightly at his masterstroke of understate-
ment, could only nod.

Their initial rush of exhilaration was dampened a moment
later when through the holes in the theatre wall they could
see the forms of struggling, dying Gremlins, grisly dancing
silhouettes rising briefly from the flames only to sink back
a moment later.

"Why did we have to do that?" Kate asked, looking away.

Billy didn't answer. No doubt he would think about it
later, but for the moment he was intent on making sure that
the job, albeit unpleasant, was at least complete. Their position in the alleyway was perfect for watching all three
theatre exits. Kate's eyes were downcast, and Gizmo ducked

down into the knapsack to avoid the flames, but Billy's eyes remained riveted on all three exits.

Another few minutes passed. The roar, at first so loud it seemed in back of them as well as in front, gradually diminished to a steady hiss. All signs of movement within the theatre also disappeared.

"I think maybe we got all of them," Billy said finally.

But the words were hardly out of his mouth when a single figure stumbled through the charred front door of the rapidly deteriorating structure, stood for a moment as if in shock, then shook its white-maned head and padded across the street.

"No . . ." Billy heard himself say. "No . . . no . . . no!"

CHAPTER NINETEEN

"Well, they're not gonna keep me away from my own home," Rand Peltzer shouted over his shoulder as he trotted out of the all-night gas station toward his car.

The attendant didn't deserve being yelled at, Rand thought, especially since he was offering friendly advice, but it had been a harrowing night and Rand's nerves were just about shot. The tension had begun during the sales meeting, when he became concerned about getting home on the snow-covered roads. Concern turned to worry when he was unable to get a call through to Lynn, and worry turned to near-panic when he began hearing the reports of strange happenings in and around Kingston Falls. Shortly after midnight Rand decided he could not stick to his original, no doubt sensible, plan of spending the night at a motel so that crews would have time to clear the roads. He had to find out if his loved ones were all right. A few minutes later, as the last salespeople were scattering to their rooms or the nearest cocktail lounge, Rand had gotten in his car and headed home.

After the stop for gas, where he received a running account of the troubles in Kingston Falls along with a recapitulation of the official warning that visitors should stay out of town if possible, Rand stopped by Lynn's mother's house. She wasn't overjoyed at being awakened at such an ungodly hour but understood that Barney had to be picked up and taken home. Realizing his mother-in-law had gone to bed very early and was unaware of the troubles in Kingston Falls, Rand decided not to cause her unnecessary worry. Apologizing for his late arrival, he took the dog and said nothing more.

Putting Barney in the front seat beside him, Rand set out again for Kingston Falls, hoping he would be able to get there by 2:00 A.M.

The journey seemed interminable. Rand had never enjoyed driving in the snow. In fact, he hated it and avoided doing so whenever possible, even if the skies were clear. Fighting bad driving conditions alone and at night was unthinkable except in the case of an emergency such as this one. Nevertheless, twenty miles down the highway he began to wonder if he had done the right thing. One detour after another sprang up, so deflecting him from his destination that several times he had to consult the road map to see where he was. Twice he made wrong turns because of poor visibility, once more because a road sign was turned the wrong way, and another time because a military policeman ordered him onto a side road he had no intention of taking. Throughout the increasingly desperate journey, his car radio issued a string of bulletins that were hardly designed to assure him everything was all right at home. Futterman dead. Mrs. Deagle dead. Stores and offices he had visited only days before nearly torn to pieces by unknown forces. Rumors of tiny but fierce aliens ransacking the town and attacking people. Most forms of communication out or intermittent at best. The majority of the town's population either hiding or on the road, fleeing like refugees during wartime. Marines on the way. Continued urgings not to be alarmed seemed only to increase his insecurity rather than assuage it. It seemed so hideously incredible. Little did he realize that he, solid citizen Rand Peltzer, was the man who was really responsible for the chaotic chain of events.

Shortly after four o'clock, his nerves jangling from the constant frustration of the detours through the snow and uncertainty of not knowing how Lynn and Billy were, he pulled off Highway 46 onto Main Street, approaching Kingston Falls from the south rather than the east, his normal route. Just ahead he could see an orange glow and considerable smoke, a situation made even scarier by the absence of fire engines, sirens, curious spectators, or traffic control guards. It was, as far as he could see, a major fire that was burning itself out while the town's population, official and otherwise, simply ignored it. Or, he thought, perhaps there was no population...

"No," he prayed. "Let them be all right. Please..."

He wanted to append the promise of some change in himself as payment if his prayer were answered, but for the life of him, Rand couldn't think of a thing God might want from him.

"I'll be better," he said finally. "I'll go to church every week."

The fire, he noted as he approached to within a block of it, was coming from the Colony Theatre. The entire building appeared gutted.

Braking so that he could get a longer view of the burned-out structure, Rand shook his head.

"I just don't get it," he murmured. "Where is everybody? No firemen, no fire freaks, not even a looter. It's crazy. It's unreal."

As he spoke, a quick and sudden movement to his right caught his eye. Crossing the street, directly in his path and only a few feet from the car, was a—

A what? Hitting the brakes hard to bring the car to a complete stop, Rand wasn't sure just what it was he had so narrowly avoided. It was small enough to be a dog, but walked upright. And the face he had glimpsed was unlike anything he had ever seen before outside of a horror movie or at Halloween. Was this one of the tiny creatures they had described on the radio?

It was gone almost before he could get a second glance, darting in front of the car at a low angle and trundling across the sidewalk to the Montgomery Ward store. In the dim early morning light, Rand saw only a greenish brown back bristling with a sort of horny plating, the sort of side view presented by some large fish or reptile. With a quick glance over its shoulder, the creature disappeared into the department store by the open side entrance door.

"What's going on here?" Rand demanded. "What was that thing? And what's Montgomery Ward doing open at this hour?"

Barney, having been jolted awake by the sudden braking of the car, broke into loud querulous barking when he caught sight of the Gremlin. Desperately trying to get even a few inches closer to it, he broadjumped into the back seat and began clawing at the left rear window.

"Take it easy, boy," Rand said firmly. "Whatever it is, it's not our job to track it down."

His head still turned to the left in order to spot the strange creature should it come out of the store, Rand heard the running footsteps before he saw the two approaching people. When he recognized who they were, his mouth fell open, his expression a mixture of complete surprise and happiness.

"Billy!" he shouted.

Bursting from the car, he embraced his son, all the while bombarding him with questions.

"What's been going on here, anyway? Is your mother all right? Why are you running?"

"Sorry, Dad," Billy replied, pulling away. "We've got to catch that— Did you see a Gremlin go by?"

"A what?"

Billy explained as quickly as possible what they were chasing, not going into why. Rand pointed toward the department store door. Nodding, Billy grabbed Kate's hand and started to run off, but Rand managed to get hold of his other arm and spin him around.

"Wait a second!" he shouted. "Don't run off. I want to know how your mother is."

"O.K., I think," Billy replied, backing toward the door as he spoke. "The phone's out but she's locked in the house. Sorry, Dad, but I've gotta catch that Gremlin."

"Why? It looks dangerous."

"It is."

"Then let the cops do it."

"No time."

"Wait. I'll help."

The offer was delivered to empty air, Billy and Kate having already disappeared into the department store.

Momentarily confused and indecisive, Rand stood on the sidewalk scratching his head. He still wasn't sure what was going on, but he knew he hadn't driven all night just to be a spectator. If Billy had a problem, it was his problem, too.

And maybe even Barney's, Rand thought, moving quickly back to the car.

"Come on, boy," he said to the impatient Barney, pushing the front seat forward so the dog could jump onto the sidewalk. "Let's go help Billy."

As he slammed the door and started to turn away, Rand's

eyes fell on an object lying in the back seat—his Bathroom
Buddy. It was perfect now, he was sure of it, and several
people at the sales meeting had expressed interest in mar-
keting it on a major scale. Knowing that, and remembering
that one door of his car still refused to lock, he made a
quick decision.

"Maybe I just better take this along," he said, reaching
into the back for the device. "I'd sure hate to have somebody
come along and steal this baby just when she's about to
make a lot of money for us."

Holding the Bathroom Buddy in front of him with both
hands, rather like a high port arms, he ran with surprising
speed into the Montgomery Ward store, followed immediately by Barney, whose flashing eyes and agitated nose
indicated he was eager for the hunt.

General David Greene was starting to become more than
a little angry and frustrated. It was now well after five
o'clock and the sky was beginning to lighten considerably.
For the better part of two hours his men had been going
from house to house and building to building in the northern
section of Kingston Falls, searching for the little green monsters. Their lack of success so far had been total.

"Well, what do you think, Medved?" he muttered to his
aide, who was never more than thirty inches away.

Major Josh Medved knew better than to respond immediately. When General Greene asked you what you
thought, it meant that he was going to tell you what he
thought.

"Tell you what I think," Greene continued. "I think either
this whole town's crazy, or they're in cahoots with the
Gremlins."

"In cahoots, sir?" Medved asked, frowning. He understood exactly what the general was getting at—any fool

could tell that—but from past experience Medved knew his superior officer appreciated thickheadedness above all other qualities.

"Sure," Greene replied. "Maybe not willingly, but I think these people may be sheltering or hiding the Gremlins. Out of fear, maybe. It was like that in Vietnam, you know. Those natives didn't help the VC because they liked 'em or believed in what they were doing. They were just plain scared."

"Yessir. That makes sense."

A lieutenant approached, looked around to see if the TV crew that had accompanied them was shooting. They were, so he saluted smartly.

Greene casually returned the salute and waited.

"Two things, sir," the lieutenant said. "We talked to some people in the next block who say they saw Gremlins at three or three-thirty. Then they all started to gravitate south, almost like they had an appointment."

"O.K. What's the second thing?"

"Sergeant Williamson called and said a whole building's on fire down at Main and Garfield. That's south of here at the other end of town. Could be the Gremlins are involved with that."

General Greene nodded and the lieutenant left.

"What do you think, Medved?" Greene asked.

Major Medved pursed his lips as if he were involved in serious cogitation.

"Tell you what I think," the general said. "I think we oughta stop beating the bushes out here and head for that fire where the action is."

"Good idea, sir."

"Stripe couldn't have picked a much better spot," Billy said with a sigh.

Her eyes flitting from side to side as she tried to adjust them to the darkness, Kate knew exactly what he meant. Montgomery Ward was spacious, with most of the merchandise spread over a four-acre, single-floor area. The aisles seemed endless—some, as the store's advertisements proclaimed, were a quarter mile long—and were jammed with displays. The illumination was minimal, coming now from small amber night lights at the intersections of the aisles.

"He could hide in here forever," Billy said.

Kate looked up at the ceiling. Billy, immediately understanding the movement, looked up too.

"Yeah," he said. "I wonder if we can find out how to turn on those overheads."

"Why don't we split up?" Kate suggested. "You keep looking for Stripe and I'll try to find the lights."

"Good. I think they may be somewhere near the office. Do you know this store?"

"Yes."

"Good. Seems to me there's a room where they have everything—lights, P.A. system, burglar alarm switches, the works."

"O.K. If it's there, I'll find it."

"Maybe you'd better take Giz," Billy said, handing her the knapsack. "He'll be safer with you, and I'll be able to move around better."

Gizmo peeked out of the canvas bag sadly, stretched forth a beseeching paw.

"Sorry, little guy," Billy said, smiling. "I'd better go on this one alone."

Kate and Gizmo headed in the direction of the office. Billy, noting that he was in the sporting goods department, grabbed a baseball bat from a nearby rack, tested it for heft, then began a systematic search of the aisles.

Alone in the semidarkness of the huge store, he was

suddenly apprehensive, even more so than when he and
Gizmo had tracked Stripe into the YMCA building. That
episode seemed a long time ago now, although the actual
passage of time was less than twelve hours. During that
brief period he had learned the essential thing about Gremlins—that their mischievous pranks could lead to violence
and death. Although he tried to drive that depressing thought
from his mind, it was definitely with him as he walked from
aisle to aisle. How much better it will be, he could not help
thinking, if I discover Stripe before he discovers me.

And how much more unlikely, another part of his mind
replied.

Annoyed and distracted by his flip-flopping mental gym-
nastics, he forced himself to concentrate on positive methods
of locating his Gremlin adversary rather than just walking
along, hoping to stumble upon him.

"What would I do if our places were reversed?" he asked
himself. The answer seemed self-evident: "I would create
a distraction so I could spring a trap."

Spring a trap with what?

With any of a hundred things, for the store abounded
with potentially lethal weapons, especially to the person
who was nervous about being ambushed. That thought having entered his mind, Billy saw the possibility of sudden
terror striking him from any part of the store. Remembering
the sports equipment section, he envisioned himself being
laid low by another baseball bat similar to the one he now
carried, shot at by a rifle, struck with weights, a tennis
racket, pool cue, or garroted by jump rope. Passing the
automotive section, he saw it presented an equally juicy
choice of weapons, including tire wrenches, snow chains,
trailer hitches, shock absorbers, or decorative hubcaps. The
Lawn Care Center presented grisly death via spading fork
or rake, and KitchenWare threatened him with mutilation
by an attacker armed with matching steak knives or barbecue

forks. Even the women's clothing section contained items that a clever or desperate attacker could use to terminate him—namely, spiked heels, belts, heavy handbags, or metal coat hangers.

"You are letting yourself get carried away," he whispered to himself.

As he spoke, he heard a whirring noise to which was soon added a faraway metallic singing voice and the rat-a-tat of a tiny drum. A moment later rock music augmented the mix into a swirl of overlapping sounds. Advancing cautiously, Billy peeked around the corner of the aisle into what was obviously the toy department.

The floor of the entire department was alive with small mechanical devices—robots, windup trucks and cars, animals, dolls and cartoon characters—each one singing or talking or making its own particular sound designed to enchant kids. Now, with all of them operating simultaneously in the semidarkness of the deserted store, the effect was eerie rather than charming, but it was difficult not to watch.

In short, a genial distraction.

The distraction, Billy thought, immediately before the—

Thwock.

—trap.

His mind completed the end of the thought even as a blindingly bright silver object passed in front of his eyes and tore into the wall behind him. Wincing in pain, Billy threw his hand to his cheek and brought down the dark wet stain he knew was blood. Disoriented, he spun around, sensing rather than hearing the approach of another flying object. Just in time he managed to hurl himself to the floor, the second object passing inches above his head.

Thwack.

Rolling behind the protection of a display at the end of the aisle, he lay on his stomach watching the second silver

object slide down the wall and come to rest on the floor
beside the first missile. Both objects were members of the
rotary saw blade family, one six and the other eight inches
in diameter.

And more relatives were on the way.

Giggling furiously all the while, Stripe leaped from his
hiding place to unleash a deadly barrage of similar blades
from a display case, quickly shredding the trash box Billy
was partially hidden behind and very nearly decapitating
him with several expertly thrown carom shots. Trapped in
a corner, Billy could do little but try to deflect the hail of
flying steel with the remains of the cardboard box. When
the saw blades were all used, Stripe continued his attack
with a variety of hammers, wrenches, small cans of paint,
and just about everything else he could get a grip on with
his claws.

Billy hurled himself backward to avoid a flying crosscut
saw and slammed into a display case, which tipped and
crashed over, trapping his legs beneath the shelves. Still
clutching the shaggy section of trash box as a pitiful shield,
he lay on his stomach in a litter of tools, accessories, and
home improvement items.

Stripe decided to finish him off while he had the chance.
Looking about for a suitable device with which to apply the
coup de grace, his eyes lit up as they fell on a wonderfully
lethal-looking heavy-duty battery. The thing was so leaden
Stripe could barely lift it, but the edge of the monster cube
felt even deadlier than it looked. He could easily imagine
it crushing his enemy's skull after the shortest of falls.

Quickly wrestling the battery to within a few feet of his
fallen foe, Stripe held it at his own chest level, poised for
the descent onto the back of Billy's head. Then, suddenly
dissatisfied at the short distance the battery would have to
fall and gain killing momentum, he decided to raise it as

high as possible so it would strike with even greater force.

Billy began to thrash free from the pile just as Stripe got the battery above his own head. Fear that his quarry was about to escape, combined with the weight of the dense object and Stripe's lack of gripping ability, caused the battery to slip. The battery bounced off his shoulder and landed squarely on Stripe's left foot.

"Yyyyeeeeggggggggrrrrrrrr!!!"

With a howl of pain, Stripe looked down at the pulpy mass of discolored flesh and shattered bone that used to be his foot and limped quickly away.

For a moment Billy could see nothing but blackness, the battery having finally come to rest not more than an inch in front of his eyes.

Pulling himself free of the wreckage, he leaped to his feet and started down the aisle after Stripe. At an intersection of four new aisles, he stopped and looked in all directions but the Gremlin was nowhere in sight.

"Darn," he sighed. "Where did he go? I sure could use those lights now. I wonder what's happening."

Gizmo shivered as he heard the noise of battle from far across the store. It sounded like someone dueling with ladders or a wall collapsing. The heavy silence that followed, however, was even more ominous, causing him to imagine all sorts of terrible things. If Billy had been victorious in that contest of flying objects, wouldn't he have cheered or shouted to Kate and himself? If the chase was still in progress or, even worse, if Billy lay injured or dying, Gizmo knew he was needed. Kate, while looking for the panel that controlled the lights, had placed the knapsack on a table just outside the store office. Gizmo knew he would be safe there, but the desire to help Billy was vastly more powerful than his sense of self-preservation.

Flipping the knapsack cover down, he crawled out of the canvas bag and lowered himself to the floor.

Not sure where to go, he padded along aimlessly for a short time, painfully aware of his lack of speed, another facility creator Mogturmen had overlooked while putting together his species.

"There has to be a better way," Gizmo murmured. "It'll take me years to get to the other end of the store on these legs."

He found what he was looking for a few minutes later in a tangle of wreckage on the periphery of the toy department. Its wheels were still spinning uselessly, the vehicle having become trapped in a corner. Gizmo approached it cautiously, located the ON/OFF switch and flipped it, causing the motor to die. Pushing it free of the fallen boxes at the end of the aisle, he rolled it to the middle of the corner and carefully pointed it in the direction he wanted to take.

"Perfect," he said proudly. "It's a perfect little—"

There being no Mogwai word for *car* that immediately came to mind, he merely shrugged and hopped inside.

The vehicle was quite sporty, nearly two feet long, pink with red stripes, a battery-operated replica of a Corvette Stingray that seemed to be crying out to be test-driven. Flipping the switch to ON, Gizmo was nearly jettisoned from the car by its sudden forward movement.

He settled back and gained confidence during the long run down the aisleway, but found he couldn't turn the car as easily as he anticipated when he came to an intersection. The result was a collision with a display of oil cans, the pyramid collapsing a split second after being sideswiped by the Stingray. The heavy thunk of the cans hitting the floor behind him caused Gizmo to breathe a sigh of relief. He vowed to take future turns more deliberately.

Whirring to the end of the aisle, he turned left and headed

up the next one. A jumble of fallen hardware supplies slowed him down considerably, but he soon regained top speed again.

As he passed through the next intersection, the sight of a figure moving down the aisle to his right caused Gizmo to swerve and brake so suddenly that the car piled into a neat line of garden tools. Ducking his head, he waited patiently until the rakes and hoes finished falling around him and then raced back toward the spot where the mysterious form had been.

The trap was so perfect and yet so simple that Stripe hardly felt the pain in his smashed foot. Because nothing complex was involved, his plan was nearly foolproof. The machine least likely to break down is the one with the fewest moving parts. So too with an ambush. The simpler the better.

The ambush Stripe now had in mind consisted of nothing more elaborate than a very long and narrow room with only one way in and out. There were no nooks and crannies to hide in, no cartons or boxes to use for cover, no closets to duck into. Called the Electronics Center, the room was simply a display area for several dozen television sets, home video games, and stereos, all neatly inset into the three walls. In the argot of the Old West, this was the box canyon into which Billy undoubtedly would come to meet his fate.

At the very entrance to the room was a small closet now occupied by Stripe. Clutched tightly to his chest were a bow and a batch of steel-tipped arrows he had found in the sporting goods department after smashing his foot. He had never used the weapon before but knew the principle behind it, the bow and arrow being the standard primitive weapon of many galaxies and therefore a residual, almost intuitive piece of knowledge. All that was required for his mastery of the weapon was a bit of practice, which would start as soon as his young enemy walked to the far end of the room. At that point, according to his plan, Stripe would step out of the closet and begin shooting. With nowhere to hide, Billy would eventually be hit by one or more of the arrows, and that would be that.

And if the young man decided to look into the closet before going to the end of the room? So much the better, Stripe thought. Then he would receive an arrow at point-blank range. The only thing lost would be the fun of using him for practice, seeing him panic and plead before succumbing to a direct hit.

Waiting patiently, it was not long before Stripe heard quiet footsteps moving down the aisle toward the room. Through the crack of the barely open door he saw the figure hesitate a moment and then continue walking. In the semi-darkness of the store he would be quite near the rear wall before realizing the room was a dead end, and by then, of course, it would be too late.

Opening the door a bit wider, Stripe peered out and was pleased.

"Just a few steps more," he whispered.

Billy went even farther than that, developing an interest in one of the pieces of equipment set into the far wall.

Perfect, Stripe thought.

Stepping quietly out of the closet, he nocked the first of his arrows and aimed it at an imaginary X between the young man's shoulder blades.

Kate was so confused she was nearly crying.

"How do you work this thing, anyway?" she nearly shouted.

For the past several minutes she had been pushing various buttons on the control panel in front of her with a total lack of success. It was not, she thought angrily, a user-friendly system, not unlike the first word processor she had tried using. Instead of labeling the buttons plainly and simply, according to their functions, the operator apparently had to punch an access code followed by the digit or digits programmed for each activity within the department store. Luckily, Kate had found the access code written on a piece of paper, but turning on the overhead lights was not so easy a matter. The closest she had come to it was when she punched the access code and the random digits 2-6, which turned on a string of permanently mounted Christmas lights near the main entrance.

"Well, what the heck," she said now. "If twenty-six does something, I might as well try sequence dialing."

With that, she punched the access code and followed with 2 and 7.

Stripe pulled the bowstring as taut as he could make it, checked again to make sure his target was lined up correctly, and prepared to loose his first arrow.

"Attention, please!" a loud voice suddenly announced.

Shocked nearly out of his wits, Stripe jerked his arm as the arrow flew from the bow, striking a television screen a foot above Billy's head.

"Attention, please," the announcer continued. "The store will close in ten minutes. Please complete any last-minute shopping you have so that our employees will be able to enjoy the rest of the evening. Thank you."

Startled by both the recorded announcement and the arrow crashing into the screen so close to him, Billy whirled. As he did so, he saw Stripe nock another arrow and aim it at him. Billy attempted to dance sideways, suddenly realizing he was the main target in a shooting gallery. Stripe responded with a fierce giggle, followed him, and loosed a second arrow. It tore through Billy's jacket at the neckline.

"That was close!" Billy muttered. "He's a good shot."

Already the Gremlin's arm was ready with another arrow. Billy licked his lips, looked around for a possible way out, but saw nothing. His only immediate plan was to continue dodging until Stripe ran out of arrows. Either that or charge, which was not particularly smart in that it made him a bigger target.

The third arrow headed his way, quicker and more accurate than the others. Falling prone, Billy heard it speed by his ear a second before he hit the deck.

Stripe giggled again, reached down for yet another arrow.

While scrambling to his feet, Billy followed the movement of the Gremlin's hand and saw it grab an arrow from a pile that must have included at least twenty more.

There's no chance, Billy thought miserably; with all those shots left he'll get me for sure.

But he could not bring himself to rush forward into the path of the flying missiles.

Kate hit the STOP button just as the store-closing announcement ended and the READY button glowed expectantly.

"Overhead lights," she said, as if trying to will the panel to obey her. "The heck with closing time. Let me have the overhead lights!"

Punching buttons furiously, she continued the numerical sequence only because she didn't know what else to do. Numbers 27 through 46 were routine announcements similar to the store's closing, and numbers 47 through 69 dealt with items currently on sale. Although she bailed out of each as soon as it failed to activate the lights, Kate was nearly beside herself. So much time was being wasted! Billy needed those lights and she was powerless to find them. All because of this complicated panel. As each number activated some insipid announcement, she pounded angrily on the desk, jabbed the STOP button, and tried again.

"Do it," she ordered. "Just do it."

"Men's Fruit-of-the-Loom underwear, now on sale for the next ten min—"

Pwing.

"A new parking lot will be open at Montgomery Ward on the—"

Whap.

"Glidden Spread Satin paint, now on sale—"

Thwong.

"Jeans for Juveniles, now—"

Twack.

In a way, the juxtaposition of sound and sight was so bizarre it was almost funny. Here he was, his life on the line as the primary target in a shooting gallery, all to the bland accompaniment of retail sales pitches and announcements that were choked off in midsentence. Except that Billy wasn't laughing. Those messages were *him*—a voice killed off by some unseen force just as it started to be heard.

Kwock.

Behind him and to his right another television screen was blasted to glass powder by the Gremlin's arrow. There was no doubt now about two vital things: Stripe was having a great deal of fun, and he was an expert with the bow. Billy knew instinctively that he was toying with him, puncturing TV screens nearby for the sheer joy of it as intermediate bits of fun prior to sending a shaft into his back or chest. So far, Stripe had used about half his pile of arrows, but the situation was made even worse for Billy when several shafts caromed all the way back to the shooter, to be used again.

"Ski poles and jackets—"

Very deliberately, Stripe broke his pattern of six shots per minute and stood grinning at Billy. Still holding the bow poised for action, he first pointed at Billy with his free hand and then pointed to his own heart.

Billy got the message. The fun and games were over and now Stripe was about to shoot in earnest. Taking a deep breath, he stood bouncing on the balls of his feet, readying himself to move as quickly as possible in any direction. But the experience of the past few minutes told him that he probably was not fast enough to avoid an arrow aimed directly at his heart.

Stripe, meanwhile, was determined to end the game, having grown weary of it. Becoming used to the store's intermittent announcements, he was able to shut out the voice almost automatically. He prepared himself now, concentrating fully on lining up the target.

"Holy cow, look at that! You hit him low, Barney, and I'll give him a jolt of this."

Stripe, barely cognizant of the background sound and certainly not realizing its content, started to release the arrow.

Gwock, plung.

The erratically loosed arrow crashed into the ceiling and ricocheted into the floor as Rand Peltzer, closing to within a few inches of the Gremlin, unleashed a flume of shaving cream from the Bathroom Buddy. It shot like a white tornado directly into Stripe's eyes, causing him to shriek with pain. At the same time Barney hurled himself at the creature's leg, snapping and growling.

Realizing what had happened and that he now had an opportunity to escape, Billy rushed forward. His escape mission was instantaneously converted into a rescue dash, for Stripe recovered from the two-pronged attack with amazing speed. Slapping Barney aside with the heavy bow as he shook the shaving cream from his face, the Gremlin grabbed an arrow and in less than a second had it pointed at Rand's torso ten feet away.

Still too far away to be of any help to his father, Billy could only hurl himself through the air, which was split by two simultaneous cries.

"Nooooooo!"

"Yeeeeechhhh!"

Suddenly Billy realized that the overhead lights of this aisleway were on, that the cry of pain had come not from his father but from Stripe.

Still recoiling with shock, the Gremlin dropped the bow and arrow and raced off toward an adjoining aisle, which was still dark. Barney started to follow, but stopped when Billy told him to stay.

Sweating profusely, Rand shook his head and smiled, looking down at the Bathroom Buddy in his hand.

"Well, I guess this was good for something after all," he said.

"Thanks, Dad," Billy said.

He started to go but his father followed.

"Wait a minute. That thing's dangerous. Why don't you wait for the cops?"

"No time." Pointing toward the office, Billy called back over his shoulder. "Tell Kate to turn all the lights on. She's in the office."

Then he was gone, racing into the darkness toward Stripe's retreating form.

When the lights went on, Gizmo was in the process of making a left turn just outside the area from which all the noise was coming. Partially blinded and gripped by a spasm of pain, he lost control of the tiny car, which raced at nearly full speed into a rack of audio tapes. Curling into a ball beneath the dashboard, Gizmo debated whether or not he should come out into the bright light and resultant pain. If he remained here, he would be all right until someone discovered him. But, of course, that wouldn't help Billy.

In this case, he thought, it's better to be sorry than safe.

Thrusting his head back into the light, he winced, but saw through the pain that the light dropped off in the adjacent aisle. If he could just get there . . .

"Lucky but dumb."

That was the description Kate gave to her last act at the control panel. And now she was stuck with it.

Totally frustrated at the array of trite announcements and failure to turn on the lights, she had abandoned her sequential-digit plan and just punched furiously at the board. Miraculously, that desperate, almost spasmodic gesture resulted in a bank of lights going on, illuminating approximately 10 percent of the floor area. That was the good news.

The bad news was that she had absolutely no idea what numbers she had punched. If adjacent overhead light systems were activated by numbers close to the one she had punched, they were still as lost to her as before.

"What was it?" she whispered, straining to recall where her fingers had gone. "What was that number?"

It seemed as if it had been something in the high nineties. Once again feeding the computer the access code, she sighed and punched 98.

"Ladies and gentlemen, we now direct your attention to the northernmost end of the store, where the Carroll B. Hebbel Memorial Fountain is being turned on for the day. This magnificent piece of free-form sculpture, the work of artist Donald Budé, was constructed so that the interplay of falling water and lights would provide maximum dramatic effect. Although relatively new, the fountain is already known throughout the state as an outstanding example of art and business working together to increase your shopping pleasure."

The significance of the announcement did not register with Billy until he heard the gentle burbling noise in the distance. Then, playing it back in his mind, he heard the all-important words . . . Fountain . . . Water . . .

"No!" he yelled at the top of his lungs, breaking stride only to scream it again as he ran a few steps backward. "No! Turn it off! Turn off the fountain!"

He realized Kate was too far away to hear him, but perhaps if his father, several hundred feet behind him, heard his plea, he would relay the message.

In the meantime Stripe continued to run ahead of him, racing as fast as he could. Billy was gaining on him, but a tiny voice in his head told him the damage had already been done. The fountain was running. There was no withdrawing the water that had fallen, and its telltale murmur was a siren song for the creature ahead who was rapidly approaching it.

Barney, well in front of Billy, was following Stripe closely, snapping at his tail and hind legs. But that was only harassment and what they needed now was containment. If Barney had been trained as a watch or attack dog, he might have been able to restrain the Gremlin. Now the most he could do was irritate and distract him while protecting himself from Stripe's slashing claws.

The northern end of the store was outfitted as a sort of greenhouse, filled with flowers of all kinds along the walls, which supported a magnificent skylight now covered by a large canvas tarpaulin. In the darkness the flowers blended together, forming an overhanging canopy, so that moving through the entrance was rather like entering a tropical rain forest.

Stripe abruptly turned at the door and gave Barney a swipe with his claws that sent the dog scurrying backward several feet. He remained at that distance, barking ferociously. Having taken care of his canine pursuer, Stripe looked directly at Billy, giggled triumphantly, and pointed to the glistening wall of water sheeting downward from the lip of the top fountain.

Billy's chest seemed about to burst from exertion, but he forced himself to continue running... faster... faster...

Then... all of a sudden it was too late.

When Billy closed to within twenty feet of him, Stripe, taking no chances, leaped onto the ledge of the fountain, teetered there one tantalizing moment, and then did a gentle backflip into the water.

The sight turned Billy's legs to strands of limp spaghetti. Leaning against the entrance wall, he allowed himself to slide slowly to the floor. Closing his eyes, he tried not to think of the past twenty-four hours, but the Gremlin's giggling, mixed with the sound of falling water, made it impossible to forget.... Four times he thought he had solved the problem... at home... in the YMCA... the theatre... and now here.... Successful each time... except for Stripe.

He took a deep breath and let the air out very slowly. Already he could hear the faint popping sounds as the bubbles that would become new Gremlins began to erupt from the surface of Stripe's skin.

Gizmo, still at the wheel of his miniature Stingray, rolled through the entrance to the greenhouse and immediately saw the worst. Billy, sitting, distraught... Stripe, laughing despite the pain of reproduction... And nothing could be done to set matters straight.

Unless—

His gaze moving quickly from floor to ceiling, Gizmo chirped optimistically, whipped the car sharply to his right, and applied full power. One thing Mogturmen had done correctly was give his creation a mind that was capable of rapidly analyzing a situation and coming up with a solution. That's why the tarpaulin, latch, and string were just objects in a big room to Billy the human, but answers to Gizmo the Mogwai. As soon as he spotted them, he knew there was still a chance to pull this one out.

Nearly crashing into the rear wall, he leaped from the car and raced for the spot where the rope was wound around the steel latch.

It was just out of his reach.

Babbling in Mogwai, he pushed the Stingray beneath the spot and leaped onto the hood. Working as quickly as he could with his clumsy paws, he slowly twisted the rope free of the metal latch. The final turn released it with such force Gizmo felt his feet lifted from the car and his body being carried upward at a breathtaking rate of speed.

Closing his eyes, he let go his grip, tumbling downward onto the hood of the car and then to the floor.

Above him he saw the canvas tarpaulin begin to roll away from the windows, the long narrow strips sliding neatly into compartments hidden beneath the sills. As they did so, a flood of bright early-morning sunlight cut a bluish white path through the middle third of the entire greenhouse.

Squarely in that path was Stripe.

Magnified and focused by the window glass, the sunlight fell across the prostrate Gremlin like a superheated girder, a searing weight he was powerless to move. Nor could he move his own body, weakened as it was by the light and the effort of reproducing new Gremlins. Soon hot fluids began to ooze from his pores, eyes, and the sides of his mouth. He tried to scream, but all that emerged was a guttural moan. Trapped in their brief moment of vulnerability before birth, the bubbles forming on Stripe's skin smoldered, blistered, and cracked. The grisly product of both the cool water and the hot violence of the Gremlin's death rose in a gray mist from the fountain and gradually dispersed, the final creation of the worst night in Kingston Falls history.

CHAPTER TWENTY

By the day after Christmas, reasonably normal patterns of living had returned to the Peltzer household and most of Kingston Falls. Newspeople from all over the state continued to pick through the wreckage—not only of buildings but of people's minds—in their efforts to dig out the grisliest details of the event, but the townspeople as a whole seemed anxious only to forget what had happened and resume their ordinary lives.

Billy managed to avoid the newshounds. He did so not because he shunned publicity or notoriety, but because he knew that any exhaustive series of questions would lead to Gizmo's part in the mess. Billy wanted to avoid that at all costs. He thought it would be difficult if not impossible because so many people knew he was involved, but preserving his anonymity was surprisingly easy.

The person who knew most about Billy's involvement, Pete Fountaine, was so terrified when he heard that Roy Hanson had been killed by an unknown creature in his lab that he ran away from home, thinking the police would connect him with the murder. Kate, of course, respected Billy's desire to be left out of it, as did his parents. Sheriff Reilly and Deputy Brent conveniently forgot that they had ignored a warning from Billy, but did accept an award for meritorious service by the National Association of Chiefs of Police. General David Greene appeared several times on local and national television, describing how he had relentlessly pursued the Gremlins until the last one was destroyed.

In any event, there being glory enough for everyone and little impetus to assign blame, Billy managed to stay out of it. As the furor began to die down, he started to believe there would be no more fallout from the Gremlin invasion.

He was correct, until the night after Christmas. Kate, Billy, and his parents had just finished dinner when the doorbell rang. Billy opened the door, revealing an elderly Oriental man. His expression was angry but controlled, like a parent who must punish a child. The wind blew through his straggly white hair, accentuating his doomsday look. Although Billy had never seen the man, he sensed immediately who he was and why he had come.

"Yes?" he asked timorously.

"I have come for Mogwai," the old Chinese man said.

He looked past Billy, catching sight of Rand. Billy indicated that he should enter and the old gentleman stepped into the room.

At the sound of the old man's voice, Gizmo, seated on the sofa nursing his sore back, immediately perked up his ears and lunged forward. Chirping excitedly, he nearly fell off the sofa in his efforts to reach the Chinese man, covering the distance in four big leaps.

Lifting the creature and nuzzling it gently, the old gentleman smiled slightly.

"I've missed you, my friend," he said.

Looking at them together, Billy was both touched and saddened. He could see that they had not only love as a bond, but many years of understanding and comfort.

Rand, feeling he should at least state his rights if not assert them, walked toward the Chinese man. "Now just a minute," he said softly. "I paid good money for him, and my boy's quite attached to him."

"I did not accept the money," the Chinese man said. "My grandson did that, and he has been sentenced to his room for a month as a result." He reached into his coat and pulled out a roll of bills. "Here is your money," he said. "I did not deduct the expenses in order to find you and get here, because you lost possible interest the money would have earned if you had kept it. We've both lost, and are even. Here. Take it, please."

Rand, his gaze alternating between the Chinese man and Billy, ignored the gesture.

"It's not that easy," he said.

"Never mind, Dad," Billy murmured. "It's all right."

"I warned you," the Chinese man said to Rand. "Mogwai needs much responsibility. But you didn't listen."

Rand shrugged. "Well, we know now. We'll be more responsible in the future."

"That is experience, not responsibility," the Chinese man corrected. "Responsibility is doing the wise thing before taking punishment, not after."

"Yeah," Rand muttered, "well..."

"Chinese philosopher once wrote: 'Society without responsibility is society without hope,'" the Chinese man added. Then he looked at Billy. "I am sorry," he said.

"I'll miss him, too." Billy smiled grimly. "But maybe this is best. I can visit, I hope."

The old Chinese gentleman nodded.

Gizmo, nestled comfortably in the old man's arms, looked at Billy and felt a terrible surge of sadness. If only he could say the human words that would let his friend know how he felt. . . . If only Mogturmen had . . . A pox on Mogturmen! he thought angrily. I can communicate. I must. And I will. I will project the human words and not be embarrassed if they come out gibberish. At least then I'll know I tried my best.

Closing his eyes, he concentrated deeply and powerfully for a long moment. Then his tiny mouth opened and human words came forth, tinged with a Mogwai accent but nevertheless completely understandable.

"Bye, Billy," Gizmo said.

Billy and his parents burst into laughter and tears at the same time. Even Kate was visibly affected, though she had known Gizmo only briefly.

"He talked!" Billy shouted, reaching out to kiss Gizmo on the top of his head.

"You have accomplished a great deal," the Chinese man said. "We will always remember you."

Billy nodded, unable to speak around the lump in his throat.

"Good evening," the Chinese man said.

As they went through the doorway into the cold night, Gizmo raised his paw in a little wave.

Billy waved back, then shut the door quickly. He did not want to watch as they moved slowly into the darkness and out of his life.